Review

Reading Josie Smith's T[...]
journey through differe[...]
descriptions of people, [...]
in unexpected and delightful ways. Sometimes I longed
to be with whatever she was describing. At others I felt
she was putting into words what I, as a musician, have
often struggled to articulate – that music is a more
natural and more important factor in our lives than we
may realise.

    Smith's story presents the idea that music can be
a constant yet almost unnoticed companion and guide.
Her words weave a connection of one special instrument
through the ups and downs of the main character's
journey to finding a spiritual master, and thereby to a
path that brings joy and fulfilment to the woman's soul
and so to her family life.

    The book is an enchanting immersion in the
power of music to support, and even help guide us to
finding our way to life's highest goals.

Joyce Wells
Singer/songwriter and vocal coach

TAMBOURA

At the heart of this book is the story of transformation, of the search for meaning in our modern world. Essentially it is one woman's answers to the age-old existential questions: Who am I? Why am I here? What is the purpose of my life? It is also a celebration of the magical way music nourishes the soul. And it is the story of Joanna and Eddie, and how the tamboura became a catalyst for change and spiritual awakening in their lives.

During the 1960s countless young people in the West looked at the world around them and rejected the materialism of their elders. They answered an inner calling: to become pioneers at the dawning of a new age, to listen to the wisdom of the ancients, to look within for happiness and fulfilment rather than expect it to come from more belongings, or higher status, or finding the perfect partner.

Some experimented with psychedelic drugs. Some looked to the East, especially to India, where spiritual knowledge and practices were still valued and vibrant. Joanna is a child of the sixties. She was at the heart of the tsunami of change that swept through that decade, and she and Eddie travelled the paths of change together into the seventies and eighties.

Yehudi Menuhin introduced the ancient art of Indian music to the West in the late fifties. George Harrison was fascinated by the sitar and studied it with Ravi Shankar. By the late sixties the exotic sound of the sitar, and the steady harmonic drone of the tamboura, were part of the culture of the times.

In 1968 The Beatles spent time in Rishikesh with Maharishi Mahesh Yogi, studying meditation. During that time George Harrison gave a tamboura to Donovan

Leitch, a British folksinger who was also in Rishikesh with Maharishi.

This is the story of that tamboura. It is a fictional story based on truth. The story begins in Miraj, in the home of the instrument maker who creates the tamboura. During the course of the book the reader travels to Rishikesh, and joins Joanna and Eddie on their journey of discovery on the Isle of Skye, and in Bristol, Kabul, Peshawar, Cornwall, West Wales and Maharashtra.

Tamboura is a book about the music of life.

To lovely Ali
with all my love

About the Author

 Josie Smith was born in London, and now lives in West Wales. Josie holds a Master's degree in Creative and Scriptwriting from the University of Wales St David's. She has written a memoir, two novels, a film script, two plays, some short stories and many poems. She has also rendered several scriptural stories for an international spiritual website. Her work has been featured in poetry collections and on the BBC.

Oher Books by Josie Smith

Diary of a Shielding Yogini (2021) ISBN:9781908146076

Tamboura

by

Josie Smith

Cowry
publishing

Published by Cowry Publishing
Gwisgo Ltd, 8 Sgwâr Alban, Aberaeron,
Ceredigion, SA46 0AD Cymru/Wales, UK

www.cowrypublishing.co.uk

First published in January 2023

Printed and bound in Ceredigion by Gomer Press
Cover design: Andy Teasdale
Book design: Karen Gemma Brewer

A CIP catalogue record for this book is
available from the British Library

ISBN 978-1-908146-12-0

I dedicate this book
to my spiritual teacher
in gratitude for her
unconditional love
inestimable wisdom
and
boundless compassion.

Acknowledgements

Thank you to my dear family, for your faith in me, for your feedback and, most of all, for simply being wonderful.

Thank you, Karen Gemma Brewer, for your courage and commitment to publishing writers from Ceredigion, and, most especially, for publishing *Tamboura*.

Thank you, Rajesh David, Joyce Wells, Dic Edwards, Jan, Gill, Rupert, Maggie and Victoria for your encouragement and friendship.

Thank you, Don, you really didn't fail me!

Contents

10   Foreword by Rajesh David

12   MIRAJ 1967

30   ST ALBANS 1964

45   LONDON 1966

54   LONDON 1967

67   MOROCCO 1968

81   RISHIKESH 1968

94   SKYE 1969

108   BRISTOL 1970

125   CORNWALL 1972

132   KABUL 1972

151   PESHAWAR Summer 1972

162   KABUL 1972

169   WEST WALES 1978-81

184   WEST WALES 1982-83

197   MAHARASHTRA 1983

223   Afterword

Foreword

The tamboura is the fundamental sound of Indian classical music, revered by musicians. It has prime place in a musician's house and is treated with great respect as a member of the family. Its sound brings joy, peace and harmony to the household. I grew up listening to the sound of a tamboura which belonged to my mother. She taught my sister and me how to play and sing along with it. It is truly a divine instrument.

Tamboura is a story about love and seeking - a deep spiritual search. Josie weaves a beautiful love story, with the sacred sound of the tamboura as an underlying witnessing presence. The lives of the central characters are intertwined with the tamboura, which was conceived in a dream state by its maker in Miraj, India. The reader will be drawn in by the sacred sound of this instrument, as was Joanna in the story.

Josie creates a vivid image of life in the UK in the 1960s. The story is based on true events, but she seamlessly moves between truth and fiction, painting a landscape which is rich in colour, music and the entire spectrum of emotions.

The central characters of the story are on a journey of discovery which takes them through three continents, ending in an ashram in India. Their journey opens up the pathway to the inner realms of their being. The tamboura in the story becomes a metaphor for the inner sound and silence which they discover at the end of their journey.

The *Upanishads*, which form part of the ancient Vedic texts, proclaim that *Sound* is the very essence of our being and indeed of the world around us. This has become a central tenet of Indian philosophy. This sound is OM, the word that expresses Absolute

Consciousness, *Brahman*.

According to the Mandukya Upanishad, the sound of OM is made of three sounds, A, U and M, which represent our consciousness in the waking, dream and deep-sleep states. Underlying the three is Pure Consciousness in which the three states of consciousness appear and disappear, like waves in the ocean. This Pure Consciousness is the Atman – our True Self.

OM in its sounding is the manifest Universe; in its silence it is *Atman/Brahman.*

The tamboura is a sacred instrument whose sound resonates with OM. Its sound expresses the three states of consciousness and symbolises Absolute Consciousness – *Nada Brahma*!

The tamboura is a constant presence in Joanna and Eddie's lives as they embark on their spiritual journey. Tamboura is a very moving and inspiring story of a seeker, written by a seeker for seekers!

Rajesh David
Singer, composer and yoga teacher

Since the one thing we can say about fundamental matter is that it is vibrating, and since all vibrations are theoretically sound, then it is not unreasonable to suggest that the universe is music and should be perceived as such.

Joachim-Ernst Berendt (1922-2000)

MIRAJ 1967

Aditya lay quietly beside his sleeping wife, savouring the moment between waking and dreaming. The *Devi*[1] had visited him again. Her fragrance lingered in the air, like the scent of gardenias. She'd spoken to him this time. What had she said? He closed his eyes to better re-capture the details of his dream, before it faded away into the mists of his mind.

Shri Sarasvati, radiant in her white garments, ethereal as she glided toward him, holding a tamboura in her arms, offering it to him. And there was music, such sweet music: flute and sitar, tabla and tamboura. Just remembering it brought tears to his eyes. He reached out to her and she placed the tamboura in his arms. He could see the exquisite designs covering it, feel the perfect balance of its weight in his arms. Her mouth opened to speak but he could not hear her words.

Still chasing fragments of dream in the caverns of his mind he rose, dressed, and climbed the stairs to the roof. Turning toward the pre-dawn glow in the east he placed both hands together over his heart and bowed his head in *namaskar*, the timeless expression of reverence for all of creation. Breathing in deeply he reached both hands high above his head, each finger extended. Relishing the stretch of his muscles he arched back. In the sky above a few bright stars still twinkled.

Breathing out he bent forward, pressing his hands flat on the floor beside his feet. *Uttanasana* – forward bending pose. Stillness enveloped his mind. He performed the familiar

---

[1] goddess

asanas of *surya namaskar,* his daily yoga practice of honouring the sun. Dawn splashed the sky with streaks of rose, gold and violet. A flock of white egrets flew west, their wings stroking the air like a blessing.

A melody resonated in his mind—the music from his dream, and suddenly he knew exactly what Sarasvati had said: "Make them for me."

Two nights ago, she had offered him a sitar. Last night a tamboura. He would make the perfect pair of instruments and dedicate them to Sarasvati, goddess of music and wisdom. He would excel himself with these two instruments, and they would be an expression of his gratitude.

At that moment the sun rose from behind the mountains, like an affirmation. Aditya completed his yoga practice with a final *namaskar.* He felt annealed to sky and earth, forged anew. A lone egret flew past him, her jet-black eye momentarily meeting his and he experienced a flash of unity. He opened his arms wide; the morning air caressed his skin. He felt invincible and utterly free.

"Aditya? Chai is ready." Neela peered up at him from the head of the stairs, her head slightly to one side, eyes bright. She reminded him of the bird. Sunlight glinted on the sequins of her dupatta, creating a sparkling ring of gold around her.

"Come here, you look like the *Devi* herself." She climbed onto the roof and he took her in his arms. "Look, the world is at our feet."

The river Krishna glimmered like a ribbon of liquid silver as it wrapped itself around the contours of the sun-scorched land below. The golden dome of the Ganesh temple swelled against the backdrop of dark hills. Rooftops radiated out in all directions, stages for the lives of the people of Miraj: women cooked on charcoal stoves, listless men lay on thin mattresses in the shade of flimsy sheets strung haphazardly between buildings, children played or wrestled. Washing hung limp in the still, hot air. Dogs rummaged for food. Cats lounged in the sun. Chickens pecked the dry earth, searching for an elusive grub.

Aditya took Neela's dimpled chin between his thumb and forefinger, tilted her face up and kissed her. He ran his hands through the rich thickness of her unbound hair, bringing a handful close to his face and inhaling the scent of jasmine and almond that surrounded her like a cloud. "I love your hair. It's like the night, dark and silky and full of mystery."

"Ha, the only mystery is how I will brush and plait it and be ready for the day. Come, your breakfast is waiting!"

Laughing, Aditya untangled himself from Neela's hair, but kept hold of her hand. "Let me stroke our child first."

Neela smiled up at him, her face alight with serene joy. She turned around, leaning her back into him, her body warm against his. He ran his hands over her softly swelling belly, then encircled her and his unborn child, his long, slender fingers gently meeting just below her navel.

"Oh, he kicked me," he said, amazed and delighted to feel the ripple of new life beneath his wife's skin.

"That's because he, or she, is hungry. Come, we must eat."

Over a breakfast of aloo paratha and chai Aditya told Neela of his dream and plans. "They will be the most perfect pair of instruments. I can see them already. It is the will of the goddess. I will go to Pandharpur to buy the pumpkins myself. None of the gourds I have here are right, and I need to re-stock before monsoon anyway. Can you be here today, in case any buyers come?"

"Yes, of course. I had planned to be here today anyway, mother is coming."

"First let's do morning puja together. I want to thank Sarasvati for her blessings, we have so much to be grateful for." Aditya looked around his simple home and breathed a sigh of satisfaction. He had grown up in this house, as had his father, Arjun, and his father before him. And now his children would grow up here also.

Golden light streamed through the small window and fell on the picture of his father hanging on the wall above the puja[2]. As he looked at his father's fine features and strong chin Aditya felt Arjun's solid presence fill the room and he fell to his knees before the family puja. "Father, I will always love and miss you. Thank you for sharing your wisdom and skill with me. Please bless me as I follow the command of the Devi. I will create a sitar and tamboura fit for gods to play."

Aditya bowed his head and felt his father's hands on him in blessing. He lit a candle and some incense, and handed the candle to Neela. In unison they waved the light and incense to the array of pictures on the puja, paying special attention to Sarasvati and Lord Ganesh, remover of obstacles. While they waved, they sang ancient mantras in praise of the goddess:

> Om Sarasvati mahabhage vidye kamalocane
> visvarupe visalaksi vidyam dehi namostute
>
> Om may we worship Goddess Sarasvati,
> the lotus-eyed goddess of wisdom, speech and music.
> You are the form of the universe, seer of all,
> please bless us with true knowledge.

They both bowed before the puja, and knelt together, enjoying the stillness that followed the potent mantras.

"You look just like your dad now, you know." Neela said, smiling up at him. 'Apart from your eyes. No-one has eyes like yours. They're neither brown, nor amber, but somewhere between, and when you smile at me like that the amber lights up like, like…. flames."

"Amber flames" he laughed, "no-one has ever described my eyes like that. People have called them strange eyes, or cat's eyes, but I like your description best. You are a poet, my love."

"Then I will write a song about your eyes while you are buying perfect pumpkins."

"Ha, and you will sing it to me when I return!"
An hour later Aditya was on his way to Pandharpur. The

---

[2] altar

journey always felt like a pilgrimage to him, and before Aditya had left Miraj he was chanting the name of Vitthal, the deity of the famous temple in Pandharpur.

Every year, in the midst of the monsoon season in the month of *Ashada*, thousands of pilgrims, the *varkari*, walked across the state of Maharashtra to the temple of Pandharpur to honour Lord Vitthal, the dark faced one. They danced and chanted for much of the journey, often lost in the ecstasy of devotion, oblivious to the rain.

They were following in the footsteps of the poet saints of Maharashtra: Jnaneshwar Maharaj, Namdev, Tukaram, Janabai and Muktabai. These lovers of God fused *bhakti*, devotion, with *jnana*, scriptural knowledge, and created the bhakti movement in Maharashtra. They composed poems and *abhangas* in the Marathi language, thereby initiating a tsunami of devotional music that opened the hearts and nourished the souls of millions.

Aditya went directly to the temple, wanting to take darshan of the Lord of Pandharpur before he bought the pumpkins. At each threshold of the temple, he rang the overhead bell, simultaneously invoking blessings and offering homage. As he approached the inner sanctuary the air around him thickened with power. Despite the constant drone of mantras from the Brahmin priests, the deep hum of humanity, the strong aromas of incense, ripe fruit and flowers, and the oven-like heat, there was a pulsating silence and stillness that drew Aditya's consciousness deep within. His heart throbbed to the pulse of silence.

Beyond the throngs of devotees, he saw the radiant dark form of the Lord, draped in red and gold, adorned with garlands of fragrant flowers and jewelled necklaces. He emanated stillness and ancient wisdom. In Lord Vitthal the formless had taken form. His presence was a portal back to the formless, back to the source of all. Aditya fell to his knees and revelled in the inner space. Once more the music from his dream thrummed through him.

A wordless prayer formed within him, intention flamed from his heart and mind, pure, and clear as crystal.

The tamboura and sitar blazed into being from the centre of his soul, and he offered it all to the Lord.

Aditya stretched out, full length on the temple floor, offering all, surrendered and overflowing with devotion. He rose, looked once more on the face of the Lord, placed some rupees in the donation box and left the temple with a joyous heart.

Heat shimmered off the baking earth as Aditya walked through a field of ripe pumpkins. This rare species of pumpkin had been grown here since the middle of the nineteenth century. Thanks to the skill and foresight of the Shikalgar family, Aditya's home town of Miraj was renowned throughout the musical world for the creation of superb Indian stringed instruments. Faridsaheb Shikalgar had pioneered the making of the tamboura and sitar from this particular inedible pumpkin. He had perfected the art of instrument making, had trained his grandson, Hussein Sahib, who, in turn had trained Aditya's grandfather, Sunil. As Aditya breathed in the earthy smell of pumpkin flesh he reflected on the centuries-old tradition of which he was a part.

Music was at the very heart of everything. The eternal vibration of the universe translated into sound, which, when listened to with focus could transport the listener far beyond the limitations of body and mind, back to the eternal vibration of being. Aditya was dedicated to music, to the creation of pure sound. It was in the steady beat of his heart, the pulse of blood flowing through his body, the rhythmic ebb and flow of his breath. It was in the calling of the birds and the buzzing of the flies, the rustle of air through dried grasses, the sigh of the trees, the steady hum of traffic and the sound of his feet on the hard-baked earth.

He entered the store house at the centre of the farm and Hassan, the owner, a small, wiry man with hands as dry and brown as the gourds that surrounded him, smiled to see him. "Aditya! Wa Salaam Aliekum."

"Aliekum Salaam, Hassan. How are you?"

"Better for seeing you, my friend. I am well, my sight

is getting weaker and my appetite is getting stronger, but Allah is good and the crop is bountiful this year."

"Yes, I walked through a field on my way here and the pumpkins look excellent. I love to see them growing. I can almost hear the sound they will create once skilful hands have shaped them into instruments."

"And what are your skilful hands shaping these days?"

"I am making a perfect pair of instruments, a sitar and tamboura. I can see them in my mind's eye and today I want to buy the gourds for them, and a few more to top up my stock."

"Well, you've come to the right place. Come, I will show you my best gourds." The two friends spent a happy time examining Hassan's collection of dried pumpkin gourds and Aditya selected a perfectly shaped large gourd for the tamboura, and a smaller, but no less perfect one, for the sitar. When Aditya had collected several more gourds of varying sizes, and settled his bill with Hassan, they sat together in the shade of the veranda, sipping chai and swapping stories.

Once Aditya was home, he soaked the two gourds in water for a day, to soften them for shaping. In the following days he prepared the wooden necks for the instruments, the *dandi*. Taking a long, slim and well-seasoned branch of red cedar wood, he carefully measured out two lengths, one for the sitar, and one for the tamboura. He cut a portion off the side of each piece of wood, then hollowed out the centre. For the sitar he transformed the slight curve at the end of the branch into an elegant swan's neck.

From a rare piece of rosewood he had saved for a special occasion, he created two matching *gullu* the flared neck which attached the *dandi* to the pumpkin gourd, now called the *kada ka tumba*. Once the gourds were shaped and cut, he fixed the *gullu* and *dandi* to them with *saresh*, a natural glue made from mucilage which he heated in a small metal pan.

The weeks past swiftly and Aditya spent every waking hour in his workshop. He began each day, as ever, with his yoga practice and puja. Neela was quietly content and supportive. She noticed a new vitality in him, his body emanated purpose, and it rose off him like musk. The amber lights in his eyes flared brighter. Even in sleep his long fingers moved as if he were plucking the tamboura. She herself was an accomplished musician and spent many hours playing the harmonium and singing *abhangas*, the devotional poems of Tukaram and Jnaneshwar Maharaj.

Most days the streets of Miraj rang with the sound of music: the silver shimmer of sarod or sitar strings, the trill and ring of tabla, the cascading notes of a singer as she explored the territory of a raga.

"I want to have the instruments ready for the Urs Festival." Aditya said one evening as they ate supper together.

"Good. There will be many buyers in town then." Neela said, her right hand absently stroking the swell of her belly. "Do you think you can finish them in time?"

"Yes, I am making good progress. The main construction is almost finished, today I'll start on sanding and polishing, and the bridges are almost ready. They just need some fine shaping. I am longing to play them."

"You will not want to part with them, you've poured so much of yourself into them. Once you begin to play the sitar..."

"And you play the tamboura..."

"We will never want to put them down."

"We will become frozen in time, eternally playing and singing."

Neela laughed "Sounds wonderful, but what about our baby? He or she will be here soon."

"He will be born a tabla maestro and will join us immediately."

"You are crazy, Aditya" Neela said, smiling at him, "and I love you."

The monsoon rains were heavier than usual. Aditya sanded and polished to the incessant sound of falling rain. Water sang on tin and stone, splashed on puddles and porches, turned earth to mud and streams to torrents. When the rain stopped everything steamed. The sun raged in the sky, clouds brooded, bodies sweated, clothes mouldered and people sighed, dragging their weary weight from place to place as if shod in lead.

Aditya worked tirelessly. The fan in his workroom whirred like a demented moth. Outside the street became a stream. Inside Aditya fashioned tiny fragments of camel bone into delicate patterns, carved pegs into lotuses, shaped perfectly curved bridges and patiently created grooves for the cotton to resonate the sacred sound. *Javari*: the ancient art of the instrument maker, creating the hollows and channels through which the vibration of strings can move to form the song of the goddess, the music of the universe.

The streets outside came alive with the name of the Lord. *Vitthalle Vitthalle Vitthalle Vitthalle.*
Jay Jay Vitthalle, Jay Jay Vitthalle.
The *varkaris* had arrived! Joyfully drenched. Faces alight with *bhakti*, devotion for the Lord. Dancing and chanting they made their ecstatic way through the rain-soaked streets. Aditya and Neela ran outside to join them as they danced through Miraj. Like a wave of love the procession moved through the town in a timeless flow of worship. The rain stopped and the sun came out. Pilgrims and citizens gathered in the town centre. Food materialised from countless kitchens: fragrant saffron rice, spicy bhajias, samosas and puris, urd dhal and fresh chappatis, mango lassi and carrot halwa. And they surged onwards. To Pandharpur. To Lord Vitthal, the incarnation of Lord Vishnu, the sustainer and preserver who inspired such devotion that the people of Maharashtra would sing and dance for him for ever.

The statue of Abdul Karim Khan looked down on the *varkaris* from his place of honour in the centre of Miraj. It said a great deal about the values of Miraj that Abdul Karim was so revered there. In the first decades of the twentieth century, he was the most influential singer in Hindustani

20

music, and founder of the Kirana *gharana* [3] of singing. Legend tells how he was dying of plague when he arrived in Miraj. He travelled directly to the Dargar Shrine [4] of Samshuddhin Mira Sahib, a Sufi saint from Kasgar, in China, to whom he was greatly devoted. Abdul Karim sat beneath the tamarind tree in the shrine and sang a poignant devotional prayer to the Sufi saint, pleading for healing. The following day he was fully recovered and he made Miraj his home for the rest of his life.

In honour of Abdul Karim Khan, the three-day Urs[5] Festival was held each year, and respected musicians travelled from all over India to play and celebrate his legacy. Many musicians and music shop owners also purchased new instruments while they were at the festival. The stringed instruments of Miraj are renowned throughout India for the quality of their construction and the purity of their tone.

Aditya had almost completed the sitar and tamboura. All that remained was the final stage of *javari* work: adjusting the bridges and tuning the strings and placing fine cotton threads along the runnels in the camel bone bridge to create the buzzing resonance of the tamboura. This was Aditya's favourite work. The sound he wanted reverberated within him constantly. It was a sacred vibration. The primordial sound of the universe: OM, the sound from which all sound arises.

When played by an adept, the harmonic drone of the four strings of the tamboura resonates through the bulbous swell of the gourd and creates a sound which can transport both player and listener to the source of all creation. This is why the tamboura is the instrument of the Goddess.

Miraj was buzzing. Bustling groups of men grappled with poles and canvas, eventually erecting a large pavilion beside the Dargar shrine of Mira Saheb. Eager traders set up stalls selling everything from flower garlands to shiny souvenirs, from crispy *puris* to spicy dhal. Musicians arrived

---

[3] school or style
[4] memorial tomb, a sacred place containing the body of a saint or holy person
[5] A festival celebrating the life of a great being

from all over the country. The Urs festival was about to begin.

In the home of Aditya and Neela two perfect instruments lay side by side before the simple home puja. Each instrument was adorned with three stripes of *bhasma*,[6] a single *bindi*[7] made of *kum kum*[8] paste, and a garland of white mogra flowers. Neela stood before the puja, dressed in her best red sari, the curve of her belly reflected in the swell of the tamboura gourd. Her outstretched palms held a gleaming brass tray, on which was a single gardenia, a lighted ghee wick in a brass holder and a neat pile of white rice, yellow turmeric and red *kum kum*. Each item held significance: the fragrance and luminosity of the divinity within all; fertility, prosperity and *shakti*, the all-pervading energy of the Goddess.

Aditya played a steady rhythm on a hand drum and rang a clear note on a small bell. The energy within the room increased as the rhythm sped up. The small flame leapt higher. The lights in Aditya's eyes gleamed. The fragrance of the gardenia filled the room and Neela felt her child moving within her to the primal rhythm of the drumbeat.

Neela raised the tray high and bowed her head. Aditya stopped beating the drum and ringing the bell. In perfect harmony they sang the ancient *arati* to the *Devi*, timeless words of worship, written in the Upanishads centuries ago. As they sang, Neela waved the tray, once to the right, once to the left, round in a circle and again. In her heart Neela was honouring everything: the Goddess and the exquisite instruments Aditya had created for her, her child who would soon be born, the gift of music and the grace of God, which filled her life with joy.

At the end of the *arati* Neela lay the tray down and they both knelt before the puja and bowed low. Peace settled over their home. Even the flame became still. Sitting cross-legged before the puja Aditya took up the sitar and carefully adjusted the mogra garland so it hung from the top peg.

---

[6] sacred ash from a ritual yagna fire
[7] a red dot, often worn on the forehead, which signifies oneness.
[8] a red powder

Neela rested the neck of the tamboura across her lap. Normally she would have held it upright, but there was not enough room for baby and tamboura. Their eyes met and they began to play an early evening raga: *kalyan* which invokes great blessings.

At first the notes were slow, aching, each note sustained, bending and willowing. The music painted longing, expressed the yearning of the soul for union. Aditya gradually increased the tempo, embroidering each note with a waterfall of sound. Neela plucked the four strings of the tamboura steadily, creating layer upon layer of harmonics as the strings vibrated and resonated. Together they created an all-encompassing mist of music, music that seeped into every molecule, bringing light, bringing peace, bringing love. They were both lost in the mystery of the raga, eyes closed, swaying slightly like a plant underwater.

Unnoticed the door opened and a tall, slender man wearing a dark red turban entered. He stood silently by the door, watching, an unreadable expression on his face. Time passed yet stood still. Only the music existed. And then the final note was played, and the vibration of the tamboura strings echoed into infinity.

After the silence had settled the visitor clapped his hands quietly and slowly. Both Aditya and Neela turned towards him, surprised. "Jaya! Welcome, we didn't hear you come in." Aditya said, carefully setting down the sitar on its padded ring and standing up to greet his guest.

"I am sorry. I could hear the music outside and didn't want to disturb you by knocking," Jaya said, walking towards Aditya. "And I wanted to get closer. That was amazing! The tamboura has an incredible resonance. Namaste Neela, you look blooming."

Jaya's presence filled the small room. He seemed to be everywhere at once. By the time Neela had laid down the tamboura and stood up Jaya was greeting her enthusiastically. She was suddenly aware of her size, the burgeoning swell of her pregnancy seemed too intimate, too close. She lowered her eyes, placed both palms together and greeted Jaya. "Namaste, Jaya, it is good to see you."

"We have just dedicated these two instruments and offered blessings for them," Aditya said, indicating the sitar and tamboura which rested before the puja.

"And what stunning instruments they are," Jaya said, kneeling down to examine them more closely, "May I?"

"Of course, that is why you are here I imagine." Aditya said.

Jaya picked up the sitar and examined it closely. "You have excelled yourself, Aditya. The work on this is exquisite." He plucked a few notes. "And the tone is wonderful."

Jaya lay the sitar back on its ring and went over to the tamboura. He turned it round, examining the fine details of the carved *patri* radiating from the *gulla*, like a ring of deep brown leaves. Then he cradled it on his lap and began to play, his forehead resting on the neck, eyes closed. Once again, the room filled with the resonant drone and an infinity of harmonies. "Perfect," said Jaya. "You have just finished them?"

"I finished this morning. This is the first time we have played them."

"Are they a commission?"

Aditya paused, meeting Neela's eye and then looking away, into the middle distance. He was reluctant to tell Jaya about the dreams, it was too personal. "No, I just wanted to make a matching pair."

"Then can I buy them?"

"You can make me an offer if you like," Aditya said, smiling, "but I will be reluctant to part with them so soon."

"Well, I can leave them here until the end of the festival. I am sure we can agree a price that will suit us both. We will talk business tomorrow. Meanwhile, can I take you both out to dinner?"

Aditya raised his brows at Neela in a silent question. She smiled and nodded slightly; it would be a rare treat to eat out. "Thanks, Jayendra. That would be great." Soon they were sat around a table, enjoying jeera rice and vegetable bhajias.

"How are your family shops doing Jaya?"

"Both doing really well. The one in Delhi is always steady, my brother, Ajit, tells me that the one in Dehra Dun has really picked up. Many travellers are coming from the West now, and Hindustani music is becoming popular there. I do not think many have the discipline to learn to play the sitar, nor to follow the dharma of classical Indian music, but many of them want to buy sitar and tabla and even tamboura."

"Yes, I read that Ravi Shankar and Ali Akbar Khan have been playing to large audiences in the West." Aditya said, pouring water into each of their glasses.

"Of course, it all began when Yehudi Menuhin recorded Ali Akbar Khan on sarod and Pandit Chatur Lal on tabla." Jaya said.

"Music of India: Morning and Evening Ragas!" said Neela, "my father had a copy. Mr Menuhin did a beautiful job of introducing the instruments. The West has finally noticed that we Indians have an ancient culture of great music. Something the British Raj never seemed to discover!"

"Some of them did," said Aditya, "but it's true, most of them had no respect for our culture."

"Well, it's different now," said Jaya, "young westerners love everything from the East, they are coming East in busloads, looking for answers to a thousand questions."

"What questions?" asked Neela.

"What is the meaning of life? Why am I here? Where am I going? What's it all about? They tell me they are looking to find themselves."

"Are they lost then?" Aditya asked, puzzled.

"In a way, yes, they are I think," Jaya said thoughtfully. "The kids I speak with have everything yet they feel their lives are empty. Some of them, many of them actually, have smoked cannabis and taken drugs like LSD. They tell me they had visions of the connectivity of all life, they've seen the cosmic dance on their 'trips.' Then they come back to earth with a thump and can't relate to the endless quest for more possessions and greater status."

25

"Yet they have so much," Neela said, "plenty of food, education, prospects. So much more than children here have."

"I know," Jaya said, "it makes no sense. Yet I think these kids are pioneers in some ways. They have seen the mess the West is in. They are the first generation in this century that have not been caught up in war. They are rejecting the values of their parents, but don't know what to replace them with. They have lost faith yet also feel there is something more, and, when they look to the East, they think we still know the answers."

"And maybe we do," Aditya said, "faith is strong here, not just following the rituals but living it, living with devotion and dharma."

"Yes," said Jaya, "and something in our traditions and in our music is calling them, is resonating with them. Maharishi Mahesh Yogi has built an Ashram in Rishikesh, and hundreds of westerners come there to learn how to meditate. Hundreds!"

"Really?" asked Neela, surprised.

"Yes, my wife's cousin works there, I've seen them. Dressed in salwar suits and kurtas, beads and bindis, sitting cross-legged in the shade of the banyan trees, repeating the mantra, singing *kirtans*[9] even. The Maharishi is touring the West now and people are flocking to him."

"Amazing," Aditya said, "so now our music and wisdom are trendy?"

"Very," Jaya said, "and we are selling more instruments than ever before. Which is great for all of us. So, which concerts are you going to during the festival?"

"All the family will go to hear Pandit Bhimsen Joshi tomorrow night, we love to hear him sing," Neela said, "Aditya and I will probably go to the final concert also. How about you?"

"I hope to attend most of the concerts, but I also have some more instruments to buy. I have started well," he

---

[9] devotional chants

smiled at them, "if everything I buy is of the same quality as yours, I would count myself very blessed. However, that is unlikely."

Aditya smiled back at him. "Well, I have some more instruments in my workshop, call by tomorrow morning and see if there is anything else you like."

"Okay," Jaya said, standing up, "I will see you tomorrow. Good night."

The full moon was high in the sky as Aditya and Neela walked home. It cast a silver sheen on the stone walls, and made the peepul tree at the corner of their street dance with light. When they arrived home Aditya polished the instruments one last time and stood them side by side against the wall. They looked magnificent, each a rich, deep mahogany that evoked earth and fire and set off the darker brown of the carved leaves and lotus shaped pegs. The intricate inlaid work along each neck and adorning every seam of the instruments was extremely fine, the white of the camel bone had a soft sheen, like ivory. Either side of the strings two ornate white peacocks with long tails and crowns perched on a delicately carved tree, and the tree was reprised in the patterns around the base of the *gullu*. A garland of tiny flowers decorated the *tabli*, the front of each instrument, with another exquisite garland embellishing the junction of *tabli* and *dandi*.

"Do they fulfil your vision?" Neela asked, standing close to Aditya as he surveyed the sitar and tamboura.

"Yes," he said, putting an arm around her and drawing her closer still, "they are exactly as I saw them in my dream."

"Can you bear to part with them so soon?"

"They were never mine. Mine are the hands that shaped them, and my part is played. They have always belonged to the Goddess, and she has plans for them, I think. Jaya arriving while we played them for the first time was no coincidence."

"There are no coincidences where the gods are concerned."

"No, you're right. What is the English word?"

"Serendipity."

"Yes, serendipity. A beautiful, musical word. I will be sorry to see them go, and I would love to know what will become of them, but now I surrender them to the Goddess. Let's go to bed."

The following evening, Aditya, Neela, her parents and a group of aunts, uncles, sisters and cousins were seated in the pavilion beside the Dargar shrine of Samsuddhin Mira Sahib of Kasgar. The pavilion was full and the atmosphere was electric. An excited buzz of conversation swirled around the hall, the concert of Pandit Bhimsen Joshi was always much anticipated and enjoyed.

The Urs Festival in honour of Abdul Karim Khan was open to all. Musicians from all over India regarded it as their *seva*, selfless service, to play here, out of respect for a much-esteemed pioneer of music. Everyone was welcome to come to the festival; Maharajas and beggars, bakers and Brahmins, brick-makers and craftsmen. Miraj had always prided itself on its egalitarianism. Music dissolved the false boundaries of status and religion. Muslims and Hindus, Jains and Christians, all played and enjoyed music together.

Aditya and family were seated behind the governor of Maharashtra and his wife. A little to their left was an Adivasi family who worked on the new railway, the women breaking rocks, the children carrying them and the men preparing the ground for rails. Everyone was there to enjoy the music.

Outside, the rain pounded on the roof of the tent. Inside it was hot and humid. The musicians took their places on the stage, amidst great applause. The excitement mounted. There was a moment of silence and then the great singer walked onto the stage and a roar arose from the crowd like a giant wave. Pandit Bhimsen Joshi bowed to the four directions and to his fellow musicians, then took his seat. Two tamboura players began creating a canvas of sound for the maestro. The sitar player painted a pattern of breezes and butterflies, followed closely by the tabla drawing raindrops of joy. And then Pandit-ji began to sing, his voice echoing the rise and fall of the sitar, the dancing notes of the tabla, transcending all and soaring like a bird, pulling the strings of every heart with him.

They sat, entranced and silent, lost in the cadence of the music, transported to the stillness of the soul.

All too soon it was over and a great sea of people surged out from the tent and into the streets: to eat at the stalls, to sit and sip chai and gossip, to wander beneath the stars and relish the silence they had been delivered to. Neela rubbed her back, wincing slightly.

"Are you okay?" Aditya asked, always quick to notice his wife's discomfort.

"I think the baby may be coming early," she said, smiling, feeling excited and scared at the same time.

"We'd better get you home quickly then. I will call a taxi." It was a long night. Aditya made endless cups of sweet chai, or sat quietly praying, while Neela, supported by her mother and the local midwife, laboured to bring new life into the world.

As the sun rose the following morning Aditya was invited into their bedroom by his tired and happy mother-in-law. Neela sat up in their bed, her eyes filled with light, a small bundle in each arm. "We have twins, my love. Come and meet your son and daughter!"

Aditya's eyes filled with tears and his heart overflowed with love as he gently kissed his wife and looked at the two tiny faces of his children. "Thank you, Neela. They are perfect, she will be as beautiful as her mummy. And he will be the finest instrument maker in the whole of India. What shall we call them?"

"How about Radha and Krishna?"

Harmony sinks deeper into the recesses of the soul and takes its strongest hold there, bringing grace also to the body and mind as well. Music is a moral law. It gives a soul to the universe, wings to the mind, flight to the imagination, a charm to sadness, and life to everything.

Plato (429-347)

ST ALBANS 1964

Mac McCleod played *Angie* on his guitar, the silvery notes flowing like a waterfall over the sibilant hiss of conversation. Someone was always playing guitar at the Cock Inn. Every table was full: girls with long hair, bright eyes, and colourful clothes; guys in polo-necks and jeans. The air was thick with cigarette smoke, beer and cider fumes, and pheromones. We all knew one another and moved easily from table to table, greeting old friends or meeting new ones. Every new arrival was welcomed with a friendly shout. Laughter rippled like a warm current around the barn-like room: concrete floor, long wooden tables and benches, windows looking out over the pub gardens at the back and a wide barn door onto the High Street.

This was our gathering space. Every Friday night we met up here to catch up, chat-up, play or listen to music, and make plans for the weekend. The musicians played in the central space, around the ancient woodstove that prevented the room from freezing during the winter months.

Mick Softley sang a song about war, his deep, earthy voice permeating the room. A couple of guys strummed along with him. Then someone began singing *Blowing in the Wind* and soon we were all wailing the chorus together, with Don and Eddie adding mournful notes on their harmonicas. Bounce shouted out for *The Times They are A-Changing*, and we all sang along. It had become the anthem for our generation. We knew change was coming, we were impatient for it. We sang Dylan's poetic prophesy with an urgent passion, born of that impatience with the ageing old road and our thirst for the new one.

One song led seamlessly into another, each musician taking a turn to play, and everyone joining in whenever we knew the words: folk, skiffle, blues, rock - we loved them all.

As we sang *Mattie Groves*, Vicky and I grinned at one another, remembering singing it on our travels. Life in St Albans was good. We'd had a wild time, hitching around Europe and then working and clubbing in London. It was our first flight of freedom since we'd finished school. But now we were content to find our fun closer to home. There was enough variety in the scene at the Cock to keep us happy and life was simpler...less work, more play.

Donovan began to play a soft, lyrical song that made me think of bluebells and woodland glades. I watched him, drawn to the way his brown curls fell across his brow, the far-away look in his eyes as he sang. He looked up and our eyes met and held. An invisible current flowed between us. My heart beat a little faster, my breath flowed a little shallower.

Later that evening I felt his gaze on me again. He was standing beside the door, empty-handed, his look a silent invitation, and I rose to accept it. Wordlessly we walked outside, across the road and into the churchyard opposite. Our hands joined. His warm and strong, mine cool and delicate. Our fingers twined together. The silence was magical, and neither of us wanted to break it.

We stopped beside the ancient Yew tree and stood side by side, admiring its gnarled girth and spreading branches. Then we turned to one another and kissed, long, sweet and gentle. Our kiss was like a poem, like a soft breeze, like a caress, like love.

We wanted more, yet knew to take this slowly, to relish the sweetness, the discoveries, the unfolding. I turned seventeen the following week. He was just eighteen.

As Spring ripened into summer, my eyes and heart opened to the beauty of love, the poetry of life. Donovan and I were together whenever possible: we walked in the grounds of the majestic Abbey, beside the lake, around the ruins of Verulamium, in wild woods and formal gardens. We talked for hours about anything and everything. We lay on grassy slopes and watched clouds billow and glide across an achingly blue sky. He played his songs to me, and I drank them in.

Mum loved him from their first meeting, he knew how to charm. His soft Scots burr gave his gentle speech an added appeal. She invited him for dinner, and he came every week. Then we went to my room—our refuge, our private realm. He was my minstrel, and I was his lady. We flew our magic carpet to mythical lands, and watched our dreams unfurl.

He arrived one warm summer evening, guitar over his shoulder. "I've written you a song," he told me, eyes shining. I took his hand and lead him to my room.

I cried the first time he sang my song to me. And the second time. Tears of love and joy. Tears of wonder. I felt I had been wrapped in velvet, and carried on a golden boat to another realm, buoyed on the currents of love.

Everything sparkled. Love coated my world in fairy-dust, covered my eyes with rose-tinted glasses. So much beauty everywhere. How could I have ever thought it was otherwise? Life was a miraculous dance. Every breath was a blessing. I lived only for love.

I thought it would last forever.

The Cops and Robbers had a gig at The Studio in Westcliff-on Sea, near Southend, and Donovan was playing in the interval. Everyone from the Cock was going to support them. The Cops and Robbers were 'our' band and they were great. All the band were regulars at the Cock: Eddie Freeman was the lead singer, he had a soulful voice, a wild energy and he played a driving, bluesy rhythm guitar. Terry Fox on Hammond organ was almost as good as Georgie Fame. Henry Harrison was a solid, creative drummer, Keith Kennadine played a mean harmonica, while young Stevie Smith lay down a steady bass.

The Studio was heaving, a dark cavern of a place that was renowned as the best live music venue on the south coast. Vicky and I made our way to the front and danced, abandoning ourselves to the heady blend of music and movement, occasionally catching one another's eye and remembering other times we had danced like this, in Wardour Street, Soho, at the Flamingo and the Discotheque.

The Cops and Robbers had quite a following. They'd been playing together for almost a year, and were going on tour in the autumn, supporting John Lee Hooker. They played a unique mix of R&B, soul and good old rock'n'roll, which was fun to dance to.

Donovan walked onto the stage and sat down, tuned his guitar and began to sing *House of the Rising Sun*, a Woodie Guthrie number. He looked relaxed, natural. By the end of his first song most of the audience were quietly listening to him. The atmosphere shifted, became stiller, softer.

I watched him from the front of the crowd. When he sang my song, I felt he was singing just to me. I was really proud of him, yet the pride and love I felt was tarnished by something darker, a sense of possessive fear, a desire to have him to myself, to keep everyone else outside, away, separate.

After Don's set I noticed one of the 'men in suits' talking to him, and then I lost sight of him altogether.

Suddenly he was by my side again, his face lit up. "Let's go for a walk by the sea," he said into my ear, sending shivers down my spine.

It was a warm night, and we walked barefoot along the sand, waves lapping at our feet. The moon was almost full, creating a pathway of silver directly to us.

"You were amazing tonight," I told him. "You looked so relaxed and happy on that stage. Everyone loved it."

"It felt really natural, Joanna. Like I've been performing all my life."

"Has something happened? That guy?"

"You don't miss a thing, do you?"

"Not where you're concerned. Who is he?"

"His name's Pete Eden. He's the Cops and Robbers manager. And guess what?"

"Donovan Leitch, stop teasing me and tell me," I said, standing in front of him and placing my hand on his chest.

Don laughed and folded me in his arms, hugging me to him.

33

"He wants to be my manager! He wants me to make a record!"

"Wow! You're going to be famous! Hooray," I yelled. We jumped up and down together, laughing and splashing water on each other like kids. "Well, I guess it was only a matter of time. Your music is special, and so are you."

"Look at the moonlight on the water," he said, "it's like a pathway to paradise."

We spent that night on the hard floor of the Studio, folded in each other's arms, and it felt like the best feather bed money could buy.

A week later Don arrived at our house unexpectedly, guitar in hand and rucksack on his back. I invited him in, delighted to see him. We went to my room. Mum was out and Dad was in the garden, as usual.

"Do you think your Mum will let me stay here for a few days?" he asked.

"Well, probably, we'll have to ask her. Why? What's happened?"

"My Mum's thrown me out. She threw my hat on the fire, I think she'd have thrown my guitar too if I hadn't grabbed it."

"Why? What's the matter with her?" I asked, shocked.

"I don't know. She was angry. I think she wants me to get a job or something." He shook his head and the skin on his forehead crinkled, making me want to smooth it out with kisses. Tears sprang to my eyes and I flung my arms around him.

"Of course you can stay here. Mum loves you like a son. You may have to sleep on the sofa though."

"Maybe I can sneak in here late at night?"

We laughed and lay down on the bed, wrapped in one another's arms.

Mum was fine, and Don stayed with us for around two weeks. My brother, Peter, was away for one week, earning his Duke of Edinburgh award on a mountain in Wales, so Don slept in Pete's room. It was a sweet time, simple, easy and fun. He played guitar on the lawn while I sewed. I showed him all my favourite places: the river, trees I had befriended, the secret glade in the woods where I was convinced that I'd seen fairies. We ate every meal together and sat up late into the night talking and dreaming.

Pete Eden invited Don to London, to discuss the next steps. Don set off the following morning and didn't return that night. He called me from Torquay the next day, telling me he needed to be by the sea, wanted some time alone. He was staying with Mac and Stella, friends from St Albans who had moved there for the summer season. I was shocked and sad. It was so sudden. So unexpected. Had he finished with me? Were we still together? What was going on?

Thoughts spun round and round in my head, robbing me of sleep. We were so happy. What went wrong?

I walked the mile and half to Vicky's house, needing to talk it all over with her, maybe to cry. The walk took me along a quiet country road. The hedgerows were bursting with life: bees, drunk with pollen, crawled out of one pink foxglove blossom and into the next, butterflies sunned their wings on delicate white cow parsley fronds, berries ripened on hawthorn, rowan and bramble, pigeons coo- cooed to one another from the trees, swallows and swifts rode the air streams, and somewhere, high above, a lark sang and soared.

Suddenly my awareness of space and time shifted. I became conscious that the reality I was walking in was only one dimension, one possibility. I sensed another version of me, walking along the same country road, at the same time, in some kind of parallel universe. She/I was so close. Merely a breath away.

Everything was crystal clear and shone with its own light: every leaf and branch, every flower in the hedgerow, every stone, and every particle of air. I stood still, entranced by the immeasurable beauty before me. I had a sense of expansion, of boundaries dissolving, of vibrant limitlessness. I looked down, and an army of ants marched at my feet, transporting impossible burdens across the road. I laughed aloud; all my sadness dissolved.

Vicky and I sat in her garden, enjoying the autumn sunshine. Donovan's desertion to the West Country took second place as I attempted to describe my experience on the road to her. It was hard to find the words, but the mere act of trying to talk about it re-captured what I had felt, and Vicky got it. We talked excitedly about space and time and the nature of reality.

Ever since I could remember I'd had a sense of knowing something in the depths of my soul. Something infinitely precious, which had somehow been forgotten. As a child I had pored over the ancient myths and legends of Greece and Rome, loving the stories and feeling that they held clues to a forgotten knowledge.

As I had grown older I had more un-answered questions: What were the Eleusinian Mysteries? Why were Mistletoe and Oak sacred? Why did we build Stonehenge? What was the secret of Long Barrow? Who was God? Where was the Goddess?

I felt I had glimpsed Truth in that moment on my walk. A chink in reality had opened, showing me boundless possibilities. I longed to travel through the chink and explore.

I also really missed Donovan. He'd been gone for three days already and his absence was like a yawning chasm in my life. Every song I heard on the radio was poignant and must have been written especially for me at that moment: words of longing, heartache, confusion and loss.

On Friday evening I met Geraldine at the lake. Geraldine and I worked near one another, and often met up for lunch or after work. She was another regular at the Cock. It was a beautiful evening and we sat under a large willow, our backs against its solid trunk, its branches wafting gently in the late summer breeze. We talked about our missing lovers, who were both in Torquay. Geraldine was with Mick, a young Irish guy with dark, gypsy good looks and a reputation to go with them.

"I can't sleep for thinking about him," she told me, her blue eyes welling with tears. "I love him and I have to be with him."

Six white doves flew across the lake, sunlight silvering their wings. A fish broke the surface of the water, sending out an ever-expanding circle of ripples. Once again, a sense of timelessness swept over me. I breathed in deeply, savouring the moment

"Maybe we should hitch down to Torquay and see them," I said, surprising myself.

Geraldine turned to look at me, her eyes widening. A breeze caught her long, dark hair, wrapping it around her face. "Joanna you are brilliant. Let's go. Now." She stood up and scooped her hair out the way, tying it in a knot at her neck.

"Right now?" I asked. "Really?"

"Well, why not?"

I laughed, "I am tempted, believe me. I am aching to see Don. But I have no money, no clothes and maybe we should at least tell our parents?"

"Good points. Tomorrow morning?"

"Great, meet you at 10.00 at the bottom of Holywell Hill." We hugged and I practically ran home, excited at the thought of our adventure. I barely slept that night, laying wide-eyed, imagining my reunion with Donovan, playing out several different versions in my mind: Don's face lights up to see me, or he turns away with cold indifference, or he is already with someone else...

Our journey was smooth and good fun, cars stopped as soon as we stuck out our thumbs, and we met some interesting people. We stopped near Stonehenge to eat our sandwiches beside the ancient monoliths.

"We always stopped here on family holidays to the West Country," I told Geraldine.

"It's amazing. I've never been here before. The stones are enormous, how did they get them here?"

"Nobody really knows," I said. "They have made up a story about them being dragged on logs, but I don't believe it. The blue stones come all the way from the Preseli Mountains in West Wales."

"So how do you think they did it?" Geraldine asked.

"I think they used telekinesis, moving them with the power of thought. They must have been a very advanced civilization; I mean this place is perfectly aligned with the rays of the rising sun at midsummer and midwinter."

"What do you think it is then?"

"A temple to the sun maybe? Or a transmitter/ receiver for cosmic and earth energy? I don't really know, but I love this place, and I can feel its energy."

"Me too." Geraldine turned to face me, her eyes serious and shadowed with sadness. "Joanna...can I tell you something?"

"Of course, what is it, Geraldine?"

"Do you promise not to tell anyone? Not even Donovan?"

"I promise I will never tell a soul, unless you say I can."

"I think I'm pregnant." I looked at her, shocked into silence momentarily, then I hugged her and she began to cry into my shoulder.

"There, there," I said, patting her back and feeling useless, "it'll be alright." But I did not even believe myself, and I'm sure she didn't. "How late are you?"

She sat up and I rummaged in my bag for a crumpled hankie. She wiped her eyes and blew her nose, then look at me with red-rimmed eyes. "Three weeks, maybe a bit more," she sniffed, wiping her nose again. "I feel different, and I felt a bit sick this morning."

"Oh...I assume Mick doesn't know?"

"He left over a week ago, and I wanted to be sure before I told him."

"So that's why you wanted to go to Torquay so urgently."

"I am longing to see him."

"Of course you are. How do you think he'll react?"

She sighed, a long sigh, weighted with sadness and fear, then shook her head, "I honestly don't know, but he doesn't really seem the marrying kind, does he?"

I looked at her and sighed also, accepting the truth of

what she was saying. "Have you thought about getting rid of it? Abortion is legal now at least."

Geraldine shook her head again. "I couldn't do that. I just couldn't. I've thought about it, but I think it would haunt me for the rest of my life." She began crying again and I held her hand silently. It was probably good to let it out. No doubt she'd been bottling it all up inside for the past three weeks, never telling a soul, worrying what to do.

When the tears stopped, I handed her another hankie, my last and grubbiest, but better than nothing.

"Let's hit the road then," Geraldine said, giving me a watery smile. I hugged her again.

"You are a brave and strong woman, Geraldine, and you can get through this. I hope he is there for you. But if he's not I will be, and you have a lot of good friends."

"Thanks, Joanna, I'll try to remember that."

We arrived in Torquay late afternoon and went straight to Mac and Stella's flat. Donovan opened the door and his face lit up when he saw me. I threw my arms around him and buried my face in his shoulder. A wave of emotions flooded through me, robbing me of words. It just felt so good to be in his arms again.

"Come in, come in," Don said, opening the door wide and gesturing us into the room with a graceful sweep of his hand. "Hi, Geraldine."

"Hi, Don."

Don made us tea while we explored Mac and Stella's flat. It was light and airy and, if you stood on tip-toe, you could just catch a glimpse of the sea from the bedroom window. "It's only a five-minute walk to the beach," Don said, "We'll go there when you've finished your tea."

"I'd love that," I said, "Where are Mac and Stella?"

"They work at the Phyllis Court Hotel, on the seafront. They'll be home around nine, after they've served the evening meal."

"And where is Mick?" Geraldine asked. I hoped that Don had not noticed the tremor in her voice.

"Ah, you just missed him. He went to St. Ives this

morning."

Geraldine managed to keep up a brave front, although I could see she was struggling. I started talking about Stonehenge, to give her time to think.

"How long does it take to get to St. Ives?" she asked.

Donovan looked at her, surprised. "About two hours," he said.

She stood up, "I'd better get going then."

I stood as well, concerned for her. "Wouldn't you rather rest here tonight, and leave tomorrow?" I asked, "Maybe you could get a bus?"

"No, I can't wait. I'm not tired and I have to see him. I'll be fine hitching."

I knew there was no point arguing with her, it was her decision and I could see that she'd made her mind up. I would probably do the same if I were in her position. I hugged her one last time, wished her luck and walked out the door with her. "Take care of yourself. And stay strong. You can do this."

"Thanks, Joanna, you've been a big help. I feel a lot stronger having shared it with you."

"I'm not surprised. Keeping something like that to yourself does your head in. My mind just goes round and round, worrying away at the situation, like a dog with a bone."

Geraldine laughed. "Yes, that's just what I've been doing. And every thought repeats itself endlessly, till you feel like you're going crazy."

"You can always talk to me, Geraldine. Please remember that."

She smiled, but her eyes remained sad. "Thanks, I will. Bye." I waved her off and stood watching her small figure walk down the hill and out of sight.

I stayed in Torquay with Donovan for about six weeks. We shared Mac and Stella's sofa bed, and even joined them working at the Phyllis Court Hotel. It was hilarious: none of us had ever done silver service before, let alone worked as waiters, and we were learning on the job. We all wore neat black and white clothes, and tied our long, straggly hair back in ponytails. Some foods, like potatoes, were relatively easy to serve, but peas and Brussel sprouts were difficult. Fortunately, most of the guests were elderly Northerners, taking a last break after the school holidays, and they were friendly and forgiving of our blunders.

It was a good life. We had two hours off between breakfast and lunch, and three between lunch and dinner, so there was plenty of time to swim in the sea, play on the beach, and enjoy the late summer sunshine. We also ate well, enjoying the same food as the guests at the end of each meal.

It was a magical time: walking hand in hand along the beach, waves lapping over our feet; watching the fiery sun sink into the water, the majestic flare of golden-red light that spread like a final gift over the western horizon and lit up our faces; the ever-changing colours and motion of the clouds; scuttling crabs and foraging birds; and the endless, restless magnificence of the sea.

I was happier and more content than I had ever been. Don was writing new songs and poetry every day, his creativity blossoming. I loved hearing each fresh creation. I told Don how I had believed that God was losing the war against evil when I was thirteen, and reading too many Dennis Wheatley books. I'd wanted to be on the winning side, and had seriously considered joining a coven of witches, if I could find one. I felt so differently now. God was definitely winning. The world was so heart-achingly beautiful, love was as endless and eternal as the ocean and my heart was flooded with gratitude.

One morning in October we woke to the sound of bells chiming all across town. I looked out the window. There had been a general election the previous day. Labour had won after thirteen years of Tory government. Harold Wilson was our new Prime Minister.

It felt like the bells were ringing in a new era. Hope had returned to our lives. Maybe we wouldn't all blow one another up after all. Maybe the world would grow kinder, and people would begin to value the real things in life: friendship, family, love, neighbourliness, rather than obsessing about new fridges, TV's and washing machines, or what Elizabeth Taylor and Richard Burton were doing, or how to get more of everything. That night there was a party in the Rising Sun. Don and Mac played until the early hours, scrumpy cider flowed freely, and the atmosphere glistened with new possibilities.

Don had been calling Pete Eden once a week, checking in how things were going. One day, near the end of October, he came back from his call excited and buzzing. It was time. Pete had booked the studio and Donovan would be making a record. There was even talk of a TV appearance on Ready Steady Go. Fame and fortune were beckoning. He left for London the following day.

Of course, I was excited and delighted for him. And yet...something in me sensed that our time together was over. I did not doubt our love for one another. It was young love, first love for me, and precious. But I could not imagine a place for me in his future. He needed to be free to fly, for his destiny to unfold as it was meant to. In essence he was a free spirit. We both were. And as free spirits we had to know when to let go. But how could I bear to be without him?

I stayed in Torquay for another week, but the magic had gone with Donovan's departure. I hitched home one cold November day. By the time I reached the junction with the A303 and the A30 the sky was dark and filled with stars. The night sky in November has a unique quality: clear and piercingly bright, carpeted with stars that beamed their light aeons ago.

I stood alone at the junction, Stonehenge a shadowy presence, and watched the majesty of the heavens: Ursa Minor and Ursa Major, Orion, and the Seven Sisters blinking and glimmering high above me. The river of the Milky Way streamed across the sky, speaking to me of eternity and my own tiny place in the great scheme of things. Out the corner of my eye I saw a streak of light. Turning I saw a brilliant light hovering above Stonehenge. It pulsed there for the space of a few breaths, then sped away like a streak of lightening. Had I just seen a flying saucer? Was it visitors from another planet? Observers of the Universe?

The first time I walked the streets of St Albans again I cried. Don's absence was like a wound, an empty space that sucked everything into it and left me drained of joy and enthusiasm. I found another job easily enough. I plodded through my days. I had no desire to go out, not even to meet up with Vicky, who was happy and in love with her latest man.

I called Geraldine's home. I'd been trying to contact her from Torquay, but her Mum told me she was still in St. Ives, so I was hoping she and Mick would work things out. Geraldine answered the phone. We met up the next day, after work. She told me that Mick had left, without a word, and she had no idea where he was. She was alone and scared, and over four months pregnant. She thought her parents would throw her out if she told them about the baby and she had no idea what to do. She planned on hiding it as long as she could.

In January 1965, Donovan appeared on Ready Steady Go, singing *Catch the Wind.* I put on a brave face in front of my family. Mum was really excited. That night I cried myself to sleep, and my pillow was still wet the following day. I'd heard from Vicky that Don was with Beverly now.

I found solace reading poetry about the pain of love. I discovered The Prophet, by Kahlil Gibran, and his words were a soothing balm for my aching heart.

> *When love beckons to you, follow him,*
> *Though his ways are hard and steep.*
> *And when his wings enfold you, yield to him,*
> *Though the sword hidden among his pinions may*
> *wound you.*[10]

I was glad I had followed love's call, and I recognised the alchemy of loss that was changing me, making me grow, and making me stronger. But it was so painful.

---

[10] Kahlil Gibran The Prophet p 10

Geraldine told her parents just after New Year, and they did throw her out. She went to a home for unmarried mothers in Brighton. I visited her there a couple of times. She was only allowed out for an hour at a time. We walked along the windy seafront. She was pale and looked smaller, apart from her swollen belly, she had somehow shrunk into herself.

She told me that all the pregnant girls had to scrub the hard stone floors on their hands and knees for hours on end. The nuns who ran the home were cold-hearted and mean-spirited. They saw it as their duty to ensure all the 'fallen women' paid for the sin of love, the sin of youth, and the nuns reminded them of their guilt and worthlessness all day, every day.

I last saw Geraldine when she was eight months pregnant. Her skin had lost its glow, her eyes were dull and hopeless. I begged her to stay in touch but I think it was all too much for her. I heard that the baby was adopted and Geraldine moved to Yorkshire.

I hope she had a good life. Like countless women before and after her, Geraldine gave herself whole-heartedly to love, and was left, wounded and alone, to deal with the consequences.

Life is a song. It has its own rhythm of harmony. It is a symphony of all things which exist in major and minor keys of Polarity. It blends the discords, by opposites, into harmony which unites the whole into a grand symphony of life. To learn through experience in this life, to appreciate the symphony and lessons of life, and to blend with the whole, is the object of our being here.

Dr Randolph Stone (1890 – 1981)

LONDON 1966

By the beginning of 1966, Vicky and I were feeling the pull of the big city again. We'd grown out of St. Albans, and it was time to realise our dream and move to London.

We found a wonderful flat in Powys Square, a garden square close to Portobello Road in the heart of Notting Hill. The flat was on the ground floor of an elegant Victorian house with high ceilings and ornate cornices. We had two big rooms, and a kitchen. The fact that the bath was also in the kitchen didn't faze us a bit. The front room, our 'sitting room', had wide bay windows overlooking the gardens of the square. The back room had three single beds, so we had space for another flatmate, if we wanted one.

We were nineteen and anything was possible. Finding work was easy. We earned good money working as temps in various offices. We went to a different club every weekend: Klooks Kleek, Eel Pie Island, The Scene, The Marquee.

Every Saturday we wandered the length of Portobello Road, which was fast becoming THE place to be on a Saturday morning. We discovered vintage clothes, feather boas, exotic jewellery and bric-a-brac on the fabulous stalls that sprang up overnight. We drank cider on the pavement outside pubs, or frothy coffee in friendly cafés. We chatted with strangers and made new friends. We were part of a growing 'scene.' We were London Girls.

I had my hair cut by Vidal Sassoon, a modern,

asymmetric style, shorter on one side with a sharply defined sweep just below my ear on the other. I loved it and knew I looked cool and trendy. I dyed my hair a rich shade of blue-black, which accentuated my green eyes. I bought a black Mary Quant dress, with laces at the front. I was very skinny and pulled the laces tight. I fell in love with a red and black coat in one of the shop windows in Oxford Street and saved up for it. The first day I wore it I bought a dramatic, wide brimmed red hat to complete my new look.

I also fell in love with a red and black Alpha Romeo Spider sports car, in a showroom in Shepherds Bush. I would stand outside that window and look at that car for ages, imagining the freedom of driving along country roads with the wind in my hair and not a care in the world. One day, I promised myself. One day.

Life was exciting and fun. Every day was filled with infinite possibilities: who might I meet in a chance encounter? What would I learn today? What role would I play this week as I walked the streets of London town, or worked in a new office? What new music would I hear that would open my mind and inspire new dreams?

Friends from St Albans started calling round. Eddie and Julian, from the Cock Inn days, moved to Earls Court and visited us regularly. Julian and Vicky had an on/off relationship in St Albans, and soon they were back together, and Vicky was in love. Julian was an artist and a musician. He looked a little like Mick Jagger, with his sensuous lips and his rubbery, mobile face. He was moody, cool and unpredictable. His sister, Veronica, also visited, and stayed every weekend, after a month she moved in with us. Veronica, with her long, long legs and short, short skirts, was light-hearted, full of energy and great fun. We met lots of people in Notting Hill, and soon our front room became a gathering place every weekend. We were at the heart of the action.

One of the great characters we met was Terry Taylor, a weathered looking guy in his thirties, who lived in Elgin Avenue and sold acid. LSD was legal, and Terry was one of the main dealers. Terry was well-travelled, and he told great stories about his visits to Morocco, Turkey, India and Kathmandu. Terry brought his empty LSD bottle round one Saturday night, washed it out with a little water, and squeezed a few drops directly onto our tongues.

That night Vicky and I took our first trip, not knowing what to expect, and surrounded by people we barely knew. I enjoyed it at first, the play of lights and colours, pulsing on and within everything, was fascinating. Then the people around me began to look strange, and slightly menacing. I went to the bathroom and the lino on the floor began to writhe, as the pattern turned into tiny snakes, slithering into and around one another. I gazed at it for what felt like hours, fascinated and horrified.

I tried going out for a walk, feeling a strong urge to be outside. At first the movement of the trees in the night breeze was a magical dance of living beings. The shimmer of every leaf held a message for me. The delicate grace of a branch against the night sky moved me to tears. But then the dark alleyways began to loom with ominous shadows. Stinking rubbish spilled from dustbins. A siren wailed in the distance and my heartbeat doubled. I went home and felt like an alien in my own skull. Nothing was familiar. Terry came over and held my hand. He re-assured me that everything was fine. He put some Indian music on and the room filled with dancing golden light. I closed my eyes and allowed the light and music to enter me, to fill me, and I relaxed and flowed with it into a lake of peace.

For weeks after that first trip, I found it hard to make conversation. There seemed to be nothing worth talking about. When I was in the local shops, I had no idea what to buy, everything looked different, and why would I need any of it? I had lost confidence in reality. I had seen that everything I thought was solid was in fact constructed of billions of moving, dancing particles of light. So, what was real? And what was the point of it all?

I took a couple more trips over the summer. I learned to make sure I was with people I knew and felt safe with. I enjoyed the sense of boundaries dissolving, the feeling of unity with everyone and everything, the sense of infinite expansion I felt. And yet I was also feeling an increased sense of unreality in everything I did. It's hard to put my fingers on, but a part of me was struggling. I had so many questions, yet I was not really sure what they were, and a lot of things I had thought were important to me now appeared empty, shallow and meaningless.

I could no longer handle being in an office, working on accounts. The hands of the clock moved in slow motion. Five minutes became an eternity. An hour was as long as a lifetime. I was SO BORED!

And so, I left. I had turned on and tuned in. Now I was dropping out. Searching for a new way to live my life. A way that was more harmonious and not dedicated to being a wage slave.

I found a job in Westbourne Grove, in a tiny café called the Safari Club. It was run by a West Indian guy called Rufus. My job was to arrive at 10.00 am, clean up, and prepare and serve lunch and drinks to the few customers who turned up. Rufus arrived around 1.00. He taught me how to cook a black pepper steak, and to make good coffee. The walls of the Safari Club were lined with African grasses and hung with painted wooded shields and spears, like relics of a safari in the jungle. It was a surreal place to work, but it suited my state.

My other job was walking three Alsatian dogs for a woman who lived in a big house on Ladbroke Grove. I have always been scared of dogs. I was terrorised by an Alsatian at the age of two, when we moved to St Albans. It knocked me down and stood over me, slathering. I had nightmares for years and crossed the road to avoid the only neighbourhood Alsatian. I have no idea why I took this job on. Maybe I wanted to prove something to myself, to overcome my childhood fears.

I collected the dogs at three o'clock every day and walked them to Kensington Park. They were big dogs and I could barely hold them. They kind of dragged me along the road and back again. Once I arrived back at Ladbroke Grove and a man was leaving the house. He looked guilty when he saw me. After that I wondered just what the woman was doing while I was walking her dogs.

Terry brought Graham round and we soon became good friends. Graham was an undergraduate at Oxford, he had a lively, enquiring mind and I enjoyed talking to him. Graham taught me to play backgammon, and I picked it up quickly, and won the third game we played. We were well matched, and I found our time together soothing and, in some ways, it helped me get a grip on reality again.

Another person I really connected with was Miss Simpkins, a very old lady who lived in the flat on the other side of the hallway from ours. I visited her occasionally. Her sitting room was so crowded with furniture and 'things,' that there was little room to move. She reminded me of a character from Dickens, Miss Haversham, without the tattered wedding dress. She had thin, wispy hair, a shrivelled, wrinkly face and she always dressed in faded cardigans that smelled of moth- balls.

Yet her eyes were bright and full of life and she fascinated me. She had a big Victorian bell jar, full of ferns, large chintzy chairs, and dusty pictures of women in crinolines and men in boater hats. I am pretty sure there was a sailing ship in a bottle as well. She served me tea in tiny china cups with matching saucers and offered me elegant biscuits on delicate plates. She told me stories about her life. I shared my dreams with her.

In the late summer we held a farewell party for Julian, who was setting off overland to India. Vicky was philosophical about his journey. She knew it was something he had to do, and she had total faith that he would return to her, once his travelling was done.

The flat was full of people, all the St Albans crowd, and most of our London mates. We danced and drank and partied most of the warm and muggy night. We opened all the windows and the party spilled onto the square.

Shortly before dawn the storm broke. Streaks of lightning flashed across the sky, followed by loud claps of thunder and torrential rain that thrummed on the windows and bounced off the pavements. I wanted to go out and dance in it, but I was too tired.

Everyone had left, apart from Eddie. Julian and Vicky had made their bed on the floor of the front room. Veronica was spending the night at her mates. Eddie stood in the doorway, about to walk home to West Kensington.

"You can't walk home in that," I said to him, looking up at the rain. "You can stay the night if you like. You can sleep in Veronica's bed."

He looked at me with relief. "Thanks, Joanna, I don't really fancy walking five miles now. And I would love to lay down. It's been quite a night!"

I laughed. "Really! I had no idea we could fit that many people in here." We settled in to our separate beds and I turned out the light.

I lay there in the dark, acutely aware of Eddie's presence in the room. I could hear every breath. I thought I would fall asleep as soon as my head hit the pillow. But I was strangely restless. The storm raged outside, making me feel tingly and intensely alive, as storms often do. "Are you asleep?" I asked him after some time.

"No. I can't sleep."

"Nor can I." The silence pulsed. We were both intensely aware of one another in the darkness.

"Joanna?"

"Yes, Eddie?"

"Can I get into bed with you?"

"Yes, I'd like that." I threw back the sheet and he climbed in with me. We snuggled down together and one thing led to another, as it does on a hot summer night.

We made love and it was like nothing I had ever experienced before. We fitted together perfectly, and every touch was tender and full of love. It felt so—right. As I lay in his arms afterwards a thought came unbidden to my mind: "This is the man you are going to marry."
This thought frightened the life out of me. I had never fancied Eddie. He was a lovely guy but he was not 'my type,'

whatever that was. He was also with Judy, a vivacious American girl. Besides, I had always thought of him as a mate. Never a lover. And I had no plans to get married anyway. I pushed the thought as far away as I could, and wriggled out of bed. "I'll get us some water," I said, wrapping myself in a shawl and walking into the kitchen.

By the time I returned Eddie was back in his own bed. As I handed him the water, he took hold of my hand. I sat down on the bed, beside him. His hand felt warm against my coolness. "Thank you, Joanna. That was…" he looked at me, and seemed as lost for words and as confused as I felt. I leaned over and kissed him on the forehead.

"Goodnight, Eddie. Sweet dreams." Then I turned out the light, climbed into my bed and fell asleep.

We saw one another again a week later, at an Indian Restaurant in Drayford Gardens, South Kensington. We were celebrating someone's birthday. Judy was there, Eddie's girlfriend. Eddie and I were friendly and natural with one another. There was no awkwardness between us, neither were there any unspoken messages. I think we had mutually decided not to mention that stormy summer night, when something inexplicable had happened between us.

Julian set off on his travels. Vicky was fine at first, but she became increasingly vague and forgetful. Sometimes she just didn't seem to be present. Instead of the quicksilver conversation we had always enjoyed, she was silent most of the time, and when she did respond to me it was in monosyllables. Vicky had lost her sparkle, and I had no idea how to help her regain it. I understood that she was missing Julian, but it felt deeper than that.

Even a night out at the Marquee didn't seem to help. We danced to the driving R&B beat of Long John Baldry and his band, but it felt like we were going through the motions. Somehow, we were not connecting either with each other or the music. Everything felt empty, shallow, somehow tawdry and desperate.

The weather changed at the end of September and

the skies were grey day after day. Portobello Road market was not so much fun in the pouring rain.

Vicky was unable to work. She was too lost inside herself. It was probably the acid. All around us there were casualties of LSD. One guy had jumped out of a second-floor window, thinking he could fly. He had broken his spine and was in a wheelchair for the rest of his life. Several people had completely lost it, and were monged out on Largactyl, or in a psychiatric unit. One girl had gone into a catatonic state and nobody could get through to her. She lay on her bed, day after day, staring at the ceiling.

Of course, there were a lot of people thriving on LSD, creating fabulous music, inspirational poetry and mind-blowing art. The Psychedelic Revolution had begun and everything was changing. However, I felt the need for home comforts. I was worried about Vicky, and, in truth, feeling a little lost and confused myself. I had no idea what life was all about, and I was tired of trying to figure it all out.

In the first week of October Rufus told me he could no longer afford to employ me. Two days later I quit the dog-walking job. We gave in our notice and decided to go home to our parents for a few months.

While we were waiting for the Green-line bus to St Albans at Marble Arch, Vicky just wandered out into the busy road. I darted out after her and pulled her back to the pavement. Her eyes were glazed. "Vicky, Vicky, what were you thinking?" I asked, my arms around her.

She shook her head, looking surprised. "I don't know, Joanna. I honestly have no idea what just happened." Tears welled in her eyes and rolled down her cheeks, unheeded. I held her in my arms, trying to convince both her and myself that everything would be fine. The bus pulled in. I loaded our bags on and we rode out of London and back to St. Albans. Vicky perked up a bit once we were back in the countryside, and seemed almost normal when we parted to catch the buses back to our parent's homes. We were both quite good at putting on an act of 'being normal.' We needed to protect ourselves with this act.

We had to live with our parents again. And we needed to re-assure them that we were okay, both for their sakes and our own. But we were not okay. Nothing felt real. The TV was ridiculous, raucous characters shouting and laughing at jokes that were not remotely funny. Our lives had shrunken back to their childhood proportions, back in our bedrooms, eating our mother's cooking, sitting with the family in the evening, trying to appear interested. But we were no longer children and this life did not fit us. We had grown out of it. Yet we were stuck in some kind of limbo, where we needed to retreat from the confusion of life and seek safe harbour—to recover our strength and sanity, to gather ourselves back together, to process what had happened, and prepare ourselves for what would happen next.

I found a job in an office. I hated it but needed the money. And I began to knit. Throughout the winter I knitted myself a new wardrobe: a bright red minidress and matching tights, in three-ply wool on tiny needles; a jumper with a modern art pattern on the front, which required intense concentration and used eight different colours; and a long, stripy dress in green and orange. Knitting helped me find myself again. Knitting was real: the clickety-clack of the needles, the comforting feel of the wool spooling out from the ball, the satisfying growth of the garment, the focus on the complicated patterns. Knitting kept me sane.

Vicky and I met up twice a week, and she also began to settle back into herself. She even started knitting as well. When the news came in early December, that Julian had been busted in Istanbul, and was sentenced to two years jail in Ankara, she did not fall apart. She found her strength again and wrote encouraging letters to him. She wanted to move back to London and find work, so she could save up and visit him. I decided to move back with her.

In early January, 1967, we found a small flat in West Hampstead. We were back in London!

Everything in the universe has a rhythm, everything dances.
Maya Angelou (1928-2014)

LONDON 1967

Friday night was UFO night, the best night of the week. Tonight, as we had every Friday for the past five weeks, Vicky and I chose clothes that the liquid lights would bring to flowing life as we danced and make us part of the mesmeric visual experience that was UFO. My favourite dress was one I'd made myself, from a length of sunset coloured, tie-dye silk. The look was floaty and colourful. We walked the short distance to Hampstead Station and jumped on a Northern Line train to Tottenham Court Road, talking non-stop all the way.

UFO, which stands for Unidentified Flying Objects, opened shortly after we moved back to London, in January 1967. By mid-February we were recognised as regulars, and often let in for free, no doubt because we were such great dancers.

We joined the line of people on the steps which led down to the UFO club. Every time the door opened the thrum of music and the tang of beer, smoke, and humans leaked up to us, which only added to the sense of excitement and anticipation. And then we were in, immersed in the colours and sounds of the psychedelic revolution that was unfolding around us. A Marilyn Monroe movie was on the screen behind the stage. Multi-coloured globules of liquid light danced to a dissonant cacophony of notes, and a visceral bass rhythm vibrated through the floor and our bodies.

We moved through the darkness, weaving our way around swaying dancers and static groups of people, settling into the unique feel of UFO: a club where anything could happen, and often did; where art and music explored uncharted ground, and where nothing mattered more than freedom.

The music gave way to a deep male voice reading a poem by William Burroughs. The words danced in my brain;

inciting images more vivid than a Disney film.

Pink Floyd exploded into their first set. I lifted off, like a rocket bound for outer space, dropping all that tethered me to planet Earth as I reached for the stars. Dancing to Pink Floyd was like flying straight to heaven: heady, transcendent and euphoric. I moved with a free and sinuous grace, like a willow tree in a summer breeze. Bubbles of pulsing lights played across my body. I lost myself completely in the music and the ever-changing patterns of light, until night surrendered to day once more.

We caught the night bus to Hampstead, and walked home, shivering against the cold February wind. Our two-room flat in West Hampstead was very basic: a sitting room/ kitchen and a bedroom with two single beds, but it was ours, and we were back in London and loving every minute of it. We were working for temp agencies again and earning good money. The weeks were a blur, we lived for the weekends and every weekend began at UFO. Pink Floyd were the resident group and their experimental and cosmic sound expressed everything I thought and felt: the wonders of inner and outer space, the yearning for something indefinable, the intoxication of rhythm and movement, and the anarchic anger of a generation that demanded change.

We, the post-war generation, were on the cusp of a revolution, an expansion of consciousness that would herald in a new age: The Age of Aquarius. The age of the elite white-mans' establishment was drawing to a close. It was time to move from war to peace, from patriarchy to equality, from fear and greed to love and generosity.

The times they were a-changin' indeed. And right here, in London, we were at the heart of it. We gathered in pubs, clubs and coffee shops and inspired one another with our visions for the future. We read Ginsberg and Huxley, Leary and Laing. We were opening the *Doors of Perception*. We were breaking down the walls that failed to box us in. We even had our own newspaper, the International Times, a source of information and inspiration that fired up our imaginations and encouraged us to act for change.

And music was our clarion call: The Beatles and the Byrds, Jefferson Airplane and the Grateful Dead. Every song fuelled the fires of change and gave witness to the blurring boundaries of reality that many of us were experiencing: John Lennon summed it all up with his classic lines in *Tomorrow Never Knows: Turn off your mind, relax and float downstream .... it is not dying...*

On February 12 Mick Jagger was arrested. On March 9 the International Times office was raided. The Establishment was fighting back, trying to silence us. A symbolic funeral was hastily convened. On Saturday March 11 a creatively-dressed group of us escorted a coffin carrying the symbolic corpse of 'International Times' and 'Freedom of Speech' along Whitehall and onto the Circle Line. Taking the coffin underground represented burial. Re-birth occurred when we triumphantly emerged at Notting Hill station and processed along Portobello Road. We sang and danced and celebrated freedom. By the time we reached Elgin Avenue there were hundreds of us. It felt like a revolution. We were taking our power into our hands. We would not be silenced and shut away. Passers-by looked at us in amazement. We were breaking new ground, making a stand for our rights. It was a heady, intoxicating feeling, and I wanted more of it.

I was riding a great wave of change and deeply grateful to be young and living in London in 1967. Finally, I had found people who felt and thought as I did. For most of my life I had felt that I was dancing to a different drum from everyone around me, apart from Vicky, Donovan, and some of our friends from the Cock. It was like being a member of a lost tribe, occasionally discovering a few stragglers and then miraculously re-uniting with the entire tribe. Suddenly, limitless possibilities opened up. A 'brave new world' based on love and co-operation. A life of freedom. An explosion of creativity.

LSD had its part to play, but it was a means to an end, rather than an end in itself. Its main role was as a key, which opened the door to higher consciousness, that Huxley had described so vividly. One friend put it very succinctly when he told me about his trip:

"I saw that everything in my world, everything that I had taken for granted as being solid, real, and totally present, was made up of constantly changing particles, pulses of light and colour. It was like seeing every electron in every atom, all orbiting around the nucleus in a chaotic yet perfect pattern. Then I found a place of total calm and stillness at the heart of the chaos, a place filled with light. All I wanted was to stay in that peace and stillness forever. As soon as I had that thought I heard a voice saying: 'Congratulations. Now go back and do it the hard way.'"

My friend knew that the 'hard way' for him was to begin his spiritual journey in earnest. He recognised that he'd had a spiritual experience, and he was reading every book he could find about spiritual awakening, meditation and yoga. Many of us were experimenting with different philosophies. We were looking to the East, which had a wealth of knowledge about the nature of reality and consciousness.

I discovered the I Ching, an ancient book of wisdom from the times of Confucius. It was both an oracle and a fountain of poetic wisdom. Every time I consulted it, the words that I read opened up my inner windows, so a little more light could enter. The words were timeless and filled with imagery: the gentle wind, the creative heaven, the joyous lake, the receptive Earth. I instinctively understood the concepts of yin and yang, the yielding, feminine nature of yin, like water that flows around all obstacles and yet has great strength, and the creative, male force of yang, solid and immovable.

My favourite was chapter 24, Return (The Turning Point.) I read and re-read these words, which made my mind expand into lakes of awareness:

The light principle returns: thus the hexagram counsels turning away from the confusion of external things, turning back to one's inner light. There, in the depths of the soul, one sees the Divine, the One.

(Chapter 24, p 504)

Then, one night at UFO I heard Syd Barrett sing: *All movement is accomplished in six stages, and the seventh brings return.* It was such a moment of affirmation, we were all on the same page, Chapter 24 to be precise, and going for the One.

My study of the I Ching also taught me to appreciate the constant flow of change, the permanent state of flux that is the essence of all. I had mind-blowing glimpses of a reality that I can only describe as being and non-being. I had flashes of understanding of the principles of quantum physics, how every particle in existence is a constantly shifting form.

How wonderful it is that modern physicists are now confirming the same truth that the sages and great beings of the East discovered, through inner travel, centuries ago: that everything is a manifestation of Supreme Consciousness.

I met a guy called Adam at UFO and we became close. He was good looking, in a lean, gangly, pale faced kind of way, and his grey eyes were deep set and hooded, which gave him an enigmatic look. He was around ten years older than me.

Adam was involved with a spiritual organisation called Subud. The movement was founded by Bapak, and originated in Java, Indonesia, in the mid-1930s. The word Subud stands for *susila, budhi* and *dharma*, which are from the Sanskrit language. Adam told me that the essential meaning was unity, or being one, living life in harmony with the energies of creation. It sounded good to me, so I went along with him to a meeting, called *latihan*, in Westbourne Park Grove.

It was like nothing I had ever experienced: a room filled with people wailing, singing, speaking in tongues, shaking, dancing or sitting in stillness in the midst of total chaos. And such a mix of people: tall, turbaned Sikhs and tiny Caucasian women, smart office workers and beaded hippies, almond-eyed women and white-haired men. A complete cross-section of London life was present in that room. Adam told me they were 'letting the spirit move through them.' Everyone was expressing themselves with total abandon and freedom.

At first, I felt shy, and merely watched. "Join in," Adam said, "let yourself go." He proceeded to do just that, and within a few minutes he was swaying from side to side, eyes closed and a big grin on his face.

I moved over to a space near the wall, closed my eyes and breathed in. The noise was overwhelming. I kept opening my eyes to see what was happening. A large man nearby threw back his head and howled like a wolf, tears streaming down his face. After some time, I felt a glimmering of energy moving through me and I was also aware of a strange inner stillness, in spite of the chaos around me.

The following Friday night Adam and I met up at UFO and we both took LSD. When the trip took off, I was unsure that I wanted to stay at UFO, it felt too much. Adam suggested I repeat 'I am Subud' to myself. I found this helped to ground me as the trip and the surreal combination of coloured blobs and bubbles of light on the screen, screaming women on the movie and the driving heartbeat of the music created a free-fall of chaotic impressions that swirled and clashed in my consciousness. It was a strange night.

A few weeks later Adam invited me to meet Bapak at Alexandra Palace. I decided to go along out of curiosity more than anything else. I was open to any experience life offered me, and never even considered consequences. The hall at Alexandra Palace was full of people, and yet the atmosphere was calm and peaceful. I was fascinated to see hundreds of different people gathered under one roof: people of all ages, backgrounds and nationalities.

Bapak gave a short talk from the stage and then he was walking amongst us. The men and women stood on separate sides of the hall. I was close to a huddle of beautiful young Indonesian women. I met the gaze of one woman, her almond-shaped eyes were a deep warm brown and full of laughter. We smiled shyly at one another.

Suddenly Bapak was with us. He stood in front of me, a small, brown-skinned man with bright eyes and an aura of intense energy. He lay his hand on my head, very briefly, and moved on to the group of women nearby.

The moment Bapak touched me, a huge surge of energy soared through me like a flame, from the base of my spine to the crown of my head. I was filled with fire, a divine heat that was both light and joy and immensely cleansing and liberating. I began moving my body in total freedom and ecstasy. I was dancing with the atoms of the air, singing with the song of the wind. I was free and yet united with everything around me.

My breathing slowed, everything became still, silent. I felt myself floating above my body, observing the play of light, hearing the sounds of people as if from a vast distance. Then I was back in my body, breathing and present, yet aware of a new lightness and stillness. A calm, still point that felt an essential part of me, and somehow made me feel invulnerable. I felt intensely alive, refreshed, renewed, and awake. I shook my head, wondering what had just happened. I looked around me, and everything seemed the same, and yet different, brighter, more defined.

Sometime later Adam found me and we travelled back on the bus to his flat. I knew I was in an altered state, and I was quietly enjoying it. I really wanted to be alone and to explore what was happening within me. But Adam was insistent, and it was too late for me to travel home alone. We shared a bed and he made love to me that night. I felt invaded. As if my skin and all that kept me separate from the world and defined who I was had melted away, leaving me vulnerable and exposed.

Had I been older, wiser, and more confident, I would have protected myself. Had he been more considerate, he would have left me alone. The combination of a spiritual opening and sex left me confused for weeks. It was hard to define my boundaries, to know the difference between love, lust, and the delicate buds of awareness that were newly forming within me.

I decided to go to *latihan* once a week. I bought a book by Bapak and read that the aim of *latihan* was 'becoming more and more you.' So, I decided to simply surrender myself to the experience, and ignore the nagging voices of doubt and British reticence that were holding me back. I really enjoyed *latihan* after that, finding a peacefulness and sense of inner calm even in the midst of the chaos of noise and movement. Soon Vicky also joined Subud and we attended *latihan* together every Wednesday night.

And every Friday night we danced at UFO. Danced to the best psychedelic bands in the UK: Pink Floyd, Arthur Brown and Soft Machine. Lost ourselves in fabulous light shows. Watched avant-garde movies and heard poetry that set our minds spinning. Being at UFO was a sensory overload. One night we were queueing on the steps to get into UFO, and a big car drew up to the kerb. A young man climbed out, walked up to our small group, and asked: "Would any of you like to be in a movie? We are filming now, near here, and will have you back in around an hour."

" What's the film about?" The guy beside us asked.

"It's an art film, directed by Yoko Ono. Who wants to come?"

Vicky and I looked at each other, and simultaneously responded: "We will." We clambered into the back, along with a few others. The car was huge and eight of us fitted in comfortably. Soon we arrived at a studio, where a small Japanese woman with long black hair welcomed us. She explained that she was making a film about bottoms. She wanted to show the beauty, symmetry and individuality of many bottoms. If we wanted to be part of this film, we were invited to strip from the waist down and walk for a minute or so on a moving dais. Our posteriors would be filmed close-up, and then we would dress and be taken back to UFO. It seemed a strange thing to do for art's sake, but we couldn't see any harm in it, and, as we were there anyway, we may as well go for it. So, we did.

Walking in the same spot for a minute, bare bottomed and British, feeling hot lights on your naked butt, and a mixture of embarrassment and avant-garde go-for-it-ness, was an unforgettable and unique experience.

Watching the film months later was also very odd. I

was amazed how different everyone's butt is, and, surprisingly, I had no idea whatsoever which one was mine.

We discovered the Macrobiotic Restaurant in Westbourne Park Road and it soon became our regular place to eat out. It was run by two brothers, American guys called Craig and Greg Sams, who had left the USA because of the unjust war the US was waging in Vietnam.

I decided to become vegetarian. I thought a lot about the phrase 'you are what you eat.' I really took it to heart, and it changed my attitude to food. I had felt uncomfortable about eating meat for some time. When I learned about the macrobiotic principles of the energy in food, based on yin and yang, I realised that I did not want to have the energy of an animal that had lived in captivity and died in terror in my body. I wanted to eat live, healthy food, to nourish both my mind and body with high vibrations, not bring myself down with dark ideas and heavy flesh.

Macrobiotic food was clean and wholesome. I learned how to cook brown rice, how to value the nutrients in vegetables and not overcook them, to enjoy nuts and seed. I discovered the thick tongue-sticking tang of tahini, the salty delight of tamari and the eye-scrunching umami satisfaction of an umeboshi plum.

Summer was a whirl of colour, music, freedom and discovery: happenings at the Round House, festivals in the park, marches and demos in which we disarmed angry policemen with the gift of a flower, shopping at Biba's, psychedelic t-shirts and flowery dresses, men with moustaches and long hair, women in flowing skirts and Indian dresses, beads and bangles, bells and bongs, hippies and head shops, talking 'til dawn, dancing barefoot on the grass as the sun rose. Loving life, the moon and stars, nature and everyone I met.

It was also a time of protest. A time to stand up for what we believe: the rights of Black people everywhere, an end to the war in Vietnam, the inalienable right of every person to be free, the miraculous power of LOVE. "All we need is love," John Winston Lennon sang, and we sang along with him, and believed the world would change.

Vicky and I continued to go to *latihan*. One week, near the end of June, we went every night. We were only supposed to go once a week. Vicky had booked her Magic Bus to Ankara for early July. She had made contact with a Subud family in Ankara, who had invited her to stay with them for a while. She planned to visit Julian first, see what Ankara was like and maybe rent a room near the prison, so she could visit him regularly and wait for his release.

We were so energised by our fifth night of *latihan* that we ran all the way from Westbourne Grove to Kensington Gardens, then ran round the pond and collapsed, laughing, on the grass. We were euphoric, buzzing with energy and joy. I knew she would be safe, even though she was setting off, alone, into the unknown. She had Subud. She would be protected.

After Vicky left, I rented a tiny room near Holland Park. It was more a broom cupboard really. The bed folded up into the wall, there was just about enough room to get undressed when the bed was down, and I had to share a bathroom. But it was very quiet. With the white walls and floaty white muslin curtains, it felt like a peaceful haven. I had never lived alone before.

The East West Centre was very near, and the Macrobiotic Restaurant had moved to Holland Park, so I had places nearby where I could hang out and meet people. I walked a lot in Holland Park, met up with friends for a meal or a drink, went to clubs and danced, had fleeting relationships that never meant much to me, worked, wrote and read books of poetry, books about the New Age that was dawning. I didn't like sitting in my tiny cupboard room to read, so I sat in the park, or in café's.

One weekend I set out to visit several friends and acquaintances, but none of them were in. I got soaked in a sudden rain shower as I walked across Wimbledon Common and arrived home bedraggled and alone.

As the leaves began to turn bronze and gold, I realised that I felt hollow, drained. The 'Summer of Love' was over and had left me empty, rather than full. I felt unsure of everything, where once I had been so confident. My own company began to feel insufficient. At times the aloneness I had been treasuring shifted into a bleak feeling of loneliness.

One wet day in late October I woke up struggling to breath. I squirted my pump into my lungs but found no relief. By lunch time my heart was beating like a frightened bird in the cage of my ribs. I called the doctor and was admitted to St Mary's Hospital, Praed Street, Paddington with a severe asthma attack. I've had asthma all my life and was very ill as a child. By the time I was fourteen I was convinced that I would not live beyond the age of thirty and had vowed to accept with both hands any opportunities life offered me. I'd had a brief respite from asthma since I'd reached sixteen, and here it was, back again to limit my fun.

During my five days in hospital, Eddie visited me. His skin was tanned from his travels in Morocco. His hair was longer and he sported a fine moustache. He brought me a bunch of dark purple grapes, silvery with bloom. His blue eyes looked full of concern. He sat beside my bed and something happened as I looked at him. I felt love, spreading through me, as warm and reassuring as it was sudden and unexpected. I was just about to reach out and hold his hand, when Veronica arrived, full of energy, enthusiasm and chatter. It was lovely to see her, and yet I kind of wished I was still alone with Eddie. When the two of them left, at the end of visiting time, I had an unwelcome premonition that they would get together.

Sure enough, when I returned to my parent's home once more, too ill to cope with life alone in London, Veronica told me she was 'having a scene' with Eddie. I struggled not to be disappointed. But I was. I had seen him in a different light, as he'd sat beside my hospital bed, and I knew I wanted to be with him. But now he was with my friend. I shrugged to myself. Just something else I would have to adjust to.

It took me six weeks to recover. I read Lord of the

Rings and immersed myself in Middle Earth, escaping from a world which no longer felt fun.

On Christmas Eve, Eddie called and invited me to go to a party with him. He told me that he and Veronica had parted ways, amicably, after a few weeks. Warm, sweet honey flowed through my veins.

The party was noisy and drunken, with bad music and naff food. But it was good to be with Eddie, we danced a bit, then went for a long walk. "Did you enjoy travelling?" I asked him.

"Blew my mind. I was robbed of everything in the first few days. By the time I left Tangier, all I had were the clothes on my back and the price of a bus fare to Marrakesh."

"Wow! That must have been tough."

"It was a baptism by fire," he laughed, taking hold of my hand.

"What did you do?"

"I learned to survive. It's a great University of Life, Morocco. I made some good friends on the Street of the Sandal-makers. They were good guys, simple and sweet, and they looked after me." His hand was warm in mine. Snow began to fall, soft and gentle.

"Tell me about the sandal makers," I asked him.

"They were like brothers to me. They make sandals from old tyres and scraps of leather. Each guy has a little shed, and they sit on low stools, or cross-legged on the floor, and stitch everything by hand. They pray five times a day, and they say 'inshallah', or 'hamdullah' every other sentence."

"What does that mean?"

"Inshallah means God willing. Hamdullah means thanks to God. They are such devout people. Genuinely. Not putting on an act. They live from day to day, if they sell a pair of shoes, they eat well, if they don't, they cope. I learned to live in the present from them and I brought them customers."

"I'd love to go to Morocco."

"You should. I am going back in January. I can't wait to get back there."

"Are you travelling alone?"

"Maybe. Dave and Jacky are also thinking of going, so I may drive down with them in their Deux Chevaux." We took shelter beneath a big oak tree. A single snowflake had landed on Eddie's moustache and was silently melting. My eyes were on his lips. We stood very close and he put his arms around me, and then our lips met and his warmth spread through me. We fitted perfectly together, there was no awkwardness, just a natural melding of our two bodies. He felt like home to me.

A week later, we went to see Liz Taylor and Richard Burton in 'The Tale of the Shrew' at the Odeon in St Albans. We sat in the back row and didn't take a lot of notice of the movie. "Can I come to Morocco with you?" I asked him. "Just as travelling companions, like brother and sister?"

He gave me a strange look. "Brother and sister?"

I met his eyes, "Look, I really want to travel and I don't want to go alone. I like you, a lot, but I don't want to rush into anything. Let's be mates, and travelling companions, and see what happens? I really don't want to spend the winter here, and I would love to go to Morocco with you and Dave and Jacky. What do you think?"

"Well, we're good mates, and there's room for one more, so why not? I don't know about the 'brother and sister' thing though. I don't think of you as a sister." He kissed me, long and warm and tender.

Who was I kidding? "I don't really think of you as a brother either," I said, laughing.

We sailed to Calais on January 15, 1968, in Dave's beat up but trusty Citroen.

People say that the soul, on hearing the song of creation,
entered the body, but in reality, the soul itself was the song.
                                        Hafiz (1320-1390)

MOROCCO 1968

The Citroen Deux Chevaux chugged valiantly across France and struggled over the Pyrenees. Eddie, Jacky and I often had to get out and push it up the steeper slopes. We had a lot of fun: we sang all our favourite songs, practiced our French on bemused villagers, laughed at the disapproving looks we received from staid matrons in Spanish hotels when we asked for double rooms; gazed in awe at snow-capped mountains and arid plains, orange trees and olive groves.

We crested yet another mountain, rounded a sharp bend and suddenly the most incredible view lay before us— the city of Malaga, glittering in the sunlight like a multi-faceted jewel, beyond the city the Mediterranean Sea sparkled, blue as sapphire, and on the far horizon, a purplish haze that might, just might, be our first glimpse of Africa.

Dave turned off the engine and we coasted down the hill to save fuel, enjoying the spice of danger as the car navigated the twisting turns of the road like a roller-coaster.

A few hours later we drove off the ferry from Algeciras and into Ceuta, the Spanish outpost in Morocco. Once we left Ceuta the scenery changed. We drove on dusty roads, past simple single-story dwellings with flat rooves. Flocks of goats meandered along the roadside, grazing on the sparse scrub. Men, dressed in djellabas, long robes with hoods, sat around tables in roadside cafes, talking, or playing board games. A few women worked in the fields.

We arrived in Tangier as the sun was setting fire to the western sky. A young boy banged on our window, demanding baksheesh. A man in a bright red Fez stepped in front of the car, forcing Dave to stop. "You want good hotel?" he asked. "Follow me, I take you."

"Cheap hotel," Dave said, winding down the window.

"But good as well," Jacky added.

"Don't follow him, man," Eddie said. "I know a good hotel. This guy will just rip us off."

Dave shook his head and wound the window up. He steered slowly through streets crowded with people, donkeys laden with straw panniers full of vegetables, and groups of children, many of the girls with younger siblings tied to their backs. We soon became accustomed to the constant clamour. We waved back at the kids, signalled no to the would-be guides, avoided the dogs and donkeys and finally pulled up in front of a small guest house.

From our room I could just see the sea, if I strained my neck out the window. We were in Tangier! I wanted to go out and explore, but everyone else wanted to eat, shower and sleep, so I reluctantly agreed.

I woke early the following morning. Eddie was fast asleep. I dressed and decided to go for a walk on the beach. The sun was low in the sky, and it was still cool. I walked barefoot, at the edge of the sea, the waves warm as they lapped gently over my ankles. The beach was empty, apart from a few fishermen dealing with the early morning catch. I was enjoying the silence and stillness, when a young boy joined me.

"Hello, Madam," he said. "How are you?"

I looked down at him, and smiled. He smiled back, and his face lit up. "I'm good thanks, and you?"

"I am also very good. Are you from England?" His eyes were a deep shade of hazel. He wore striped shorts and a tee-shirt, and I guessed he was around eight.

"Yes, I live near London."

"Oh, I would like so much to visit London one day," he said.

"Well, maybe you will. Your English is very good. Do you learn at school?"

"Yes, and I also speak French and a little German."

"Goodness."

"When did you arrive in Tangier, Madam?"

"You can call me Joanna, I don't really feel like a 'madam,' and I arrived last night."

"Thank you, Joanna. My name is Hassan. It's your first

time here?" I smiled at him again, he was cute, and I was enjoying his company. We'd walked a fair way along the shore by now. I stopped walking and looked back at Tangier, seeing it properly for the first time, set against the backdrop of an azure sky and turquoise sea, its white buildings gleaming in the bright sunlight.

"Pleased to meet you, Hassan. Yes, first time. It is very beautiful."

"It is beautiful where you live also?"

"Yes, and very different, colder, greener, the sky is not so blue, nor the sea so warm."

"This sea is very warm. Will you swim?"

"Maybe, I hope so. It depends what my friends want to do."

"Where are your friends?"

"They are asleep still, at the hotel."

"Look, here is my home. You can come in and meet my mother." He pointed to a low apartment building on the edge of the beach.

"Thank you, Hassan, but no, I should go back now, my friends will wake up soon."

He took hold of my hand and gazed up at me, his eyes huge and pleading. "Please come, Joanna. My mother will be so happy to meet you. You could have some mint tea with us, and a little yoghurt. You must be hungry by now."

I suddenly realised that I was hungry, and the thought of mint tea in a local home was very tempting. It would be good to meet a Moroccan woman, Hassan could interpret for me. It would be an adventure, and I would have a lot to tell Eddie about when I returned. "Okay, Hassan. You've persuaded me. Are you sure your mother won't mind?"

"Quite sure," he said. "She'll be very happy." Hassan led me up two flights of stairs into his home. His mother was out, but his father, a small man wearing a green and white striped djellaba, welcomed me and invited me to sit on the sofa. The sitting room was large, with a big window facing the sea. I noticed that the television was still covered in clear plastic. Every shelf was crammed with ornaments and pictures. A large gilt-framed picture of Mecca hung on one wall. Hassan brought me some sweet mint tea and a plate of small, home-made biscuits. "My mother will soon be here," he said, sitting beside me and taking one of the biscuits.

After around ten minutes there was a knock at the door and another three men arrived. They joined Hassan's dad, whose name I had already forgotten, in the kitchen. I sipped my tea and began to feel tired. Maybe I should go back and sleep some more.

The men joined us in the sitting room. One of them took out a small clay pipe with a long, thin handle. He took a pack of green kif out of his pocket, packed some into the pipe, lit it and passed it to me. I was too embarrassed to refuse it, so I took a quick draw, then passed it back to him. He refused it and indicated that I should smoke it all. I held the smoke in for a moment and released it as I breathed out. My head felt cloudy already.

I sipped the rest of my tea, and ate another biscuit, while the men shared several pipes. "When is your mother coming, Hassan?" I asked. "I should get back to my friends now."

"I will go and get her, please do not leave before she is here. She will be very sad to miss you." And he left. I leaned my head back against the sofa, feeling very drowsy.

I don't think I fell asleep, but something happened to the time and, when I opened my eyes, it was much later, so maybe I did. I stood up, feeling groggy, and went to the bathroom.

When I came out one of the men was standing outside the bathroom door, blocking my way. He grabbed me and tried to kiss me. I pushed him away, but he held me close. I felt the heat of his body pressing into me, and I struggled to get free from the hard grip of his arms. I suddenly realised how stupid I'd been, and the danger I was in. Fear flooded through me, bringing with it a surge of adrenaline, and I pushed harder against the man who was holding me. I was vaguely aware of the other men behind him. I had to escape.

"J'ai une bebe," I cried, unsure whether I was saying 'I'm having a baby,' which was my intention, or 'I am a baby.' I was hoping that if they thought I was pregnant they would let me go.

My voice rose, along with my panic. Beneath the shrillness of my "J'ai une bebe," I could hear the rumble of their male voices. The guy holding me backed off and I ran to the front door, opened it, flew down the stairs and out into the glaring sunlight and heat. What had happened to the day?

Tangier glimmered in the distant heat-haze, like a mirage and I started walking along the beach towards it. My heart was pounding in my throat and I kept looking behind me, afraid they were following me. My legs felt like lead as I dragged against the sucking pull of the sand. Sweat dripped down my back and my head throbbed. I wondered whether they had slipped something into the tea... or the biscuits? Hassan was just a slimy little con artist, working the beach for stupid, naive tourists like me. I wanted to kick myself, but didn't have the energy.

Suddenly a huge guy appeared from nowhere in front of me. I stopped in my tracks and stared at him. His big arms reached out for me and I ducked beneath them and tried to run away, but he caught me and threw me to the sand. I screamed, loudly, as I fell, and drew my knees up to my chest, trying to create a barrier between us as his body dropped onto mine. I fought with a strength I never knew I had. I was utterly determined that I was not going to be raped. No way. Some part of me silently called out for help as I felt the weight of him push me into the sand, his hot hands pushing my legs apart. I screamed again and one of his hands smothered my face. I kicked and struggled with every ounce of my strength.

And then I heard other voices, calling out urgently in French, felt the thump of feet, running on sand. Hands pulled him off me and a kindly face in a police uniform helped me to my feet. "Ca va, madam?" The policeman asked politely, his eyes wrinkling in concern.

"Oui, merci," I said, panting with relief, and slightly dazed.

"Comment t'appelles tu?"

"Je s'appelle Joanna Jenkins," I replied.

"Ah, nous vous cherchez," he said. The policeman spoke rapidly in Moroccan to his two companions, who had hand-cuffed the man who'd attacked me. They marched the man towards the road and escorted me back to the hotel, where Eddie paced anxiously outside.

"Oh, thank God you are safe," he said. "Where the hell did you go? Are you alright?"

"I'm sorry," I said. "I just went for a walk on the beach."

"This is Tangier, Joanna, not Southend. It's not safe for a woman to go out alone here."

"Yes, I realise that now," I snapped. I was beginning to feel very shaky.

"Merci, monsieur," Eddie said to the Policeman, who was looking on with some amusement. Eddie signed some paperwork and the two men shook hands. I felt small, stupid and vulnerable.

"Au revoir, Madam, soyez plus prudent a l'avenir.

I nodded, feeling sheepish. "Au revoir monsieur. Merci beaucoup."

We went back to our room. "Are you really okay?" Eddie asked.

"Yes, but I could do with a hug." He wrapped me in his arms and the tension of the past hours dissolved. I started to cry. Not huge, shoulder-shaking sobs, but tears of grief and relief. "That could have been so much worse," I said.

"I'm glad it wasn't."

"Did you call the police?"

"Yes. When I woke up and you weren't there, I went out to find you. When there was still no sign of you by lunch time, I asked the hotel to call the police."

"I'm glad you did. They rescued me on the beach. If they hadn't come at that moment..." I started crying again, and he held me close.

"You must have a guardian angel looking out for you. Shh, it's okay now. You're safe." I hugged him tight, finally relaxing and allowing the nightmare to slip away. "Shall we go and find some food?" He asked.

"Yes, please," I said, wiping my eyes and blowing my nose. "That was a strange way to begin our journey."

"Well, at least you learned not to go out without me." I nodded, but felt a slight qualm at the realisation that I was no longer safe to move around freely.

After three days in Tangier, we'd had enough of the constant hustling and clamour every time we went out. Dave and Jacky wanted to travel to Casablanca, while Eddie and I wanted to go straight to Marrakesh, so we decided to go our separate ways. We had been good travelling companions, but now we wanted to begin our own adventures.

We caught the early bus and arrived in Marrakesh eleven bumpy hours later. The first we saw of Marrakesh was the dark tower of El Koutoubia, silhouetted against the rose-purple twilight sky. The first sound I heard, as I stepped off the bus, was the Mullah calling the faithful to prayer. The air was infused with the scents of cedar, spice, leather, woodsmoke and something I could not define, something exotic which I later came to call the fragrance of the desert: hot, dusty and vibrant with promise.

Eddie grinned like a Cheshire cat, happy to be back in his favourite city. He looked completely at home. He led me along narrow streets, confident as a local, and stopped outside an ancient ironwork gate, set into an elegant blue and white tiled arch that could easily have graced the Alhambra. He pulled on the bell and we waited. Soon a small man with bright, bird-like eyes arrived and his face lit up when he saw Eddie. "Mon amie," he said as he ushered us in and took my bag. "Tu es revenue. Bien venue."

Eddie dropped his bags and threw both arms around his friend. "Zaahir, this is my friend, Joanna. Joanna, meet Zaahir, he was very, very kind to me when I lived here last year." Zaahir's smile became even brighter, as he welcomed me with a warm handshake and the offer of freshly brewed mint tea.

We walked into the smallest and most beautiful courtyard I had ever seen. The floor and walls were tiled in blue and white mosaics. A tiny fountain rained steadily into a miniature tiled pool. A vine, bearing fragrant orange flowers, grew up one wall to a balcony above, where it twined and trailed around the balustrade. A low table and four cushioned chairs stood invitingly in the shade of the vine.

I sank thankfully into the chair and sipped the sweet tea that Zaahir served us. I was aware that a silly smile had settled on my face. I felt relaxed and happy, as if every discomfort and challenge of the journey had simply melted away. I was home, and all was well with my world. I think I fell in love with Marrakesh at that moment.

The following morning, we climbed the stairs to the flat roof and I saw a sight that made me gasp in awe—the city of Marrakesh spread out before me, a symphony of red and ochre sandstone, stately palm trees, dominated by the elegant tower of El Koutoubia, the warm tones disappeared into a mauve-blue mist, and, rising above the mist, a crest of snow-covered peaks soared majestically into the clear blue sky— the High Atlas. They looked close enough to touch, and yet they also looked ethereal, like another world, a world of mystery and ancient stories, a world of secrets and of knowledge. A world I longed to visit.

Eddie pointed out the parapets of the old fort, a stone's throw away. A stork flew over us, his great wings ruffling the air, and landed gracefully on one of the red turrets of the fort. He folded his wings and stood stock still, one leg folded elegantly under his body, his long neck silhouetted against the backdrop of the mountains. "I've never seen a stork before," I said, taking hold of Eddie's hand.

"They're fabulous, aren't they? Almost prehistoric."

"And magical. No wonder there are so many stories about them."

"They live in the fort. I think there's a nest on each turret. I love watching them."

"I think I will too, they are so big and kind of detached."

"Yes, that's a good word for them. Maybe it's because of their long necks, they seem to be looking down on us all."

"But in the nicest possible way, no judgements!" Eddie laughed and kissed me. His lips were warm and soft.

Desire flamed between us, hot as the sun.

Later we explored Marrakesh. The first place we visited was the street of the sandal makers. Every man on the street welcomed Eddie with smiles and hugs. We sat in tiny shacks and watched them work goat leather into sandals and *babouche*, soft shoe-slippers in a myriad of shades from fuchsia pink to midnight blue. We drank copious glasses of sweet mint tea, chatted in broken French, comic mime and the international language of laughter.

I saw a different side of Eddie with the sandal makers. He was always relaxed and friendly, but with these guys I could see his natural bonhomie, his warm-hearted good nature. He responded to their own gentle, devout manliness with his innate humour and unaffected openness.

For lunch we ate *bisa*, a delicious dish made from butter beans, skinned and mashed, with added olive oil and paprika. Then we rested in our room.

In the late afternoon we ventured into the souk. Every narrow street was crammed with vibrantly colourful stalls: spice stalls, sacks overflowing with aromatic spices— paprika and cloves, cumin and anis, nutmegs and cinnamon; pottery stalls displaying tagine pots and ashtrays; leather stalls with bags and babouche; lantern stalls, silks and wools and woven baskets; hand-made mirrors from the Tuaregs of the desert; sweets dripping with sugar, succulent oranges and sticky dates. The colours, sounds and smells were fantastic and overwhelming. I loved every chaotic moment of it.

We emerged from the souk two hours later and made for the terrace of the Café de France. We ordered mint tea and a salad and surveyed the square below us. Now it was cooling Djem El Fna, the Place of the Dead, was full of life. Smoke spiralled into the air from the food stalls. A few early customers sampled the cornucopia of delicacies on offer: kebabs, chicken wings, aubergine, fish, French fries, egg sandwiches, rice, salad, tagine, a whole side of lamb, a myriad of unidentifiable objects fried, spiced and no doubt delicious. The smells mingled and drifted in the evening air.

A kalash and driver sat patiently waiting for the next

passenger, his horses motionless but for the occasional flick of a tail or toss of a head. A water seller, in his multi-coloured clothes: tasselled hat, brass encrusted belts and empty animal bladders, posed with a tourist, then held out his hand for payment. A man in a white cap wavered across the square on his bike, the front carrier laden with a dozen trays of eggs.

To the east, a thin veil of cloud shrouded the High Atlas. In the west, El Koutoubia Mosque and a lone palm tree created charcoal silhouettes against an azure sky wisped with flamingo pink cloud. A crescent moon rose in the north, Venus in her arms. The Mullah's cry echoed across the plain. Peace washed over me. Eddie smiled and reached over to hold my hand. "Beautiful, isn't it?"

"I think it's the most amazing place I have ever been—it's crazy and chaotic, yet deeply peaceful and spiritual. It feeds every part of me, body and soul."

"Wow, Joanna, you've expressed it perfectly. Now you know why I love this place?"

"Yes, and I love it too. I want to stay here forever."

Eddie laughed and the look in his eyes made warm joy ripple through me. "That's just how I feel about Marrakesh."

The cacophony of sound rising from the square soon called us to join in. We paid our bill and wandered around Djem El Fna, hand in hand. We watched the Gnaui drummers, from Senegal, dressed in white robes, spinning the long tassel on their red fez hats round and round as they danced, drummed, clanged their cymbals, jumped high in the air and squatted low like Cossacks. They were mesmerising and their rhythms spoke to every part of my body.

At the heart of another circle of people, a cobra swayed sinuously, hood flared, black eyes hungry for prey. A six-foot python writhed away from the circle towards the crowd. The white-turbaned snake charmer guided the python back with a well-placed foot, not missing a note on his pipe. A storyteller held a small crowd spellbound. Two men-women minced and pranced in veils and skirts. An old man sat on a plastic box selling single cigarettes. Then we heard a sound like the blues and discovered a silver haired man sitting beside an up-turned bicycle, playing a guitar and singing in a deep, rich voice. He had an attachment at the end of his guitar, which added a percussive rattle as he played. His music was full of soul and rhythm. We tapped our feet and moved in time with his song, feeling the music seep into us like honey.

"How amazing that guy was," Eddie said, as we ambled contentedly back to the hotel. "His music could have been played by John Lee Hooker. He was singing the blues."

"Well, I guess it all comes from the same roots...they are all from Africa. Maybe the blues originated here?"

"Maybe. That guy was unforgettable though."

The Hotel was too expensive to stay in for long, so we found a room in the medina. Our room was on the top floor of a three storied building, built around a central courtyard, which was criss-crossed with washing lines and full of women and children talking, playing, working and laughing together. We were the only non-Moroccans living there.

The room was basic and unfurnished, with a blue and white tiled floor and white-washed walls. We bought a rush mat to sleep on, a quilt and pillows for bedding, a clay pot and one pan to cook on. And so, our life together began.

We slowly settled into our own rhythm: woken by the call to prayer from the nearby mosque, a simple breakfast of fruit, a walk to the old fort to see the storks, or around the medina, or a visit to the street of the sandal makers, *bisa* and bread for lunch, coffee and socialising in the Café de France, shopping for the day and cooking the evening meal, and then the magic of Djem El Fna. I learned to cook two one-pot meals: vegetable tagine and pea omelette. Eddie learned to make excellent mint tea.

We even had regular visitors: Ron, a bearded and bedraggled American guy, and El Rubio, an albino Moroccan. He was alabaster pale; with hair the colour of peeled carrots and the lightest eyes I've ever seen. His body was all angles, like someone had stitched his bones together haphazardly. El Rubio had a vulnerability about him which made me want to look after him. He felt comfortable with us and I had the impression that he was always an outsider. Ron was a poet. He was much older than us, had been on the road for years, and he too seemed to feel at home with us. We bought a bigger pot and I made supper for the four of us twice a week. Ron read his poetry, Eddie had borrowed an old guitar and we sang Beatles and Dylan songs together.

Our life was simple, peaceful and glorious. Eddie and I adapted to one another naturally, enjoying long conversations or companionable silence. We are both strong-minded people, so there were inevitable clashes of will, which often erupted into fiery rows where neither of us was prepared to back down. And every time we made up was like swimming in nectar—sweet, tender and infinitely precious.

Marrakesh wove her magic around us: the taste of desert sand in the air; the flight of the storks; the music and aromas of Djem El Fna; the majesty of the High Atlas, which stood like sentinels on the horizon just out of touch, or hid behind clouds allowing tantalizing glimpses of their peaks if you looked up at the right time. Marrakesh is like a song that plucks the strings of your heart, her rhythm enters your soul and re-arranges the tempo of your being.

Days turned to weeks and our money dwindled. We started to earn a little, helping tourists to find what they wanted. We learned to buy enough food for each day: a small pat of butter, two eggs at a time. We discovered how little we really needed. The people in our part of the medina recognised us now, greeted us as we passed by and enjoyed our attempts at speaking Arabic.

My parents sent us some money, enough to keep us going for another month. It was getting too hot in the South. Reluctantly we agreed that it was time to move on, to slowly make our way back to the UK and earn some more money, so we could travel again. We really wanted to spend some time in the Rif Mountains and decided to head for a small village we'd heard about—Chefchaouen.

I cried as I watched the tower of El Koutoubia Mosque disappear from sight through the back window of the bus to Rabat and we both vowed to return as soon as we could. This place felt more like home to me than anywhere I'd ever lived.

From Rabat we travelled on to Fez and then took a bumpy bus ride over the Rif Mountains to Chefchaouen. We saw Berber women carrying enormous logs, or working in the fields, their children strapped to their backs. They looked free and independent and I wondered where all the men were. In the next village I saw groups of men in tea shops, sipping mint tea and smoking pipes of kif, so my question was answered.

Chefchaouen perches high on the side of a mountain, and the Ras el Ma waterfall rises within the village and cascades through it. Chefchaouen is a poem of water and stone. Everywhere you go you hear the sound of water as it gushes through courtyards, trills beside most homes, pools and gurgles and flows ever downwards, towards the sea.

Chefchaouen radiates peace and calm and the ever-present motion of nature. The houses in the oldest part of the village are painted blue. Some streets sing in colour with red, orange and yellow dyed wools and rugs hanging from shop doorways. Other streets sing a restful song, against the backdrop of grey rocks, scorched earth and the sapphire sky.

We celebrated my twenty-first birthday swimming in the river below Chefchauouen. The air was so clear we could hear the children playing in the school two miles away. I stood beneath a waterfall and watched rainbows form and dissolve as the water tumbled over me. We sat on smooth rocks, bodies entwined, breathing in the beauty and revelling in love.

I had come of age. I felt so well I threw away my asthma spray. I was done with struggling for breath. I had never felt so happy nor so free.

Too soon we had to leave our mountain paradise and begin our journey home. We had enough money for the bus to Ceuta and the ferry to Algeciras, then we hitched to Torremolinos, a small fishing village beside the Mediterranean Sea, which was just beginning to develop into a tourist attraction. Eddie played in a bar one night and the owner invited him to play each evening in exchange for a meal and a space on his roof where we could sleep.

We lay beneath the stars every night, lulled to sleep by the sound of the sea lapping against the shore and breakfasted on fresh figs from the tree that overhung the roof. Nothing fazed us. In Morocco we'd learned to live in the moment. I had realised that there was no point in worrying about what would happen next. And I'd developed faith that everything would work out fine. All we had to do was believe in the innate goodness of the universe and take the opportunities that presented themselves—fearlessly.

One night, as we lay wrapped in each other's arms, Eddie whispered in my ear: "I knew from the first time we made love that we would be together."

"Really?" I asked him, amazed and delighted, "and what did you feel?"

"Scared. I tried to ignore it, but we fitted together so perfectly, and I felt I'd known you all my life...for ever really." He kissed me and his lips were warm and soft and slightly salty. Our bodies knew each other so well by now that our limbs naturally folded around each other, creating union.

"I knew I was going to marry you," I told him. "And it frightened the life out of me. I had no plans to even get married." He sat up and looked at me, his eyes wide. Somewhere out at sea a ship's horn sounded.

"Wow. That's amazing. So we both knew we were meant to be together that night."

"Yes, and we both wanted to run the other way."

He laughed, then bent and kissed me again. "So how do you feel now? Still think of me as a brother?"

I kissed him back, harder. "Well, you're starting to grow on me."

"What, like a wart?"

"No, more like... like a lover, like a friend, like my best mate in all the world."

He pulled me closer. "I'm really glad I didn't walk back to West Kensington that night," he said, burying his face into my neck.

"So am I," I sighed, as I surrendered to the heat of his body.

The music is not in the notes, but in the silence in between.
Wolfgang Amadeus Mozart (1756- 1791)

RISHIKESH 1968

The sight of the new moon rising over the Valley of the Saints brought tears to Nuka's eyes. Her heart swelled within her, surging with a sensation that she struggled to name. Love? Awe? Gratitude? Perhaps a mixture of all three, heightened by her conscious awareness of the sacredness of her surroundings and filtered through the clarity of her mind.

The weeks of meditation and the teachings of Maharishi Mahesh Yogi had purified Nuka's mind and connected her to a deep and satisfying stillness. She breathed in the clear, cool mountain air. Below her the holy river Ganga flowed majestically onwards. Countless thousands of people worshipped this mystical river. Surely, she thought, every drop of its water carried blessings across the land.

The town of Rishikesh twinkled in the distance. Ancient mountains rose like silent sentinels in all directions. Above her a sea of stars glinted and glimmered in the velvety darkness of the sky. The milky way streamed like a heavenly river across the universe, echoing the majesty of Mother Ganga.

The crescent of the new moon, a fine sliver of silver, hung in the sky like a wish, balanced on the peak of a mountain and cradling Venus in her arms.

Nuka scanned the constellations, trying to recognise familiar shapes. She saw the Plough, now appearing more like an upside-down shepherd's hook than the question mark she always saw in the Danish sky.

A peacock screeched sharply into the silence of the night. A sweet fragrance drifted on the air, some night-blooming flower, blossoming in the cool light of the moon. Jasmine perhaps?

"Beautiful, isn't it?" Nuka turned towards the voice, startled from her reverie with nature. Donovan stood behind her, wrapped against the cold in a big blanket. "Sorry if I surprised you," he said, "I often come here to drink in the magic of the place."

"Yes, it's one of my favourite places too," Nuka responded. "Look at the new moon. Isn't she gorgeous?"

"Totally beautiful."

"They call her Chandra," Nuka said, "I love that name. I've been learning a song to her."

"Really? Can you sing it to me?" Donovan asked.

"Well, I...I'm not sure."

"C'mon. Don't be nervous of me."

"I only know the chorus."

"I'd love to hear it."

Nuka drew in a deep breath, gathered her courage, gazed at the rising moon and sang in a sweet, clear voice:
"Chandrashekara, Chandrashekara, Chandrashekara Pahiman,
Chandrashekara, Chandrashekara, Chandrashekara Rakshaman."

"Wow, I love it. You are worshipping the moon. I don't know what the words mean but I can sense the worship."

"Yes, me too. Being here makes me want to worship everything. The beauty I see makes me cry."

Donovan smiled gently. "I know just what you mean. Maharishi is teaching us to 'understand the mechanics of creation.[11]' Perhaps we are beginning to understand, becoming aware of reverence."

They watched the moon slowly rise. After a while Nuka turned to walk back to her room. "Goodnight, Donovan. Sweet dreams"

"Goodnight, Nuka. Thanks for singing to me."

"You're welcome," Nuka said, laughing.

The following day Nuka was practicing some hatha yoga stretches on her veranda when Jenny Boyd walked past on

---

[11] 'All You Need is Love' p 182

her way to breakfast. The two women smiled shyly at one another. They had not yet spoken, but Nuka knew that Jenny had arrived with her sister Pattie, wife of the Beatle, George Harrison, a week ago.

As far as Nuka was concerned the Beatles and the other 'famous' people who happened to be at the Chaurasi Kutia Ashram, otherwise known as The International Academy of Meditation, for the course were simply fellow seekers. She knew that some of the other course participants resented the crowds of press that had accumulated at the gates of the Ashram. She, however, believed that the visiting celebrities deserved some peace and quiet, the same as everyone else. And, although she was a little shy when she met them, she wished to treat them normally.

So, Nuka smiled warmly at Jenny when she sat beside her at breakfast. "How are you getting on?" she asked.

"Well," Jenny said, "I love listening to the Maharishi, and it is very beautiful here."

"I am sensing a 'but,'" Nuka said, her eyes twinkling.

Jenny laughed ruefully and rubbed her leg. "Yeah, well, it's hard to like mosquitos. And the food..."

"Is bland and boring." Nuka added, smiling, "apart from this porridge which is delicious when you add plenty of honey and buffalo milk." Both women laughed. "My name is Nuka, I'm happy to meet you."

"My name is Jenny. How long have you been here Nuka?"

"I arrived from Denmark at the end of January, so almost four weeks now."

"Wow. Are you doing the whole three-month course?" Jenny asked.

"Yes. I hope I will be chosen to be an initiator. I would so like to introduce Transcendental Meditation to people in Copenhagen."

"Have you been meditating for long?"

"Well, I started trying to meditate over twelve years ago, when I was eighteen. I found it very hard to get my mind to be quiet. I learned hatha yoga, and that helped. When I lay in *shavasana*, flat out on the floor, at the end of the practice, I often experienced stillness. I wanted more of it but didn't know how to connect with it. Then I met Maharishi six years ago, and I realised that what I'd needed all along was a teacher. And a mantra. And now I'm here. What about you?"

"My sister, Pattie, introduced me to Maharishi two years ago and I've been meditating regularly since then. It has helped me a lot."

"How do you think it helps?" Nuka asked.

Jenny put down her spoon and considered Nuka's question for a moment, her gaze focused on the river Ganges, flowing below them. "I think I feel more connected to myself, less like a leaf blown about by the winds of life. There's something very nourishing about just being still, isn't there?"

"Yes," Nuka responded, "I think stillness is what the world needs right now, it's certainly what I need."

"Nuka, I noticed you doing yoga this morning, as I walked past your hut. I would really like to learn how to do it. Would you teach me? I think it would help me to meditate."

"I would be happy to. I teach hatha yoga in Denmark, although my day job is in advertising. When can we fit it in though?"

"How about after lunch?"

"It would be better later," Nuka said, "maybe around 3.30? It's good to have an empty stomach when doing hatha yoga."

"Fine. Would you come round to our bungalow? I'm sure Pattie would like to join in as well."

"Sure. See you then Jenny." Nuka said, surprising herself by experiencing a shiver of excitement that she had been invited round to the bungalow where George Harrison also lived. She'd seen the four Beatles at the evening lectures of course, they always sat in the front row, along with Donovan, Mike Love from the Beach Boys and Paul Horn. They often ate meals with everyone else also, yet she had not wanted to intrude on their privacy and had kept her distance.

It was different with Donovan. The gentle Scottish troubadour lived in the hut just in front of hers, so they had met on his first day at the Ashram. She enjoyed hearing him singing and playing his guitar every evening. His music was soothing and somehow familiar, it struck a deep chord within her, like an ancient tribal memory of sitting round the fire with loved ones, sharing tales of long ago. He already felt like an old friend, or a younger brother.

Nuka meditated for three hours after breakfast. Maharishi was encouraging everyone to sit for longer sessions each day. He had told them that prolonged meditation would uplift their consciousness, so that his knowledge could 'flow into them.'

Many of the other course participants were struggling with the longer meditation sessions. Some were re-experiencing past traumas, such as the death of a loved one. Others claimed to be re-living past lives. Nuka had doubts about that, although she firmly believed in reincarnation. Somehow the tales people told from previous lives did not ring true, and either way she believed that the past was over and done with, why return to the troubles of another life when it was hard enough to cope with this one?

For Nuka meditation was mainly calm and nourishing. Yet she still felt she was at a threshold and that a sense of fear was holding her back. She wanted to maintain the discipline of long daily practice in the hope that she would eventually overcome her fear.

After lunch she took a short rest, then meditated for another hour. At three o'clock she had a 'shower' with the help of a cup and a bucket of cold water. The 'bathroom' was far from luxurious.

Nuka walked along the path to block six, where the Beatles were all housed. A peacock strutted proudly across her path. Once he was safely on the other side, he proceeded to fan out his magnificent tail. The peahen, who was the object of his display, was nonchalantly pecking away at some grubs near the trunk of a teak tree. Nuka stopped to watch them. Every feather in the peacock's tail quivered, even the soft, downy ones on his back. It was as if he was stretching every fibre of his being, silently shouting: "Look at me! Aren't

I amazing?" He strutted his stuff quite grandly. Yet the peahen took no notice of him, so he folded up his glory and walked away, head high.

Jenny was sitting on the veranda, dressed in a loose pair of white cotton trousers and a colourful top. "Nuka," she said, throwing her arms around her, "I am so glad you came." Jenny led Nuka into the bungalow. George sat cross-legged on the floor, playing an acoustic guitar, long hair covering his face. He looked up and smiled at Nuka.

"This is Nuka, George, she's a hatha yoga teacher from Denmark and is going to teach Pattie and me."

"Hi Nuka," George said, "maybe you can show me a few stretches as well. Me knees are killin' me sittin' like this for hours on end."

Nuka laughed. "I'd be happy to, George. A lot of us have problems with our knees. We're all spoiled in the west, so used to sitting in comfy chairs that our bodies have forgotten how to sit on the floor."

"Yeah," George said, "I've seen little kids an' old ladies here in India, squattin' on their haunches, feet flat on the ground. They make it look easy."

"I think it is for them," Nuka said. "They've sat like that all their lives."

Pattie came in from another room. "Hello Nuka," Pattie said. "We are both really looking forward to learning some yoga moves from you. Shall we go round the back? It's cooler there."

The three women walked around the bungalow to a flat and fairly smooth piece of ground that was well shaded, yet still open to the gentle breeze. A couple of squirrels chased each other around in circles, oblivious to the presence of the women. A tribe of monkeys chattered noisily in the trees above. "All the animals are so tame here," Pattie said, spreading three mats on the ground.

"I think they feel safe with us," Nuka responded.

"Maybe they like the meditation vibes," Jenny added, helping Pattie to straighten the mats. "The monkeys always come close when I'm meditating."

"Yeah, I've noticed that too," Nuka said.

"Good good good, good vibrations." Pattie sang to the melody made famous by the Beach Boys. As she sang, she twirled around, her wide-opened arms lifted up to the sky.

They all laughed and Nuka was amazed how quickly she had become at ease with the two sisters. They spent some time practicing simple breathing techniques and some basic hatha yoga asanas, like the cat and the mountain pose. Nuka taught them down faced dog, encouraging them to hold the stretch and gradually lengthen their spines and allow their heels to move down towards the earth. Finally, she talked them through the relaxation pose of *shavasana*, consciously softening every muscle in the body.

The sight of three women laying quietly on the ground was too much of a temptation for the cheeky monkeys, who quickly surrounded them and started pulling at their hair and chattering manically. Laughing, they all rose to their feet, rolled up their mats and beat a hasty retreat to the bungalow. As they rounded the corner, they saw two Indian men unloading large bundles wrapped in cloth from an ambassador car which was parked outside. Donovan and George were watching from the veranda.

"Hi girls," George said. "Mr Singh from the music shop in Dehradun is delivering the instruments we brought the other day." Turning to a small and wiry gentleman wearing a green turban, George placed his palms together in the traditional Indian greeting of Namaste, and bowed his head. "Mr Singh," he said, "this is my wife Pattie, her sister Jenny and Nuka, from Denmark"

Mr Singh greeted each woman gracefully, with a short bow and folded hands. "Namaste," he said, "please call me Ajit. This is my nephew, Prahlad."

Soon everyone was inside the bungalow and the instruments were carefully unpacked. First to emerge from its cocoon was a splendid sitar. It was a deep, shiny red-brown colour, inlaid with intricate designs of birds and flowers in white on the round body and slim neck. George lifted it lovingly and gently plucked a few strings. "Beautiful," he said, "such a pure tone, and it's almost in tune."

"I will adjust the tuning very soon Mr George." Ajit said, "If you will allow me."

George smiled at Ajit and nodded his head slightly. "Of course, Ajit, but only if you call me George. No-one calls me Mr. George," he laughed.

Meanwhile Prahlad had unwrapped the tamboura and he stood the instrument beside the sitar, steadying each one on stuffed cotton rings.

"Wow," Donovan said, "they are a perfect pair. Were they made by the same craftsman?"

"My brother, Jayendra, bought them in Miraj, a town in Maharashtra which is famous for the best Hindustani musical instruments." Ajit said, a note of pride in his voice. "This pair were made by a particularly fine craftsman. They are the best you can buy."

Ajit tuned each instrument in turn while Prahlad unwrapped a pair of tablas that George had bought for Ringo. Nuka had been watching the arrival of the instruments with fascination, but now she felt like an intruder. "I'll see you later," she said to Jenny, as she prepared to leave.

"Oh, please don't go, stay for a drink with us," Jenny said, "Wouldn't you like to hear what the instruments sound like?"

"Well, yes, I would love to, but...."

"No buts. Here, sit beside Pattie and I will make us all some tea." Jenny was hard to resist. And Nuka really wanted to stay, so she sat down as directed and watched as Ajit handed the sitar to George.

George tentatively plucked the strings and then began to play a cascade of notes that brought images of waterfalls and sunlight to Nuka's inner eye. "Hey Don," George said, "Have a go at the tamboura. It's quite easy, Ajit will show you."

Donovan sat on a floor cushion and Ajit placed the tamboura on his lap, facing forward. Soon Donovan was creating a carpet of sound that filled the room. Nuka closed her eyes and let the sounds wash over her. The tamboura had a mesmeric drone that reached into her heart and mind, soothing her and encouraging her to turn inwards. The sound of the sitar traced patterns of light onto the steady stream of harmonics created by the tamboura. Then Prahlad joined in with a dancing rhythm on the tablas, a sound that infiltrated her blood and fused with the steady beating of her heart. Ajit began playing the vichitra veena, a magnificent instrument consisting of a long, fretless body supported by two gourds, with a peacock carved into its up-curved neck. Ajit used a round paper weight as a slide and created a magical sound of bending notes and singing strings. The music took flight, like a flock of bids soaring into a perfect sky. The sounds swooped and dived, flying in circles and cycles of indescribable joy. Tears fell from Nuka's eyes as her heart swelled with an inexplicable longing.

In the pulsing silence, after the music, the room shimmered with love. Nuka opened her eyes and looked around. Everyone else still sat with eyes closed. She had no idea how long they had been playing, nor how long they'd sat in silence, time was irrelevant. She felt like she did after a very deep meditation, centred and still, yet tingling in every pore.

Donovan cradled the tamboura in his arms, his head against the long neck. His eyes met George's and they simply looked at one another, a silent communication passing between them. "It's yours, man," George said, "just come round and play it with me often."

"Thanks, man," Donovan said, "I think me an' this instrument are gonna get along jus' fine!" Everyone laughed at Don's attempt at a southern accent and Jenny stood up to get the tea, which had been entirely forgotten.

The days passed in a golden haze of Maharishi, meditation, monkeys and music. Just as the magnificent and sacred river Ganges flowed beside the Ashram, so too a river of creativity flowed through everyone. People were writing, painting, dancing and singing. Every evening Nuka lay in bed and listened to Donovan singing and playing. He'd written a song called 'Happiness Runs' which everyone, especially Maharishi, loved. There were times when Nuka found herself singing it when she was trying to repeat her mantra. Not that she minded.

Sometimes she heard Donovan playing the tamboura and singing another new song about love and a hurdy gurdy man. It reminded her of the excitement of the circus, and made her feel like a child again, listening to her mother sing her nursery rhymes.

John, George and Paul were also buzzing with creativity, and writing new songs daily. Nuka often saw them all playing together and longed to sit close and listen, but she didn't want to intrude. Like the Maharishi, Nuka felt protective of them. She imagined what it must be like to have hundreds of screaming teenagers and nosy press men watching every move. She knew she would hate it. How great that they had the freedom to just be in the Ashram, to eat simply, breathe in good air and find some peace in their crazy lives. The brightness in their eyes and smiles showed how good this time was for them. Sometimes, after the evening meal, their songs and laughter rippled through the Ashram like sunlight on water.

Jenny invited Nuka round every other day, and the three young women enjoyed their informal yoga sessions and often sat chatting afterwards. Cynthia Lennon joined them a couple of times, but did not come regularly. Although Cynthia always appeared relaxed and happy, Nuka sensed a deep sadness in her, yet felt unable to reach out to her. She reminded Nuka of a wounded animal who had retreated far into her shell and was pushing everyone away.

One afternoon, as they rounded the corner of the bungalow after yoga, they found John playing a haunting song to Donovan and George. Cynthia sat alone in a corner of the veranda, watching John sing. Pattie, Jenny and Nuka joined her and listened quietly. "He's singing about his mum, Julia," Cynthia said softly, "she deserted him."

"I can hear the pain in his voice," Pattie said, "that poor little motherless boy will always be a part of who John is." Nuka said nothing, but inwardly she was offering thanks to Maharishi for the gift of transcendental meditation. She recognised in the raw emotion she heard in John's voice that he had gone deep inside himself and was beginning to heal a wound that had affected his entire life.

Nuka understood. Her twin sister had died in a car accident when they were both thirteen. It was only when Nuka had begun to meditate that she'd had the courage and the inner strength to look into the dark space her sister's loss had left within her. Meditation had supported her to heal the anger, guilt and resentment, to recognise how Astrid's death had created a suffocating blanket that had virtually smothered the joy from her family for years.

Now, whenever Nuka thought about Astrid, she remembered the laughter and the fun they'd had together; nights spent huddled under the blanket with a torch, blonde heads bent over the same enthralling book, racing one another down ski slopes, diving into the ocean, finishing each other's sentences. Through meditation Nuka had discovered that Astrid lived on in her, she had forgiven her sister for leaving her and she nourished Astrid's presence in her heart and mind. Her eyes filled with tears as the final notes of John's song faded into the jungle.

On the night of the full moon in March, Maharishi invited the entire Ashram on a moonlit journey along the river Ganga.

Shortly before sunset the excited procession of assorted meditators from all walks of life followed their Guru through the winding paths of the jungle and down to the riverside village of Swaragashram. Like olden day minstrels John, George, Paul and Donovan followed in Maharishi's footsteps, strumming their guitars and singing *When the Saints Come Marching In,* and *You Are My Sunshine.*

It was a joyful occasion. All the villagers lined the path to watch the procession. Several enterprising families had set up tables bearing ghee and sugar rich sweets: milky white *rasmallai,* caramel *moticheer ladoo,* golden *cham cham,* bright orange carrot *halva,* sticky red *jalebi.* Unable to resist

the temptation of a sweet treat, all but the most austere
yogis bought more than they needed, ending up with sticky
fingers and the short-lived euphoria of a sugar rush.

Two flat bottomed barges awaited them at the
landing. Maharishi boarded first and took the place of honour
on an elevated bench at the rear. Maharishi's celebrity guests
boarded next, the Beatles and their wives, Donovan, Mia,
Prudence and Johnny Farrow, Paul Horn and Mike Love. Jenny
insisted that Nuka board with her, so she found herself sitting
in the third row and could see Maharishi perfectly. He looked
magnificent, like an ancient Maharaja: seated on gold satin,
dressed in flowing white silk, adorned with several garlands of
marigolds, his long silvery hair flowing into his beard and his
eyes twinkling with delight.

Once everyone was settled, the barges raised anchors
and drifted sedately side by side down river. As if on cue, the
red sun set behind one mountain and the silver moon rose
above the opposite peak.

Two Brahmin priests stood either side of Maharishi
and began reciting sacred texts from the Rigveda. The ancient
sounds washed over the travellers as they floated
downstream. Temples nestled in the trees, rose-pink in the
afterglow of the setting sun. The silvery orb of the moon
travelled majestically across the sky, creating a glistening path
of light on the dark waters of Mother Ganga.

After the Brahmin priests had finished chanting, Paul
Horn played his flute. The notes danced on the moonlit
water, argent, magical, full of devotion and a subtle longing.
Donovan strummed his guitar and began to sing, "Happiness
runs in a circular motion, happiness runs, happiness runs."
John, George and Paul sang a medley of Donovan songs:
Catch the Wind, Mellow Yellow, Josie, Sunny Goodge Street
and ended with *Jennifer Juniper*, the song he'd written for
Jenny. Donovan and Paul Horn sang classic Beatles songs: *She
Loves You, Strawberry Fields, I Want to Hold Your Hand, and
Tomorrow Never Knows*. Then someone began to chant *Hare
Krishna, Hare Rama* and the *mahamantra* enfolded them all
in the sounds of love.

The barges drifted from one side of the river to the other, no particular place to go, simply floating in the light of the moon. Everyone was mesmerised by the beauty of their surroundings, the magic of the night, the wonder of the moment. Within and without. Perfect harmony.

Nuka looked around her and wondered whether she was dreaming. Here she was, in one of the most sacred valleys in India, floating down the holiest river in the world, with her Guru and some of the most famous musicians of the western world. She closed her eyes, to drink in the moment, to anchor it in her heart and wrap it in the golden tissues of remembrance. As she relished the moment, she sensed an inner dissolving. She was no longer Nuka, or a devotee of Maharishis, or a Danish woman. She was the water and the moonlight. She was the music and the love that made the music flow. She was the starlight and the darkness that supported the stars. She was infinite and she was tiny. She was all things and she was nothing.

Hare Rama, hare Rama,
Rama Rama, hare hare
Hare Krishna, hare Krishna,
Krishna Krishna, hare hare

*After silence, that which comes closest to expressing the
inexpressible is music.*

Aldous Huxley (1894-1963)

SKYE 1969

"*Speed bonny boat like a bird on the wing over the sea to
Skye.*" I had always loved the Skye Boat song, and now I was
singing it to myself as we drove onto the ferry-boat to Skye.
We were not carrying the man who was born to be king, true,
but we were carrying my best mate, Vicky, and her new-born
baby, Jasmina.

As soon as Eddie parked our ancient Rover 90 on the
narrow ferry we piled out and made our way under the bridge
to the prow. We were a colourful group: Vicky and I in long,
flowing skirts and bright knitted jumpers, Eddie and Julian
both wearing embroidered Indian shirts and denim jeans.

I noticed the disapproving glances we received from
the other, more conservatively dressed passengers. We were
used to those looks and didn't care. So what if they thought
we were hippies? We were living our lives according to our
values now, bringing back the magic, colour and music to a
world that had become obsessed with possessions and was
slowly turning grey. We were blazing a new trail based on
love and freedom and rejecting the war and greed that had
poisoned the twentieth century so far.

Vicky wrapped another shawl around Jasmina and
hugged her into the warmth of her body, turning her back to
the sharp wind blowing in from North Minch. Julian put his
arm around the two of them. "Ah, it's good to breathe in the
fresh air of the islands after Inverness," he said.

His long, lank hair flapped around his pale face; a soft
smile played on his full lips. I took a picture of the three of
them, to capture the memory of Jasmina's journey home.
Vicky looked tired but happy, her auburn hair a mass of wild
curls blowing around her heart shaped face.

"How are you feeling Vicky?" I asked.

"Pretty good actually, I'm glad to be outside. I've

been stuck in hospital since Jasmina was born, what's the date?"

"November 15," Eddie said.

"She was born on the 10th, so that's five days, and the only walking I've done is round the maternity ward. Thanks for coming to bring us home. How long did it take you to drive from Hertfordshire?"

"About nine hours," I said, "we left the caravan at Don's and slept for an hour or so in the car on the way here."

"You must be knackered, man," Julian said, turning to Eddie.

"Yeah, looking forward to sleeping in a bed again," Eddie said, yawning. He looked wide awake to me, his blue eyes as clear and bright as ever. Tying his long brown hair into a pony tail he turned into the wind to look ahead.

The boat juddered and the air filled with diesel fumes as we pulled away from Kyle of Lochalsh and set off for Kyleakin. The hills of Skye looked like a sleeping animal, covered in green fur. Beyond them the jagged peaks of Sgurr na Coinnich and Beinn na Caillach pierced the horizon like an accusation.

The hairs on my neck and arms goose-rippled as a wave of ancestral memory washed over me. I knew this place, felt it in my blood. I was coming home as well, even though I'd never visited Skye in this lifetime. I sang the Skye Boat song into the wind as we chugged across the narrow neck of Loch Alsh. The sun shone pale and watery in the west. A flock of seagulls flew behind us, shrieking and squabbling. One dived into our wake, coming up with a small silver fish in his crooked beak.

In less than thirty minutes we were driving down the side ramp. We drove North. Vicky nursed Jas in the back seat and I sat beside her. The boys were fooling around in the front, singing Beatles songs and making up daft words. Vicky prised the sleeping baby off her nipple and held her out to me.

"Would you like to hold her, Joanna, while she sleeps?" she asked.

I took the precious bundle in my arms and snuggled my face into her soft skin. The dark curtains of my hair fell either side of her, creating a private space for the two of us. She smelt of milk and talc and damp wool. Delightful. I held her warm cheek against mine and a pang of sadness stabbed through me, making my breath catch in my chest and hot tears spring to my eyes. I wiped them away and breathed in deeply. Vicky reached out and squeezed my hand.

"You'll have another babe soon; you have to grow a friend for Jasmina." We looked at one another, both remembering that day in June when I'd miscarried. Vicky and Julian had travelled south to visit us in Hampshire. We'd gone for a long walk by the river. Summer sun, golden iris, blue skies and the joyful song of the blackbird. It was idyllic until I suddenly felt intense cramping and the baby I had only just become aware of slipped out of me.

I smiled at her. "Thanks, love. I'm fine. This is no time for sadness. You rest and we'll soon be there."

I sat back and watched the spectacular scenery pass by. To my left the sea glittered silver grey, and misty islands floated on the horizon. Ahead sharp angled mountains rose majestically, reaching for the mottled light of the sky. Ancient rock faces, gnarled, wind bent trees, placid sheep, weathered faces and whitewashed crofts passed by. The light had a unique quality, soft, yet bright, misty distances and crystal-clear skies. Magical. I looked down at the sleeping baby in my arms and felt peace.

"There's Waternish ahead," Julian said, "Go slow here, man, the road is narrow and full of holes." Eddie slowed to a crawl as I strained to see the tiny hamlet we were considering making our home. We pulled up outside a grey stone house with a bright red door and Julian leapt out. "Welcome to the auld school hoose," he said, bowing theatrically.

As I stepped out of the car the salt tanged wind hit me in the face. The low-slung sun on the horizon was colouring the western sky in shades of salmon pink and slate grey. The sea reflected the changing clouds, adding purples and mauves to the palette. A pathway of shimmering gold stretched from the sun to our feet, welcoming us.

The door opened directly into the kitchen: red quarry tiles covered the floor, in the centre of the room was a scrubbed wooden table, which looked like it had stood there for years; an old Rayburn stove was set against one wall, and beneath the only window was a deep china sink, with a stained wooden draining board supported by rusty iron brackets. The pots and pans hanging from the ceiling and the mixed smells of salt, wood, earth and something organic, felt homely and welcoming.

A door from the kitchen led into a cosy sitting room, with a fireplace, two easy chairs, a beat-up sofa and several cushions and rugs scattered around the floor. It was colourful and messy, with washing draped on a stand in the corner and Julian's guitar resting beside a chair. A flight of stairs led up to the two bedrooms and another door opened into the simple bathroom. Against one wall a small wooden sideboard was covered in papers and art material. Several bright paintings hung on the walls. One was a portrait of Vicky, one a seascape and one a stormy sky."

"Are these yours?" Eddie asked Julian.

"Yeah man, I've been painting a lot since we moved here."

Eddie smiled, "When I first met you, in the little studio in Bushey, you were painting every day."

"Yeah, I was at art school then, all I had to do was paint and play. Times have changed, man."

Eddie laughed. "Good to see you painting again." We busied ourselves lighting fires, unloading our cases and making food while Vicky settled Jas. Within an hour we were sitting by a warm fire eating cheese on toast and baked beans.

The kitchen door opened and Ben, Lucy and Nicky arrived with a swirl of wind and the smell of the sea. Eddie and Nicky hugged liked long-lost brothers. Not that they looked remotely like brothers: Nicky over six foot tall and beanpole-thin, pale faced with a shock of unruly black hair;

Eddie short and stocky with a ruddy, weathered complexion. "Man, the last time I saw you was your wedding day," Nicky said.

"When was that then?" asked Ben, a fine-boned man, slight and gentle.

"January 29," I said. "I remember how shocked my mum was when we both climbed into the back of your Land Rover, Nick, to drive from our flat in Elgin Avenue to the registry office in South Kensington."

"Yeah, brides are supposed to travel in limos, not Land Rovers." Nicky said, laughing.

"Let's see the new arrival then," Lucy demanded, hanging her coat over a chair and rubbing her hands together to get warm. "God it's cold in here. I should have lit the fire for you but I had no idea what time you'd be arriving." Lucy had a brisk natural energy, her warm hazel eyes darted everywhere, taking us all in and somehow knowing what each person needed.

"Jas is sleeping in our room," Vicky said, "you can come and see her, Lucy, but the rest of you will have to wait until she wakes." She led Lucy up the stairs while we all found seats as near the fire as possible. Julian added another log and poked the smouldering wood to create a fresh blaze. A gust of wind filled the room with smoke.

"Great to see you Ben," Eddie said. "It's been a long time."

"Yeah," Ben replied, "we moved up here as soon as Donovan bought the land and neither of us have left since. We love it. I've learned to fish and sail and already feel more at home here than I ever did in south England."

"I know what you mean, Ben," I said, "I was never at home in St Albans either. I felt like a square peg in a round hole."

"Do you think you'll settle here then?" Nicky asked.

Eddie and I looked at each other. "Hmm, we don't know yet," I said. "We've moved around so much this year we feel like we have wheels on our feet."

"Yeah, and I kind of like being a gypsy really," said

Eddie, "I get restless if I stay anywhere too long."

"So where have you been this year?" Ben asked.

"Well," Eddie said, "after the wedding we just wanted to return to Morocco, so we caught a boat to Casablanca and travelled south again, to Marrakesh."

"Oh man, I love Marrakesh!" Julian said, "The sounds and smells of Djem El Fna, sitting in the Café de France, sipping mint tea..."

"Sunset over the Atlas Mountains and the call of the muezzin from El Koutoubia," I added, seeing it all in my minds' eye.

"Did you go south to the Sahara?" Ben asked.

"No," Eddie responded, "we rented a room by the old fort, watched the storks nesting, walked to Djem El Fna every night and listened to the Gnaui drumming."

"And the old guy playing blues on guitar," I said. Eddie smiled at me, his blue eyes sparkling in the firelight.

"It was a good life," he said.

"When we were in Morocco, we crossed the High Atlas and lived with the blue people, the Tuareg, in the desert," Julian said, piling more logs onto the fire, which was blazing nicely now.

"We went west to the coast at Essouera," Eddie said, "it was peaceful there, but we had to leave in May, it was too hot."

"We sailed back from Casablanca," I said, "met some people from the New Forest on the boat and ended up living in Hampshire for a few months, we bought a caravan to live in. At the end of the summer, we towed it to Hertfordshire, thinking we'd stay there for a while, but it was impossible to find anywhere to site it. So, we asked Don if we could come here. We left the caravan in his yard. And now here we are."

"Great to have you," Ben said, hugging us both, "welcome to Waternish."

"Thanks man, it's good to be here," said Eddie.

It was good. Outside the wind howled and the sea crashed on the shore. Inside we sang folk songs while Julian and Eddie played guitar and Ben added rhythm on an old clay pot. Vicky's face glowed in the firelight as she nursed Jasmina and rocked slowly on the old wooden chair. I had a sense of time and space merging, as if we'd been sitting by fires together, in other times and other places for centuries, singing and at ease in one another's company.

"It's like the old days in St. Albans," Nicky said, "what was the name of that pub we all met in?"

"The Cock Inn, believe it or not," Julian said, prompting a ripple of laughter.

"We made some great music there," Eddie said, "Mac MacLeod, Mick Softley, Donovan and Micky Lenahan. We sang and played for hours on end."

"Yeah, and sneaked off to the church yard for a smoke and a snog, when we got the chance," Julian added.

"It was quite a cool scene, looking back," I said. "We were an arty bunch."

"What do you mean 'were'?" Julian asked. "We still are!"

"Yeah, look at us now, five years later," Nicky said, "Don's a famous folksinger, Mick's songs have been sung around the world, Eddie's a legend in his own time, lead singer of the Cops and Robbers, on stage with the Who, Georgie Fame and John Lee Hooker, Julian will be a famous artist..."

"Yeah, when I'm dead and buried" Julian said morosely.

"Let's raise a glass to the Cock Inn," Eddie said, re-filling everyone's glasses.

We all stood and raised our glasses high. "To the Cock" Julian said

"And to friendship," I said, looking at Eddie "most of us met there."

When I went to our room that first night, I noticed an instrument leaning against the wall in a corner. It was over four feet tall, with a round base and a long neck, ornately decorated and the most beautiful shade of mahogany. I plucked each of its four strings and the sound it made filled the small room with an exotic, discordant resonance that spoke to my soul. I turned the finely carved pegs and tuned it as best I could, then played it again, plucking the strings like a double bass. The sound transported me, sending my consciousness spiralling into a vast, still space. I put my head against the round, warm wood of the neck and plucked the strings again. The vibration of the notes resounded through my body.

"Wow, what's that?" Eddie asked as he entered the room.

"I have no idea, but I love it. Listen to this sound."

"Maybe it's a sitar?" he said.

"Maybe, it certainly looks Indian, doesn't it?"

"We'll ask Julian tomorrow. Are you warm enough? I'll stoke up the fire." He added several logs to the fire and secured the guard.

"Thanks, love," I said, "I've filled the hot-water bottle and we can snuggle up." We lay curled up in one another's arms and I fell asleep to the sounds of roaring wind and crashing sea.

The next morning dawned clear and frosty. After a bowl of porridge, Eddie and I went for a walk. The tide was out and the beach was covered in sea-smoothed stones. Occasional pools of water reflected the pale blue of the winter sky. Three islands stood, mist shrouded, on the western horizon.

"Look," Eddie pointed out to sea, "there are seals." I looked out in the direction he was pointing, and there, sure enough, I saw four dark, dog like heads bobbing in the sea.

"Wow, first seals I've ever seen," I said.

"Congratulations," he said, folding me in his arms.

A little further along the shore Ben was dragging a dinghy over the rocks. We ran to help him. "Fancy a ride?" he asked, "I'm off to catch lunch for us all." We didn't need asking twice and clambered aboard. Ben started the motor and we sailed out into Loch Bay.

Once we were a fair way from shore Ben cut the motor and we drifted quietly on the tide while Ben cast his fishing rod and waited for a bite. From this vantage point I could see the sweep of the shore and the rising hills beyond. Ben pointed out landmarks; the village of Stein, the islands of Isay and Mingay in the foreground and the distant mountains of North Uist beyond.

"What's over there, to the south, where that cloud is?" I asked.

"Dunvegan castle," Ben said.

"Is that rain?" Eddie asked, pointing to the murky greyness falling from the cloud over Dunvegan.

"Yeah, you often see that here, especially from the sea. You can be in sunshine and watch a cloud bursting over a nearby village. It's one of the many things I love about this place." The line went taught and Ben reeled in a fat, wriggling mackerel. He expertly prised it from the hook and threw it on the floor of the dinghy, where it thrashed about and slowly died.

I had been mainly vegetarian since I had learned about macrobiotics in London in 1967. Although I had eaten no meat, I did occasionally still eat fish, however, seeing this fish die made me question whether I even wanted to eat it. Within thirty minutes Ben caught another seven mackerel and we headed back for lunch in Ben and Lucy's caravan, which was further up the hill from the schoolhouse.

By the time Lucy had gutted the fish, coated them in oats, fried them in oil and served them up with fresh baked bread I had lost all my qualms and thoroughly enjoyed the meal.

We spent the afternoon exploring the area. We visited Nick's tiny, but very tidy caravan and also the beautiful gypsy caravan that Donovan and Enid used when they visited. I loved the solid woodwork and fancy mirrors.

Julian showed us the village of Waternish, which consisted of a few houses and a pub, all standing in a line near the shore. Finally, we visited Loch Bay Boathouse, which Ben, Julian and Nicky were renovating for Donovan. We could see how much work remained to be done before it was habitable.

"I'm no good at building, man," Eddie said to Julian.

"Well neither were we, but we're learning, and so will you." Julian responded.

"Hmmm," said Eddie, and I could sense his doubt.

"How else could we make a living up here?" I asked.

Ben and Nicky laughed. "Winkles," Nicky said.

"What?" Eddie asked, puzzled.

"Winkles, man, little black sluggy things that cling to the rocks. We get a quid for a bucket full." Nicky said, still laughing.

"A quid?" I said, "How long does it take to pick a bucket full?" Now everyone laughed.

"Depends how quick you are," Ben said. "We'll go out tomorrow, when the tide's low, and you can pick some."

Later, when we were sat by the fire with Jules, Vicky and Jasmina, I asked about the instrument in our room. "It's called a tamboura," Julian said, "Donovan brought it back from India last year."

"Does he play it?" I asked.

"He used it on *Hurdy Gurdy Man*, but I'm not sure whether he played it on that recording. I think he did. He doesn't play it now though, or he wouldn't have left it here. He hasn't been here for about five months."

"Well," Vicky said, "he's been too busy. Enid's been here though. She gave me this cradle for Jas, little Donno was in it before. Isn't it beautiful?" Vicky rocked the oak cradle Jasmina was laying in. She looked like a fairy tale baby, asleep under her pink covers, with glittery stars dangling above her from the cradle's hood. Just at that moment her eyes popped open and she stared at us peacefully. "Little darling, come here and let me cuddle you," Vicky said, bending into the cradle and scooping Jasmina up in her arms.

"I really like the sound the tamboura makes," I said, "it's soothing and hypnotic. It takes me somewhere."

"Where's that then?" asked Vicky, smiling.

"I don't know. I'll go and play it again and then maybe I can tell you." I went upstairs to our room and lit the fire, relishing some time alone. I sat on the floor and cradled the tamboura in my lap. It felt so right in my arms, like we fitted together. Even though the instrument was huge and slightly uncomfortable, I loved it. I adjusted the tuning until it felt right and played the four strings over and over. The constant strumming created multiple harmonic overtones that washed over me like a river of sound. I was lifted beyond myself, floating in another realm, like a cloud or a bird, surrounded with soft colours and a heady fragrance. I played for a while, then lay the tamboura down and simply sat, relishing the expansive state I was in, the subtle vibration of the silence as the notes of the tamboura slowly faded away and were replaced by the sound of the restless sea, crashing on the shore below me.

The following morning, we picked winkles for three hours. Eddie and I gathered two buckets between us and our fingers were frozen. Every time I closed my eyes all I could see were winkles. We walked the shore, turning over rocks and stones, scraping off the limpet-like creatures and throwing them in the bucket.

Ben had shown us what to do, then gone to work with Jules and Nick on pointing the walls of the boathouse, so it would be weatherproof before winter truly arrived. If this wasn't winter then I dreaded to think how cold it would get. The only time I was warm was in bed or in front of the fire. The days became weeks, each day indistinguishable from the other. There were no shops on Waternish. Once a week a small blue van arrived with a few tins and some tired looking vegetables. Our diet was oats, fish and brown rice, with occasional vegetables, and bread when Lucy baked. It was a simple life and we loved it.

Most evenings we gathered round the fire at the schoolhouse and sang. Songs like *The Cuckoo, Jack of Diamonds, Blowing in the Wind, She Loves You* and the Donovan favourites, *Mellow Yellow, Catch the Wind* and *Season of the Witch*. Julian also liked to play the song Don had written for me when we were teenagers in St Albans.

The landscape was endlessly wondrous: the quality of

the light; the starkness of the mountains; the eternal movement and colours in sea and sky filled me with awe every day. Living on Skye was living close to nature, being at one with the elements. We saw eagles and seals, sparrow hawks and gannets. When it was too wet to go out, I would sit by the window, play the tamboura and watch the constantly changing dance of nature.

And every day we picked winkles. When the moon was full the entire village joined us on the beach. They brought shovels and went home with bulging sacks, making our buckets look very meagre indeed. We earned about ten pounds a week, almost enough to live on, frugally.

Occasionally we went to Portree for a shopping trip, a round trip of about fifty miles through stunning countryside. The town, though tiny, felt noisy and busy and an assault on my senses after the peace of Waternish. I could not imagine what a city would be like.

Jasmina grew bonnier each day and we all fell in love with her. She was a happy child and was content with whoever was holding her. I still longed for my own child, but the tamboura consoled me. I played it every day and discovered cotton strings on the bone bridge. When I adjusted the cotton, the strings buzzed in a delightful way, extending the drone effect.

One evening Donovan phoned. After he'd spoken with Julian about the house I asked for the phone. "Hey Don, it's beautiful here. Every day is a miracle."

"I know, one of the crofters at Lustin told me 'God was showing off when he made Skye.' I've been thinking of writing a song about it."

"Good idea. I really love playing the tamboura, it's magical and takes me into zones I've never travelled in before."

"You can have it, Joanna. I knew I'd taken it to Skye for a reason. Enjoy it."

"Really?" I asked, breathless.

"Yeah. I want you to have it. No point in it laying there unloved. Instruments need to be played. I look forward to hearing you play it when you come back."

"Thanks Don, you really are a star." I said, feeling like crying I was so happy. That evening, as I cradled the tamboura on my lap and plucked the strings I felt I was holding a precious friend, someone who would be with me for the rest of my life.

Four days later we were searching for winkles for three hours in freezing rain and a sharp north wind. We gathered half a bucket full! Eddie came back with four half crowns and threw them on the table. "A measly ten bob!" he shouted, "My fingers are almost dropping off and all I ever see is winkles. Winkles when I eat, winkles when I sleep, winkles when I wake up in the morning. I'm sick to death of winkles!"

Jasmina, who'd been feeding, reared back from Vicky's nipple, opened her tiny mouth wide and cried like a banshee.

I jumped up. "Calm down, love. Here, sit by the fire and I'll make you a cuppa."

"I don't want a cuppa tea. I don't want to see another winkle. Ever! I want to go to a pub and have a beer. I want..., Oh I don't know what I want. But I don't think I want to be here anymore. It's too quiet and too cold and too hard to make a living. What am I gonna do? Pick winkles for the rest of my life?" He sat down and looked at me, his fire turning to sorrow as he gave voice to the frustration that had been building up in him.

"I didn't know you felt like that."

"Nor did I, 'til I said it." He reached out and held my hand. His hand was warm, in spite of the hours on the freezing beach. Mine was still icy.

Vicky had tactfully moved into the kitchen and was walking around with Jas, singing softly to her.

"We can't go on like this," he said, squeezing my hand.

"But I love it here."

"I know, so do I, at least I think I do. I love being with the guys and making music with Jules and Ben. But what am I going to do? We can't live on the money we get from winkles. There's no other work. I really don't want to ask Don for a handout and I can't work on the house. I'll smash my hands up for sure and then I won't be able to play." He sighed and put his head in his hands. I put my arms around him and we just sat there, silently.

"We'll go back South," I said, after some time.

He leaned back and looked me in the eyes. "Really?"

Our eyes held one another's and the love between us was tangible. I knew nothing else mattered. I smiled and nodded, "Really. We're all that matters. We'll be fine wherever we are. Maybe we're not meant to stay in one place just yet."

Eddie leaned forward and kissed me, his lips warm and soft. "I love you, Joanna Freeman."

"I love you too, Eddie Freeman. When shall we go then?"

"Monday."

"Okay, that gives us a couple of days to say goodbye. I'll tell Vicky."

Three days later we sailed away from Skye on the same ferry boat. The tamboura was wrapped in blankets in the back of the car. As we drove ashore a giant double rainbow formed ahead of us, the road passing directly under it. "Somewhere under the rainbow then," I said, as we drove South.

"Each celestial body, in fact each and every atom, produces a particular sound on account of its movement, its rhythm or vibration. All these sounds and vibrations form a universal harmony in which each element, while having its own function and character, contributes to the whole.

Pythagoras (569-475)

BRISTOL 1970

The walk home was uphill all the way. The bags I was carrying were heavy and I stopped for a rest outside an elegant red brick house. Cotham was full of houses like this, built during the Georgian era, when Bristol was an affluent port serving the far reaches of the British Empire. I noticed a pram outside a neighbouring house and peered in at the sleeping baby.

I had a sudden impulse to grab the child and run. I felt like two people. Sensible me was shocked by the primal urge to hold a child, any child, that crazy me was feeling. "You can't do that," I told myself. "Think how her real mum would feel when she came to get her baby."

"Just pick her up then. Feel her soft cheek against yours. Go on." I hesitated, standing over the pram, my arms aching for the child in spite of myself.

"No!" I told myself. I turned away and picked up my shopping. I was still shaken when I reached the bed-sit we called home. I dumped the shopping on the floor, lit the gas under the enamel kettle and collapsed onto the sagging easy chair beside the bay window.

Fat, resinous buds grew on the Sycamore tree outside. In the garden opposite golden daffodils nodded in the breeze. School kids hurried home, heavy satchels on their backs. The kettle whistled and I made myself some tea and sat down again. I had to stop being so obsessed. Every month, when my period started, I felt a disappointment so raw it was like having my skin scraped off. Like something had died inside me. Which it had in a way.

I spoke to no-one about this, didn't even write it in my diary. There was nowhere to go with it and nothing to say.

My only consolation was playing the tamboura. When I sat on the floor and cradled it in my lap, my arms tenderly holding its round body, my head resting on its neck, I felt peace. As I plucked the four metal strings, I became lost in the vast ocean of sound. Loosing myself I found something so much greater.

I put down my empty cup and picked up the tamboura, adjusting the tuning and the cotton strings on the bridge. I began to play, slowly plucking the strings. The resonant harmonics created layer upon layer of sound, a rippling, ever expanding wave of music that engulfed me.

The door opened and Eddie burst in, threw his conductor's hat and bag on the table and flopped down on the bed. "Phew," he said, "I'm knackered. I must have walked miles on that bus today. We were really busy."

"What route were you on?" I asked him, putting the tamboura back in the corner.

"41, Temple Meads to Clifton Zoo. Lots of tourists going to the zoo today."

"Nice day, it's getting warmer so I suppose everyone wants to get out."

"Yeah, how was your day?"

"Oh, pretty routine really. Maisie moaned about her husband all morning. I entered loads of figures into the machine, had a sandwich, went for a walk at lunch time and did the shopping on the way home. Just another day at the office!"

"Better than picking winkles in the freezing rain though," he said, hugging me.

"Yeah, much better, and pays well too," I said, laughing. "Fancy omelette for tea?"

"That would be great. Do we have any cheese?"

"Yep, cheese omelette it is then. What time's the gig?"

"We should be there for the sound check at 7.00. They open at 7.30."

"Ok, I'd better get moving."

Once we'd eaten, we changed our clothes and made

our way to the bus stop. I carried the guitar and Eddie carried the tamboura, wrapped in blankets and tied up with string for protection. People stared at us when we climbed aboard the bus with our instruments, but we didn't care. I sat beside the tamboura, hugging it protectively, leaning the neck towards me so it didn't bang against the luggage rack. Eddie sat on another seat, the guitar in his lap.

Paul and Stash were already in the back room of the pub when we arrived. Stash was tuning up his double bass, Paul was fiddling with the P.A.

"Hi guys, how's it going?" Eddie asked, unzipping his guitar case.

"Great," Paul said, "I think it'll be a good night. Lots of people told me they're coming. Hi Joanna, I thought you could sit on this stool, what do you think?" Paul indicated a low stool, which looked just the right height to sit on and play the tamboura.

"Looks perfect, Paul, thanks." I unwrapped the tamboura and began to tune it while the guys set up. "Can you fine tune it for me, Eddie?" I asked. His ear was much better than mine and I found the tamboura stayed in tune longer after he'd tuned it.

After the sound check I made a nest of blankets for the tamboura at the back of the room and bought a round of drinks while the guys played. We'd met Paul and Stash at a New Year's Eve gig, shortly after arriving in Bristol and Eddie had played with them ever since. About a month ago, I began playing tamboura with them on a few numbers, like *Norwegian Wood* and *Sunny Goodge Street*. I'd never performed before and was quite shy. I worried if I would know that the tamboura was out of tune while I played. But the exhilaration I felt when we played together was worth going through the nerves beforehand. Tonight, I was really looking forward to playing.

The pub filled quickly and at eight o'clock Stuart, the landlord, introduced us and the guys began the set with *Hoochie Koochie Man*. The music was an eclectic mix of R&B and folk with funky jazz undertones, and some mind-blowing improvisations. Halfway through the set I joined in with the tamboura and played for around half an hour.

The tamboura added an exotic foundation to the music, allowing Paul to improvise on his twelve-string guitar. Eddie provided the vocals and a driving rhythm with open-chorded strumming, and Stash's fingers danced on the bass notes, bringing a visceral physicality to the music.

After I played, I joined the throng of sweaty bodies jumping and gyrating to the music. Every face I saw glowed with the joy of music, dance and the sheer freedom of self-expression. The tribal connectivity was tangible, like a silken thread that joined us all together. I'd experienced this at festivals, gigs and parties for most of my adult life.

Throughout the late sixties there had been a lot of talk about the dawning of the Age of Aquarius and the new age of enlightenment. Many people explained the changes of the times as a result of experimentation with LSD and other psychedelic drugs. However, I felt it was much more than that. We were riding a tidal wave of change, a massive expansion of consciousness; an unprecedented expression of the power of youth— the explosive energy of a music which merged the rhythms of Africa with the esoteric beauty of the East, the liberation of breaking down boundaries and barriers. We were a new generation and we had money and power. We vehemently rejected the materialism of our parents and were determined there would be no more war. We valued life and nature and loved the multi-cultural rainbow coloured world we lived in. We danced to the rhythms of the world, and fearlessly blazed a new trail.

After the gig we sat around chatting, too buzzed up to go home. "Why don't we have a festival on the downs?" Paul suggested.

"Great idea," Stash responded with enthusiasm. "We can be the headline act."

"Well, we can play and I'm sure we'll get loads of other bands," Paul said. "Maybe we need to get someone people have heard of as well."

"Some people have heard of us." Eddie said.

"It doesn't have to be a big deal," I said, "we could just do it and spread the word and even if a few hundred turn up it'll be fun. We can keep it simple."

"Do you fancy organising it, Joanna?" asked Stash.

"Maybe," I said, "I'll think about it."

That night I couldn't sleep for thinking about it. The idea had grabbed my imagination and I was excited. Over the following weeks I spoke with everyone I knew and by the end of April the 'Clifton Downs Midsummer Festival' was a reality. As the word spread, musicians were clamouring to take part and the line-up was settled by early May.

I woke up one gorgeous May morning, sunlight streaming in through the yellow curtains and the blackbird singing its heart out on the Sycamore tree. The moment I sat up a wave of nausea washed over me. I wrapped a towel around me, ran down the stairs to our shared loo and was violently sick. Eddie was still fast asleep when I returned to our room.

After washing my mouth out with cold water, I drew back the curtains, sank into the sagging easy chair and stared out the window, my heart fluttering like a bird. I looked at the calendar and realised I was three weeks late. And I'd just been sick. I rested my right hand on my stomach and smiled. At last, a baby was growing inside me again. This one would be strong. I mentally welcomed her, reaching out my awareness to the delicate group of cells within me that was dividing and multiplying as I breathed in and out. Life! What a miracle.

I picked up the tamboura and sat on the floor with it on my lap. Softly I played the strings and serenaded the new life within me, knowing this sound would sooth her. How did I know she was a girl I asked myself? Then shrugged because, although I did not know the answer, I knew my daughter was growing inside me.

Eddie woke, yawned, stretched and smiled at me.

"I think I'm pregnant," I said.

He jumped out of bed and wrapped me in his arms, "Oh Joanna, wow. Oh wow. When will it come?"

"Not sure yet, I've only just realised." We smiled joyfully at each other and clung together, relishing the magic of the moment.

I walked around in a warm glow for the rest of the week. Each morning I was sick but it didn't last all day and I was so happy it didn't matter. When I saw the doctor, she confirmed that I was, indeed, pregnant. The baby was due on December 21. I stopped at a phone box on the way home and called mum. She cried with joy when I told her.

"Come and see us soon, love. I miss you," she said, "how about coming for your birthday at the end of the month? I want to mollycoddle you."

I laughed. "I don't need mollycoddling Mum, I'm a grown woman."

"Ahh but you're still my little girl, you always will be. You'll understand once you become a mum as well."

"Ok, maybe we can come for a few days over the bank holiday, I'll talk to Eddie. And you can always come and visit."

"You've got no room for me there. Maybe you should look for a bigger place now."

"Good idea," I said, "Another room would be great. I'll get the papers and see what's around." That afternoon I bought the local paper and found a flat in Montpellier that was affordable. We went to see it that evening, loved it and moved in three weeks later.

Our new home in Albert Park Road was on the ground floor, with a small garden, our own front door, a tiny hall, a living room, kitchen and bedroom as well as our own bathroom. Luxury indeed! We painted the living room a warm shade of apricot. I was home-making for the first time in my life. We'd never stayed anywhere long enough to bother with decorating before.

Many families from the Caribbean Islands lived in Albert Park Road and the kids played freely in the quiet street outside. I loved seeing the ladies, dressed in their best, walking to church on Sundays. They wore such brilliant colours: bright pink dresses with scarlet hats, or vivid emerald and sunshine yellow. Their gardens were full of colourful windmills instead of flowers, and we bought windmills for our garden too. There was something exotic about living in Montpellier, walking past the whirring windmills, seeing the guys gathered on the street corner, smoking and chatting, the unfamiliar aroma of spices in the air.

While planning for the festival I'd met Mark, who played sitar. I invited myself round to play the tamboura with him. Eddie and I set off one Friday evening, catching a bus from Cheltenham Road to Clifton.

'Hi, come in,' Mark said, ushering us into his living room. We sat on his bright red sofa and admired the geometric prints on his walls. There was no carpet on the floor, simply plain pine floorboards, sanded and varnished to a light gold. The room had an open, uncluttered feeling with large floor cushions and minimal furniture.

Mark served us tea in thick pottery cups and proceeded to talk about Indian classical music for over an hour, telling us about ragas and tuning and performances he'd heard. We made interested noises now and again, fidgeted, drank our tea and tried not to meet each other's eyes in case one of us started giggling. When were we going to play? I wondered, but didn't like to ask.

Eventually he took the sitar on his lap and adjusted the tuning. I moved onto a floor cushion and Eddie fine-tuned the tamboura and handed it to me. I plucked the strings and the magic of the sound captured me once again. Then Mark played a cascade of notes on the sitar and we travelled into a new soundscape: desert dunes, palm trees, terracotta palaces and stark blue skies, camels and elephants, tigers and monkeys arose and dissolved in my mind's eye as the music saturated us. When Mark finished, I plucked the tamboura strings for a few minutes more, letting the resonance of the notes drift off into the ether. The silence that followed was profound and full, pulsating with stillness.

"Phew," I said, "that was powerful."

"Music is the doorway to the soul." Mark said. After that there was nothing to say.

On our way home we were both quiet, recapturing the magic in our minds. I hugged the tamboura close to me on the bus and felt the roundness of its body pressing against the small swell of my stomach.

Midsummer's day dawned fresh and bright. We arrived on the downs a little before 10.00am, Stash and Paul were already setting up with some mates they had roped in to help. Over the next two hours a steady stream of people arrived and by mid-day the festival was well underway. An enterprising ice-cream van pulled up on the pavement and was doing a roaring trade.

A group of young girls in flowing tie-dye dresses danced to the music of a psychedelic synth player and a manic drummer. People lay around on the grass, happy to simply be. The sun was hot, the sky blue, an occasional fluffy cloud floated by. In the distance the elegant span of Clifton suspension bridge stretched across the gorge to Leigh Woods.

We played for an hour and people loved it. I had never performed in the open air before and there was a quality of freedom to playing beneath the skies that bordered on ecstasy. The vibrations of the tamboura radiated upwards and outwards, seemingly re-arranging the molecules of the air around us. Wherever I looked I saw joyful faces, eyes bright with light, with love. This is unity and peace I thought. This is what harmony looks like. Each person present was expressing his or herself in their own, unique way. One guy, wearing shorts and a bright yellow Indian shawl, was dancing alone with a look of utter absorption on his face, his hands tracing intricate patterns through the air. A young girl sat cross legged, intently drawing. A couple lay entwined on a blanket, gazing into each other's eyes.

The band that followed us sounded like the Byrds, with ethereal harmonies, virtuoso guitar solos and the best drummer I have ever heard. I danced barefoot, embracing sky and earth with my movements. Nobody wanted to go home and we spent the rest of the balmy evening gathered in small groups talking, singing, playing guitars and watching the sky darken and stars appear. The entire event was effortless and easeful. People even cleared away the rubbish and we left the downs cleaner than when we had arrived.

We made many new friends that day. I felt part of a community of like-minded people again. Maybe, just maybe, we could make a difference and change the world for the better. We gathered in one another's homes most evenings, our animated discussions ranging from art and music to politics, non-violent revolution and the Vietnam War.

We dreamed of a world where all were equal, where no one went hungry, where each person had what they needed and did not want more. We railed against the old men who tried to control everything: Ted Heath and the Tories who personified capitalism and consumerism to us. We had grown up with Harold MacMillan telling us we'd never had it so good. Lived in net-curtain-twitching suburbs where envy and greed defeated the generosity and good-neighbourliness of the times of poverty and war.

The times were changing and we were that change. It was exhilarating and heady. Anything was possible.

One hot day in August I stepped out of the bath and my foot was covered in hundreds of fleas before my other foot even reached the ground. I screamed and Eddie came running in. The bathroom was alive with fleas. They had appeared out of nowhere and transformed the brown lino into a black, seething mass. I wrapped a towel around me, tried to wipe the army of fleas off my feet, and ran into the kitchen. We spent hours spraying and scrubbing and eventually called the council in to fumigate.

"It's an epidemic." Bill, the council pest-control man told us. "They're all over Montpelier. I've never seen anything like it. You'll have to move out while we spray."

We stayed with some mates in a commune in Hotwells, an area at the foot of Clifton Hill, and, when a room on the fourth floor became vacant, we decided to move in. Even though the fleas had gone our flat stank of chemicals and we wanted to try communal living.

The commune rented the entire house, which was on a busy and noisy corner on the main route to Bristol docks. On the ground floor was a shop, which we all took turns to work in. We sold candles and incense, hand-made leather goods, tie-dye shirts and dresses, bongs and chillums and second-hand books and miscellanea.

It was fun working in the shop, there was always something going on: people passing through on their way back from India, offering us cotton caftans and mirrorwork from Rajasthan, or a guitarist singing in the corner, or a group of people animatedly discussing politics. The shop was a meeting place, a hub for the community. It was the place to hear about what was happening and to connect with others. Half of one wall was always covered with posters and adverts for everything from kittens to caravans.

The kitchen and bathroom were on the first floor, along with a tiny cupboard of a room occupied by Fred. He was a pasty-faced macrobiotic vegan who had so many foibles about food he rarely ate anything and he was the most miserable person I had ever met.

Jo and Jessie lived in a front facing double room on the third floor. Our room was directly above theirs. Jessie and I hit it off immediately. She was from Liverpool, like my mum, and had a down-to-earth practicality and relentless energy. Jo, on the other hand, was permanently stoned and utterly useless. He had no conversation, no opinions and all I ever heard him say was 'yeah man' and 'pass the joint.' I couldn't understand what Jessie saw in him.

The other two single rooms on the third floor were occupied by Henry and Mandy. Henry was an artist who spent hours every day on the downs, sketching surreal pictures of trees and nature spirits. Mandy was a textile student at Bristol Poly and was responsible for all the tie-dye in the shop. She also made a terrible mess in the kitchen every time she cooked and was somewhat scatty and dis-organised.

We were the only room on the top floor. It was a converted attic, with the roof sloping down to the floor and tiny windows that looked out over the rooftops.

Life in the commune was chaotic, crazy and occasionally hilarious. We were all so 'free thinking' and worried about appearing 'uncool' that no one organised anything. Eddie was the only person working. I stopped work in October and spent hours crocheting colourful squares each day which I sewed together to make cushions, bags and occasionally bedspreads. I sold these in posh craft shops in Bath and Bristol, earning about a shilling an hour if I was lucky.

Either Jessie or I cooked a main meal most days, mainly because we wanted to eat something nourishing. We usually cooked brown rice and vegetables or a hearty stew. We were all vegetarians and had agreed to be a 'no meat' household. Henry cooked a good spaghetti and sauce sometimes and both Eddie and Fred washed up, but Jo never did a thing. I became used to cleaning the kitchen before I cooked and tried to ignore the mess the rest of the time. It wasn't easy. The sink was always full of dirty cups, the surfaces covered in breadcrumbs, jam, Marmite, smears of butter and general debris.

I loved being pregnant, I walked with a new pride, holding my shoulders back and head high. I had never felt so healthy in my life. I sometimes stood in front of the mirror, admiring the curve of my belly. It was getting hard to fit the tamboura on my lap, and I started laying it horizontally across my knees. The baby wriggled and kicked inside me most of the time, but she always slept when I played the tamboura. It was a lullaby for both of us, bringing us back to stillness and peace with each stroke of the strings.

In December Eddie took on extra work delivering the Christmas post. We were spending most of our time in our room, the novelty of communal life had quickly worn thin. I baked bread every day and barely ate a slice of it. Most of the food we bought disappeared and we had given up asking everyone else to contribute fairly. I reluctantly came to the conclusion that human beings are basically selfish and thoughtless. It takes becoming responsible for another life to induce us to the path leading to maturity. It is hard enough to live with someone you love, let alone try to live with people you barely even like.

On December 15 I woke at five with a sharp cramp in my stomach. I walked down the three flights of stairs to the loo and my waters broke all over the floor. I wiped it up, made two cups of tea and climbed back up the stairs to our room. I gently shook Eddie awake. He opened his eyes and looked blearily at me. "The baby's coming. You'd better wake up and phone the hospital."

"What?"

"The baby's coming. My waters have broken."

"Are you in pain?"

"Not really, a bit of cramping but we need to tell them. I'll probably have to go in."

"But you're not due for another week."

"Maybe she's impatient. Drink your tea and then you can call them."

By seven a.m. we were in Southmead hospital. I had been examined and told that it would be several hours until anything happened. I was having weak contractions every forty minutes. "You may as well go to work then," I said. "You can phone up during the day and come in when it gets close."

"I don't want to leave you." he said, putting his arm around my shoulder.

"Well, I don't really want you to go, but they won't even let you stay on the ward with me, and we really need the money! I'll be OK."

"You sure?"

"Yes, sure, love you. Call every two hours and check in though."

"Of course. I love you too. Good luck!" My eyes filled with tears as he walked away. He stopped by the door and waved back at me, I smiled weakly and waved. Another contraction made me catch my breath, then I remembered what I'd been taught and focused on breathing through it.

Throughout the day the contractions came regularly, intensifying with every hour. Around me the daily life of the ward went on. Visitors came and went. Nurses and doctors did their rounds. I felt I was in another world. The voices around me seemed distant, blurry. Someone offered me food, but I refused it. "You need to keep your strength up, my love," the nurse said in her thick Bristolian accent.

"I'd love a cup of tea, and maybe a banana? Can I get out of bed and walk around? It hurts my back lying here all the time."

"Better not. You're safe in the bed. We wouldn't want you falling over, would we?"

"Well, I need the loo."

"I'll bring the bedpan."

"Please let me walk."

"Oh, okay, come on then." I clambered out of bed and walked to the loo, nurse hovering beside me. Why didn't they let me move around I wondered? Surely women had been giving birth for centuries and it did not feel natural to do it lying down. My lower spine was burning and I felt so much better moving around.

A contraction gripped me and I bent over and clutched the nurse's shoulder, breathing into the pain. "You see, you'd be better off in bed," she said, grasping my arm.

Reluctantly I allowed her to lead me back to the bed. "I'll just sit on it for a bit. You can leave me now, I'll be fine." I said, knowing I had a good ten minutes before the next wave of pain.

Time passed in a blur of pain and breath, bright lights and unfamiliar voices. Eddie came back around five that evening. He sat beside me and held my hand, his strength flowing into me and lifting my spirits. All too soon they hustled him away. "No visitors allowed during meal times, Mr Freeman. I'll show you to the waiting room. You can come back at seven, during visiting hours." I heard his footsteps receding and felt alone and abandoned.

As the ward became busier the noise became more surreal. I was drifting in and out of realities. The spiky, red world of pain. The blurred stark white world of meaningless words and vague apprehension. A cold blue world of emptiness and fear. Finally, I heard someone say: "She is in a lot of pain; she should be in the delivery suite now."

I was moved onto a hard stretcher and wheeled down a cold corridor, then left alone again. The pains were stronger and closer. Inside I was quietly screaming for Eddie.

A porter came and wheeled me into another room. Bright florescent light dazzled me. My legs were strapped up in stirrups and a doctor wordlessly examined me. His rubber coated hands felt hostile. A nurse put a smothering black mask over my mouth and nose. "Breathe in lovey. This will help with the pain." The gas flowed into me, softening the scarlet pain into shades of pink and purple. "You can use this when you need it," she said, placing my hand on the mask.

"She's dilating nicely but has a way to go yet," the doctor said to the nurse.

"Can my husband come?" I asked.

"He can pop in for a few minutes if you feel up to it dear," the nurse said. "We'll be back in a while. Don't forget to use the gas and air." The door closed. I was alone again. My stomach squeezed and hardened creating a burning pressure that made me want to scream. I reached for the gas and air. Breathe in. Whirr. Breathe out. Pain. Breathe in. Whirr. Breathe out. Relax. Endure.

The clock ticks slowly on the wall. The familiar tightening as the pain escalates once more.

Eddie is there, warm hands, stroking my brow,

Breathe in. Whirr. Breathe out. Pain. Breathe in. Whirr. Breathe out. Relax. Endure.

Pressure between my legs. Unbearable. Has to be born. Born. Baby. Coming. Hold on.

Breathe in. Whirr. Breathe out. Pain. Breathe in. Whirr. Breathe out.

Eddie is gone. Alone again. Clock. Tick Tock. Nine o'clock.

Nurse: "Sorry love, we are short staffed and there's a breach birth next door. Here's the bell, call us of you need help." Presses something into my hand. Leaves.

Pain. Breathe in. Whirr. Breathe out. Pain. Breathe in. Whirr. Breathe out. Clock. Tick Tock. Ten o'clock.

"She's in third stage."

"Put her in the stirrups again."

"Pant now dear, don't push, baby's not quite ready to come."

Breathe in. Whirr. Breathe out. Pain. Breathe in. Whirr. Breathe out. Pain. No break between. The world is pain and I must push. Don't push. Pant. Pant. Pant. Pant. Pant.

"Right, now you're doing really well. On the next contraction I want you to push."

Push push push. Red face. Straining. Impossible! Push! Push!

Breathe. Rest. Push. Push. Push. Can't push. Rest. Push! Push! Push! Clock. Tick Tock. Ten forty-five.

"Forceps."

Cold steel. Warm liquid. Pain.

"Baby's head is here, one more push now." She slithers out of me and the nurse holds her. Open mouthed she yells her indignation at the world. Joy floods through me. Busily they clean and wrap her and briefly place her in my arms, then lay her in a cot, and leave.

Clock. Tick Tock. Eleven o'clock.

I am still in stirrups.

I long for a cup of tea.

I want my baby. She sucks her hand noisily. She sounds strong.

I want Eddie.

I want to be out of these stirrups.

I feel cold and wet and sore and alone.

Baby sleeps.

I ring the bell.

"Yes?"

"Can I have a cup of tea please?"

"You have to be stitched up. You have a rip from the forceps. Doctor will come as soon as he can. Then you can have tea."

Clock. Tick Tock. Twelve o'clock.

Clock. Tick Tock. One o'clock.

Baby is gone. Still alone.

"Right, let's get you stitched up and back to bed, eh? You've done really well."

Clock. Tick Tock. Two o'clock.

Finally, back in a ward by three thirty. Eddie has gone home. They would not let him in. He was in a waiting room alone all evening, while I was left alone because they were too busy. Barbaric!

We call her Molly Rebecca Freeman. She is the most beautiful baby anyone has ever had. She is always hungry and sucks hard. Her eyes are blue. I love her so much it hurts. I hold her close and gaze at her in total wonder. She has grown inside me, yet she is already her own person. She is strong.

After four days we are transferred to the Clifton Laying-in Hospital. All new mothers have to have the recommended ten days bed rest before being allowed home with their baby.

This is where we learn how to look after our child. I am sitting up in bed, trying to breast feed, a shawl wrapped around my shoulders and Molly. Nurse comes in. She is big boned and heavy chested. She takes one look at my small breasts. "You'll never be able to breast feed with them," she says, "Better give the poor mite a bottle or she'll starve to death."

I feel my worthless breasts shrivel. Molly opens her mouth and howls. The woman takes her away from me to give her a bottle and I curl up into the bed and cry. Why is this so hard? Every part of me hurts. My nipples are sore from Molly sucking, my womb is cramping unbearably, my fanny burns from the stitches and I cannot sit comfortably. I am bone tired and yet cannot sleep because it is too light and too noisy. I long for my mum and for Eddie.

Mum drove through the night and arrived to meet Molly the day after she was born, but now she is back in Cornwall. Eddie is at work. I am a useless mother who can never feed her child because her tits are too small.

That night Andrea, a motherly Caribbean nurse, is on duty. She brings Molly to me for a feed around 4.30am.

"I can't do it. Nurse Morris says I am too small to breast feed."

"What nonsense yo' speakin', chile? Yo' have perfec'ly good titties for yo' babby. Look, just put yo' teat in her mouth and relax."

I do as she says.

"Relax, ah said."

I breathe in deeply and look at my baby. Molly sucks hard, and I feel the warm liquid flowing out of me and into her. My womb contracts gratefully. Molly's tiny, oh so perfect hands stroke my breast and I look up at Andrea and smile.

"Yo' see, yo' a perfec' mother. Size does not matter. All that matters is a loving heart. Believe in yourself girl."

"Thanks Andrea."

We come home on Christmas Eve. I sit on our bed, my baby in my arms and my darling Eddie beside me and feel like the luckiest woman in the world.

The ear collects the spiralling energy from the cosmos, this energy gives life to man and we see this vitality in the light which shines forth from our eyes.

Anonymous Tibetan Medical Doctor

CORNWALL 1972

Dear Mum,

Happy New Year!

Winter in Kabul is so beautiful! Thick, white snow covers everything. The mountains look magnificent. The sky is cornflower blue, the sun so dazzling I have to wear sunshades. Even though it's minus twenty it's dry and the cold doesn't seep into your bones like at home. The new house has a brilliant heater which burns sawdust, and we have a big log fire in the sitting room.

Molly loves the snow! She toddles around in the garden, laughing and rolling around in it. We made a huge snowman yesterday, bigger than she is. We have thick, brightly embroidered sheep-skin coats, woolly hats and gloves, so we stay very warm.

I love living here, each season is different, the hot dry summer, the perfect autumn with sunshine every day, and now this glorious, sparkling winter.

We take a daily walk to Chicken Street, stop to chat with a few shopkeepers and admire some Turkoman jewellery, or a Baluchi carpet, take tea in one of the cafes and visit the post office to collect our mail.

Speaking of mail.... thanks for our Christmas presents! Molly plays with her dolly every day and the Marmite was VERY welcome. We had just run out!

Everyone loves Molly, her big blue eyes and blond hair are such a novelty here. But they all call her bacha, which means boy. I suppose the naffers (Afghans) can't handle calling Molly a girl. I've given up trying to correct them.

The women here are completely covered up in grey or black burkas which look like tents. They have only a small net grid to look out from. None of the women ever speak to anyone.

So strange! I still can't get used to it. I've heard that in Afghan homes the women serve the men first and never eat their own meal until every man in the house has finished eating. Can you imagine that!

We went across the Khyber Pass and into Pakistan to visit Peshawar last week. We stayed with Mohmeen, a business associate who helps with exporting the handcrafts. The journey was fantastic, it was spring in Jalalabad, which is only a two-hour drive from Kabul, and summer in Peshawar! I had to stay within Mohmeen's compound all the time we were there. Mohmeen said I would attract too much attention, which could be dangerous. Women do not travel around freely at all.

One of Mohmeen's servants lives in a tiny hut at the back of the compound with his wife and three children. I did see them, and we waved shyly at one another, but I don't speak any Pashto and she doesn't speak English, so we just smile, wave and nod in a friendly way.

Eddie went into the mountains around the Khyber Pass with Mohmeen and the guys. He told me it was wild up there; everyone carried a rifle over one shoulder and a bandolier of bullets over the other. Not surprising the British had so much trouble trying to invade Afghanistan.

The naffers are proud people. They have so little, yet they walk tall, hold their heads high and act as if they own the world. The guys dress strangely, in baggy cotton pants and western jackets, which they buy cheaply from the aid markets. You can see some of them in the photos. They insisted we take a picture of them with Molly.

Juma, one of the salesmen who comes round our house with a big bundle of embroidered susanis and agate studded jewellery, is from the North, Uzbekistan, I think. He is sweet, gentle and kind and a delight to do business with. He has deep brown slanted eyes and a round, open face. He looks like he's descended from Mongols. There are a lot of men like him in Kabul, and they seem much gentler than the sharp-faced and volatile Afghans.

Molly is chattering away now, although we don't understand most of what she says. I wish you could see her, Mum. I will

try to come home this year. I'm sending you the latest pictures
from her first birthday and Christmas, and I've taught her to
say Nana when I show her your picture. She's having trouble
with saying Grandad though.
Please give Dad my love, I will write to him soon.
Sending you big cuddles and a wet kiss from your
granddaughter.
Love
Joanna

Humph! What's the good of her saying Nana if I never hear
her? I've read and re-read this letter so many times I know
every line. Yet it's still only words on paper. I want to hold my
grandchild on my knee, sing to her, cuddle her, and hear her
say each new word as she learns it. The photos are lovely
though, at least Joanna sends me a bundle of pictures every
month. But it's no substitute.

She always was selfish and thoughtless. What kind of
mother drives five thousand miles with a six-month old baby?
I stayed home when she was born, pushed her in the big
pram to Kew gardens every day to feed the ducks. Mind, my
mum wasn't around either. Well, she died just after Arthur
and I were married at the end of the war. But Sadie I mean,
my real mum who gave me away to her sister when I was
two. She wasn't much of a mum, nor a gran. So, I didn't owe
her anything did I?

Am I saying Joanna owes me then? Is being a parent
like a deal, a job, a contract? 'I'll look after you for sixteen or
more years, then you have to make sure I'm happy and
fulfilled for the rest of my life.'

No, she doesn't owe me anything. Good luck to her. If
she has the opportunity and courage to travel and have
adventures then I admire her for it. No thought of
consequences.

No 'Will you be okay, Mum, if I leave you and take
your only grandchild half way across the world? Oh, and can
you look after my junk while I'm gadding around the planet?'

This bloody sitar thing, taking up all the space. How

long will I have this here? Still, it's quite exotic and, for some reason, sitting here in the spare room with this weird instrument makes me feel closer to her.

Donovan gave it to her. Saw him on the telly yesterday, singing and strumming his guitar, just like he used to do when he stayed with us. He was a nice, polite boy, bit of a dreamer, suppose that's why she liked him so much. Used to sit and play his guitar for hours on end, the two of them shut up in her room. God knows what they were up to. I was too trusting, too innocent.

Yet I have to admit I do admire her. She never let fear stop her doing anything she wanted to do. Climbing out the window and going up the West End to dance all night when she was sixteen. And leaving us a note saying she'd gone fishing. Gone fishing! I was so naïve. I even believed her! I'll never forget the night the police came round to tell us she'd been arrested. Arthur had to go up to London and get her out from West End Central police station. Then they had to go to the Flamingo Club to get her handbag and asthma pump. She and Vicky had been picked up on Wardour Street at three in the morning, arrested for being out late and 'under age.' What kind of a charge is that anyway? Arthur said the blokes who opened up the club looked like right gangsters. We grounded her after that. Didn't last long though. She soon wheedled her way round us. I never have been able to refuse her anything.

All those years when she was little, sitting by her bedside, holding her hand as the breath wheezed in and out of her. How could I deny her? I get the feeling she's been trying to cram as much life as she can into whatever time she has.

I felt like that in the blitz. Bootle was bombed every night and the air raid siren brought both fear and excitement with its deafening wail. Mam and Da always went to the Halliwells' basement, next door. But I went to the Blair Street Shelter and felt free for the first time in my life.

The nights we spent in there were the best of my young life: playing the piano, everyone gathered around singing their hearts out. "Come on Julia, give us another tune, you know you want to."

Me Mam was so strict I'd barely spoken to a young man, other than my brothers. My life was work, work, work and study, study, study. Every Saturday morning, I scoured all the doorsteps on Blair Street to earn a few coppers, and I gave them to Mam to buy food!

I was the first in our family to pass my eleven plus and get into the Grammar School. I was studying to go to college, but Sadie wanted me to start work at fifteen. She threw all my books on the fire!

In the air raid shelter, I sang and I danced, I tried smoking ciggies and I met my Arthur. I did my fair share of sneaking out as well after that. Mam wouldn't let me go to the Palais on a Saturday night. So, I lied to her. Told her I was going round to Flo's to set her hair. Flo's mum was in on it. I kept my dancing shoes there and my only half decent dress. Flo and I danced all evening.

I've always been light on my feet. Love dancing. We'd dance with the boys on leave from the war: soldiers, sailors and airmen. There were even Yankee airmen sometimes. Tall, clean-shaven and handsome. Flo fell in love with one, I think his name was Bill. He always had silk stockings and coca cola. He gave me my first orange. Wonder what happened to him? So many people came and went in the war.

I used to go out with me Da, after the raids. He was in the home guard. We'd go round together, finding bodies and seeing if anyone had survived. I would identify the children and young people, if there was anything left of them to identify. Sometimes, when I close my eyes, I see them still.

Here I sit again, staring at myself in the spare room mirror. I've just been to Port Quinn. I love going there, watching the sea crash against the rocks, the seagulls screaming overhead, salt spray in my face. I thought of getting another dog, they're good company, dogs. But I cried for days after Pookie died, I don't think I could go through that again.

The brass was so clean that week. I always clean the brass when I'm sad. There's something about cleaning and rubbing that soothes me. Not working now though. I've cleaned the brass every day this year and the ache inside never gets any less.

Look at yourself, Julia Jenkins, you're not even fifty and you look like a sad old woman. Pull yourself together, it's not like you to get maudlin.

What's it all about? That's what I can't work out. One minute you're wrapping presents for pass the parcel and saving up all year for train sets and dolls prams. Next minute you're driving them to Cheshunt to see where their favourite pop star lives, or dropping them off at the station to go train-spotting.

Your days are full from the moment you open your eyes to the time you lay your head back on the pillow: cooking, cleaning, taxi-ing, consoling, cajoling, loving, cuddling, laughing—mothering! Then they are gone, grown, independent and walking their own sweet path. As it should be, as it should be.

But who am I now? What's the point of it all anyway? The dogs die, the kids leave, the husband carries on gardening or snoozing or watching the wrestling on a Saturday afternoon. How long is it since I've danced and sang and played the piano?

So, whose fault is that? The piano is still downstairs, out of tune but that can be fixed. I've never been one to lie down and moan, so I'm not about to begin now. I'll write a list!

Julia's to do list January 1972
Call piano tuner
play piano every day
join the ramblers
look for a dance class
have my hair done
do something I've never done before.

What would I really like to do? Hmmm. Well, I've never really travelled, I mean the furthest I've travelled is Aberdeen in the north and Land's End in the south. Most of my life I've been looking after other people. Me Da, cousin Muriel, Arthur and the kids, the boys at work. Maybe now I should put myself first for a change! Ha! That's a thought. What would I really like to do?

130

Well, the first thought that came up was 'go to Afghanistan and see Joanna and Molly.' But that's impossible.

Why is it impossible?

Well, it would cost a fortune.

How much?

I don't know.

Well find out. What about those endowment policies you've been paying into for years? They must be worth something by now. And you've got a bit of money stashed away, 'for a rainy day.' Look outside. It's raining. If not now, when?

Hmmm.

Dear Joanna,

You'll never guess what I've just done! I've cashed in all my insurance policies and booked a flight to Kabul!!!!! Yes! I'm coming on April 18 and staying until May 2.

I am so excited, and longing to see you all. Dad is happy for me to go. I'll cook him lots of pies and put them in the deep freeze. Alan has given me the time off work with full pay as a bonus, I can still have my two weeks holiday later in the year.

I've made an appointment with the doctor to work out what jabs I need, and I've even begun filling in my passport application.

I think the only thing that was stopping me was fear, and now I've started organising it I can't imagine what I was scared of. I've always wanted to travel and I really think this will just be the start of my adventures.

I'm flying with Turkish Airlines, with a three hour stop-over in Istanbul.

I haven't told anyone else yet. I wanted to share it with you first. I can't believe how easy it feels now I am actually doing it. I wake up every morning with butterflies in my stomach. I am so excited. I feel like a new woman.

I can hardly wait to see you. Write back and let me know what the temperature will be and what clothes you think I'll need. What do you want me to bring you?

Dad sends his love, as do I! Please give my love to Eddie and a big kiss and cuddle to Molly.

SEE YOU SOON!!!!!

Love Mum
Music is the art of the prophets, the only art that can calm the agitations of the soul.

Martin Luther (1483-1546)

KABUL 1972

My heart was pounding and I hugged Molly's warm body to mine as I watched the Turkish Airlines plane taxi to a stop in front of Kabul airport. After an interminable wait people began descending the stairs, which had been wheeled up to the plane door. I screwed my eyes up against the bright sunlight, trying to recognise Mum.

"There she is," said Eddie, pointing excitedly. Sure enough, there was Mum, dressed in slacks and a loose top and looking so much smaller than I had remembered her as she stood on top of the stairs and looked around.

"Quick, take a picture," I said. We had become experts in capturing moments to share with the family. Mum looked over to where we were as I spoke, as if she could sense us.

"Look, Molly, there's your Nana," I said, tapping the window and waving frantically. Of course, she couldn't see us. She was too far away. Nevertheless, Molly joined in the fun and waved as well. We watched as the passengers walked toward the terminal building. When I could no longer see Mum, I put Molly down and grabbed her soft, warm hand. "Come on, let's go and meet Nana!" Eddie and I looked at each other, sharing the excitement and slight trepidation we both felt. He smiled and reached out for my other hand.

"It'll be fine. Julia's going to love it here!"

I breathed in and nodded. "Of course she is."

We made our way to the arrivals door and waited, alongside an Afghan woman with a baby in her arms and two small children clinging to her burka, an official looking soldier and a group of hippies.

Soon Mum appeared in the doorway and next minute she was in my arms, her eyes brimming with unshed tears. I hugged her tight, unable to speak, it was so good to see her.

"Welcome to Kabul, Julia," Eddie said, enfolding us both in his arms.

Mum wiped her eyes and squatted down to greet Molly face to face. "Hello, little one. Can I have a cuddle?"

Molly melted into her Nana's open arms, responding naturally to the love streaming out to her. Mum buried her face in Molly's hair, breathing in her scent. When she looked up at me her eyes glistened with tears of joy. Soon we were all in the car on our way home.

"How was the journey, Mum? Did you manage to sleep at all?"

"Not really, I'm too excited to sleep. I'm longing for a cup of tea and a shower though. I almost got arrested in Istanbul, they nearly didn't let me back on the plane."

"What happened?" Eddie asked, his forehead wrinkling in concern.

"We had a long wait between flights and I was bored so I went exploring, I think I must have gone somewhere I was not supposed to. An angry policeman started shouting at me in Turkish and took me to his office. I couldn't understand a word he was saying so I just kept saying sorry and smiling and eventually they let me go."

"Were you scared?" I asked.

"A bit. More scared of missing the plane really. All my luggage was on it."

"You're amazing, Mum. You've never left Britain before and now you've flown half-way round the world."

"I can't believe I'm here. The view from the plane as we were landing was incredible. I've never seen such enormous mountains."

"I know, Kabul is on a plateau and it's only when I am above it that I can see the mountains properly," I said.

"And they seem to go on for ever, they were covered in snow."

"The snow has only just melted on the mountains surrounding Kabul," Eddie said, "but the Hindu Kush, to the north will be covered in snow well into July. Maybe we can take you into the foothills while you're here."

"I'd love that. What I most want is just to be with my darling granddaughter and you two. I've missed you so much." Mum cuddled into Molly, who was drowsing on the seat beside her. Molly opened her big blue eyes and reached out her hand to stroke Mum's face.

"Nana," she said, laughing happily.

"Well, it was worth travelling five thousand miles just to hear that." We all laughed.

"Now we're in Shahr-e-Nau, which means New Town really," Eddie told Mum. "This is where our house is."

"Are there walls around every building then?" asked Mum, observing the stark twelve-foot-high walls that hid every building from view.

"Most of them," I said.

"It's a comparatively affluent area," Eddie added. "The embassies are all here and mostly westerners and government officials live in this district. People like to keep themselves and their property safe."

Mum looked thoughtful but didn't speak. We pulled up outside the walls of our house. I got out to open the big double gates, closing them again after Eddie had driven in. "Welcome to our home in Kabul, Mum," I said, opening the car door for her.

She climbed out and stood silently for a moment, taking in the bungalow with its sunny, wide veranda, shady garden and tranquil setting. "It's beautiful Joanna, so much bigger than I imagined, yet still cosy."

"Yes. We both love it, much cosier than the huge house we first had. Come on, let's get you settled in."

Soon we were relaxing on the veranda enjoying our tea. Molly was fascinated by her Nana and insisted on sitting on her lap, much to Mum's delight.

Once Mum had looked all around the house, exclaiming over the large, bright sitting room and surprised by the relatively modern kitchen and bathroom, she went for a shower and sleep.

The following day we walked to Chicken Street. It was a bright, sunny day, the blue sky a perfect backdrop for the soaring mountains which graced every horizon. Mum was fascinated by everyone and everything she saw. She nodded respectfully to a group of women dressed in full length burkas, and they each nodded back in return. We stopped at a cart which was heaped with enormous watermelons. A man, wearing a light grey turban, baggy charcoal-coloured pants and shirt and a tweedy western jacket, smiled warmly at us. Mum smiled radiantly back at him.

"As Salama Alaikum," Eddie greeted him.

"Wa Alaikum Assalam wa Rahmatullah," the stallholder responded.

"I've never seen so many melons," Mum said, "Are they good?"

"Good," the stallholder nodded enthusiastically. Eddie mimed that we'd buy one on the way home and we walked on.

"There's been a drought here for over three years," I told Mum. "The South, around Kandahar, is all desert, and most of the rest of Afghanistan is mountainous, and yet the melons and grapes are the most delicious fruit I've ever eaten. They are so juicy."

"It's as if God has given them juicy fruits to make up for the dryness everywhere else," Eddie said.

We passed an emaciated cow, so thin you could count her ribs, grazing on a pile of rubbish. "Is there no grass?" Mum asked.

I sighed. "The only grass I've ever seen in Kabul is in the gardens of Shahr-e-Nau."

A young father with his two-year old stopped to greet us. The two children smiled at one another, communicating in the universal language of childhood, while the adults struggled with minimal Farsi and English, creative mime and generous smiles.

By the time we reached Chicken Street I had the feeling the Afghans really liked seeing three generations of us together. Afghans are family people. The man is the head of the house, but we had learned from our interactions with the traders that family always comes first.

Most of the westerners that passed through Kabul were on the ever-expanding 'Hippie trail,' travelling East to seek answers to questions they had barely formed. Some became stuck in Kabul, trapped by the easy availability of hashish and hard drugs.

Eddie and I had a child to care for and we lived a very domestic and simple life. I never wanted to go to India. I had a dream once, the only part of which I remembered when I woke was a warning that if I went to India I would die. So, I was content to stay in Afghanistan, with occasional forays over the Khyber Pass to Pakistan.

We walked to Chicken Street most days, looked in the shops, went to the Post Office to collect mail, cooked, ate, played with Molly and did our work. In the ten months we'd lived in Kabul we had become known by the traders along our daily route. They all loved Molly and were now delighted to meet another member of the family.

Chicken Street was the hub of Kabul for visiting westerners. Each shop was vibrant with colour, their wares hung on every wall, window and post available: hand knotted carpets in natural shades of maroon, red, amber and orange; flat woven kilims with geometric designs in the colours of earth and nature, Turkoman jewellery in silver and brass, studded with coral and agate, carnelian and lapis lazuli; wall and tent hangings, *susanis*, each exquisitely embroidered with flowers, birds and intricate patterns; ancient camel dressings, cross-stitched tent bags, engraved brass work, lacquered boxes in jewel colours, ikat-dyed silk chapan robes and vintage Kuchi wedding dresses in rich silk-velvet, embroidered with gold and silver.

Anything and everything was for sale. For a price. Which usually began very high and could come down dramatically if you played the game well and the time was right. Haggling was an art and we were still learning it.

Every shop keeper greeted us and wanted us to come in and share a glass of tea with them. Mum was welcomed warmly over and over again. We stopped in our two favourite shops and Mum bought a carved wooden box for Dad. We left the bargaining to Eddie, who had become very good at it.

"My face aches from smiling," Mum said as we started walking home. "What amazingly friendly people. I know they want a sale, but they seem to be genuinely pleased just to see us."

"They are," Eddie said, "the Afghans are great people. Proud and somewhat wild, yes, but such huge hearts."

"Do you ever meet any women?" Mum asked.

"Not really," I said, "I've heard that the hammam's, the hot baths, are places where women hang out together, but I've never been to one. I'm a bit nervous to try it actually."

"Well, I'm not surprised," Mum said, "is everyone naked?"

"I'm not sure," I laughed, "That's why I'm a bit nervous about going. Not sure how comfortable I'd feel in a room with a lot of naked strangers."

"I can understand that. Think I'll give it a miss for now too."

We spent the rest of the day in the shade of the garden. Eddie went to the airport to meet our next group of visitors, a couple of Americans called Bill and Matthew. Molly was asleep on a charpoy, a wood-framed bed with a surprisingly comfortable woven base.

"Remind me how you came to be here?" Mum asked. "It's so different from your life at home, and you left so suddenly I never really understood what was happening. One minute you were living in a caravan on the Welsh borders, next you were driving to Afghanistan."

"I know, it was very sudden. Well, we went to the Glastonbury Festival in June last year, and when we returned to the caravan there were two letters on the doorstep. One was from Eddie's agent, telling him EMI. wanted to offer him a recording contract, the other was from my friend Graham, asking me to call him about some work that involved travel."

"Graham's the guy from Oxford Uni who you met when you lived in London isn't he?"

"Yes, and his wife, Sarah, used to commission me to

make crochet bedspreads when we lived in Bristol. They've been good friends to us."

"I never even visited you in the caravan." Mum said, sipping her tea, "I was planning to come in July."

"We weren't there that long, were we? It was better than Bristol because it was our space, but it was hard to earn any money from Eddie's gigs."

"What happened when you called Graham?"

"He asked us if we wanted to look after his interests in Kabul. Do you remember I told you that he has a carpet shop in Maida Vale?"

Mum nodded. "What did he want you to do?"

"He needed us to deal with the export end here and to look after his clients when they visited Kabul to buy antiques. They are mainly American; Graham has a store in Southern California now."

"Was that a hard decision to make? Eddie has been waiting for the 'big break' as long as you've known him. Why didn't he go for the recording contract?"

"It was a really hard decision, Mum. We talked about it for hours. It was a real crossroads in our lives. In the end the call of adventure won. We are both gypsies at heart I think and we love exploring new places."

"Yes," Mum agreed, "you are both well suited in that respect, always restless."

We looked at one another silently for a moment. I could sense her sadness that we'd left, but I didn't want to take on any guilt for living my own life the way I wanted to. "Well maybe you'll do more travelling now you've started Mum. It's a big world out there."

"I'd love to, but your dad isn't keen. Anyway, get on with your story."

"Well, when we talked about it, we thought the Rock'n'Roll lifestyle might not be so good for Eddie anyway, and we wouldn't really have been sharing it. He wasn't sure that 'fame and fortune' would actually make him happy."

"Probably wouldn't have. Even the Beatles split up, and there seems to be someone dying from some excess or other every month. Cliff Richard is still going strong though. Do you remember when we went to see where he lived in Cheshunt?"

"I was only about twelve, Mum! I did love him though. You were a great Mum, driving us all over Hertfordshire to go to gigs."

"Or sit outside pop stars houses." We both laughed and at that moment Molly woke up. As always, she was wide awake as soon as her eyes opened. She sat up and held her arms out to her Nana, who was decidedly her new favourite. Mum picked her up and cuddled her on her lap.

"I'll go and get her a cold drink and a snack."

Haaroon untied the huge bundle carefully. Bill and Matthew were sitting on the sofa, bright eyed and enthusiastic. They had slept most of the previous day, the journey from California was long and punishing, even for their surf-fit bodies. Mum looked comfortable on an easy chair, Molly was on her lap, as usual, and they were looking at a picture book together. Eddie and I sat at our dining table, watching as the evening unfolded.

Haaroon was our most regular trader, and we were both very fond of him. A Tajik, he was tall, thin, with bushy eyebrows, sharp, piercing eyes and a distinct nobility in his bearing. He always wore a brown turban, and dark brown loose trousers and shirt.

The first item Haaroon presented with a flourish was a purple silk *susani* with an exquisite border of flowers, birds and leaves in every colour that vegetable dyes produced: bronzes from Himalayan rhubarb, crimson from teak leaf, yellow from pomegranate rind and blue from indigofera leaves. A collective sigh went around the room.

Haaroon smiled to himself and produced a bright tent bag, one side of which was covered in cross-stitch, a double carpet bag, a variety of small prayer rugs with intricate designs, more colourful *susanis* and several silk-brocade *chapans*. Bill and Matthew questioned him about prices while Eddie served drinks and I handed round plates of snacks.

139

Mum looked like she was thoroughly enjoying herself.

Then Haaroon delved into his bundle and brought out a small leather pouch which he emptied onto a piece of black velvet. Uncut rubies, chunks of gold-veined lapis lazuli, aquamarine, emeralds, garnets and sapphires glinted on the dark cloth. I could not resist kneeling beside Haaroon and dipping into the pile of gemstones. I selected a large, uncut emerald the size of my thumbnail. Light danced within it as I moved it around on my palm.

"This is gorgeous Haaroon. Where was it mined?" I asked.

"This is from the Panjshir Valley, near my home," Haaroon said, pride colouring his voice.

"Are your family living there now?" Mum asked.

"Yes, my wife and children live with my parents in the mountains outside Bazarak. It is best country in the world."

"How many children do you have?"

"Three, two sons and a daughter, *hamdullah*."

"You must miss them," Mum said.

"Yes, I go home for Eid," Haaroon said.

I placed the emerald back in the pile, knowing it was beyond our budget. Bill and Matthew took my place on the floor and examined the gem stones. I looked over at Molly. Her eyes were drooping. "I'm taking Molly to bed," I announced, "you're welcome to join us Mum, if you like, or stay here."

"I'll stay," Mum said, "it's not every day I get to see such exotic treasures."

By the time Molly was settled and I returned to the sitting room, Haaroon was packing everything away. He looked very pleased with himself. Eddie and I exchanged glances which confirmed to me that sales had been good. I smiled to myself, happy that the evening had been a success.

We were driving into the centre of Kabul, with Bill and Matthew behind us in a taxi. We drove across the Kabul River, which hardly deserved the name of river as it consisted of a few muddy puddles in a dry and stony bed. Afghan men thronged the roads on either side of the river, most of the men wore a large turban with a loose piece of cloth hanging down below their shoulders.

The vivid blue of the sky provided the only colour in a landscape of brown and grey. The mountains offered several shades of brown, un-alleviated by any morsel of greenery. The men wore greys and brown, with an occasional off-white turban and most of the buildings were dirty white, fading to grey. And yet I had grown used to the colour-scape of Kabul and found beauty in the stark contrast of the jagged mountains against the perpetual blueness of the sky.

We parked the car and walked along the 'river' bank to the building which housed the money changers. This was one of the busiest areas of the city. We climbed the stairs to the first floor, which was divided into small cubicles, each opening onto the corridor. I was carrying Molly, and both Mum and I were at the centre of our group, with Eddie in front and Bill and Matthew bringing up the rear. Eddie had arranged it that way. The women had to be seen to be protected. It was a matter of honour.

A man sat inside each cubicle, sometimes on a chair, but more often on the floor. There were no women around, other than Mum and me. Eddie entered a cubicle and we all piled in behind him. "*As Salamu Alaikum,*" Eddie greeted the thin-faced man sitting on the floor.

"*Wa Alaikum Assalam wa Rahmatullah,*" Arsalan responded, eyeing us all with sharp, bright eyes. His nose was long and slightly hooked, and, as I met his piercing gaze I was reminded of a hawk. I lowered my eyes. I had learned to play the part of 'little woman' when out and about in Kabul. It was more important that Eddie was respected.

"*Hal e shoma chetore?*" Arsalan asked.

"*Khobas, tashakur,*" Eddie responded.

"What's he saying?" whispered Mum.

"Arsalan was asking how I am," Eddie said. "I told him good, thank-you." Eddie introduced Mum, Bill and Matthew to Arsalan, and they nodded respectfully at one another.

"Exchange good today?" Eddie asked, sitting cross-legged opposite Arsalan.

"Good rate," Arsalan responded, with a slight incline of his head "Pound or dollar?"

"Both," Eddie responded. "What rate?"

Arsalan reached for a piece of paper, wrote on it and passed it to Eddie. Eddie nodded and took a bundle of notes from his pocket. First, he counted out the pounds, and slid them over to Arsalan, who recounted them and secreted them into his waistcoat. Then Arsalan counted out a large bundle of Afghanis. Eddie watched carefully, re-counted the bundle, folded it and placed it in his inside pocket.

Then the procedure was repeated with a pile of dollars. Once the dollars had been pocketed Eddie stood. Placing his hand over his heart he looked directly into Arsalan's eyes. "*Tashakur. Khodafez*," Eddie said, lowering his head slightly.

"Well, that sure was different to any bank I've ever been in," Bill said as we walked out into the bright sunshine. We all laughed.

"I don't think anyone changes money in banks in Kabul," Eddie said.

"You certainly handled yourself well in there, man," Matthew said, "I felt I was in safe hands."

"Thanks," Eddie responded, smiling, "I've been here long enough to learn the ropes. It's all about respect with the Afghans. They are immensely proud people and I love them for that. I think that's why the British never managed to defeat them or cross the Khyber Pass. Their pride is their strength."

"We need to visit the tailor now," I said, "then we can go to the Khyber for a coffee."

"Lead on then," Matthew said. We put Molly in her Maclaran buggy and walked the short distance along the road to the tailor's district. In Kabul all the artisans and traders worked together. It was simple and effective and reminded me of Morocco, with its streets of tanners, dyers and sandal makers.

The tailors of Kabul also occupied an entire street— stall after stall of dark-eyed men hunched over sewing machines or sat on small stools in the sunshine putting the finishing touches to garments. The street was far more relaxed than the money-changers floor, which had thrummed with static tension and subliminal danger. A group of ragged children played ball in the street, some women in burkas were bartering in one stall, and a street vendor was frying something spicy on the roadside

We entered Sajid's stall and he looked up, his face wreathed in smiles. "Salam Sajid," I said, "how are you?"

"Good! Very good Mrs Joanna. *Tashakur*. And you?"

"I am very happy, thank you. This is my mother, Mrs Julia, who has come all the way from UK," I said.

"Salam," Sajid greeted Mum, his smile revealing several missing teeth.

"Salam," Mum responded. "You speak very good English."

"*Tashakur*, thank you. I like very much English people," Sajid said.

"Are my dresses ready, Sajid?" I asked.

"All ready Mrs Joanna," Sajid said, breaking into rapid Farsi as he directed his son to get the dresses.

The young boy staggered back with a bundle wrapped in brown paper, which he lay on the counter. I peeped under the brown wrapping at the neatly folded pile of dresses. I noticed that the top dress, a deep purple material, was stitched in pink cotton.

"Matching cotton?" I asked, knowing what the response would be.

Sajid shrugged comically, his eyes widening and his hands opening in the universal sign of bewilderment. "Good cotton. The best," he assured me.

I had attempted countless times to persuade him to sew each dress in matching cotton, but he preferred to use the same colour thread for every dress, it saved time and he could not see the problem.

I shrugged also and laughed.

"What do I owe you, Sajid?" I asked. He rummaged under his desk and produced a tatty invoice. I paid him, touched my hand to my heart, and thanked him once again. "*Khodafez*, Sajid, see you soon," I said.

Eddie picked up the bundle of dresses and we walked

back to the car and put the dresses in the boot. Soon we were seated on the terrace of the Khyber Restaurant, drinking coffee and watching the world go by in Pushtunistan Square.

Several hippies sat on the low wall of the central fountain, dusty rucksacks beside them. A group of heavily bearded men walked purposefully across the square, rifles slung casually over their shoulders, bandoliers of bullets glinting in the sunlight. Children played, goats meandered, a donkey, harnessed to a cart laden with furniture, ambled across the square. Smoke spiralled upwards from the fire of a street food trader. Another group of turbaned men squatted on their haunches playing a game of dice.

The sun glinted on the roof of the Royal Palace, turning it to gold. A line of people formed outside the Ariana Cinema next door. Vivid posters advertised the films to be seen, in Farsi and English. Mum stared at everything, drinking it all in and sipping her coffee quietly. Bill and Matthew looked equally fascinated. Molly was fast asleep in her buggy.

The muezzin called the faithful to prayer and a steady stream of devout men filed into the mosque. The Mausoleum of Amir Abdul Rahman gleamed white in the sunlight, its minarets and gold cupola adding an oriental air to its stately lines. The mountains brooded silently in the distance. Well-groomed men in suits chatted outside the city's two banks.

Three Kuchi women walked boldly past us, their heads high. They were dressed in flowing black dresses, heavily embroidered in bright colours and mirror work. Each wore a loose scarf over her head. They stopped nearby and stared directly at us. I touched my hand to my heart and smiled at them, lowering my head slightly. The youngest smiled back at me, taking in the family scene of sleeping child, mother and husband. They spoke excitedly, then the elder of the three tossed her head, turned and led the group away.

Mum looked questioningly at me. "They are Kuchies," I told her. "Nomadic tribespeople who travel from North to South and back again. Aren't they wonderful?"

"They look very different from the other Afghan women I have not really seen," Mum said, referring to the ladies in full length burkas with even their eyes concealed by mesh.

"I love the Kuchi women. They are so free, so wild. One woman walked into our garden in the other house. Cool as a cucumber she was. Walked in, looked around, looked at me then walked out again."

"They look very proud," Mum said, "I could sit here all day watching Kabul life, but I'm getting hungry. Shall we go home for lunch?" Eddie settled the bill and arranged where to meet up with Bill and Matthew and we made our way back to the car and drove home.

Eddie was busy with Bill and Matthew over the next two days, so Mum and I had some precious time alone. We pottered around the house and gardens, playing with Molly and simply enjoying one another's company. I noticed a shift in our relationship, probably due to the fact that I was now a mother. Mum was treating me more as an equal and fussing over me less. She had Molly to focus her mothering instincts on now so I had graduated to adult status at last. Mum also seemed genuinely impressed with our life in Kabul, and seeing her reaction helped me realise how much we had grown in the time we'd been here.

I was in my workroom, measuring out materials for another batch of dresses when Mum came in. "I've settled her down for a short nap. Can you show me what you do?" Mum asked.

"I'd love to," I said, putting the scissors down and hugging her. "First I buy rolls of materials from the material bazaar," I said, showing her the stack of rectangular bales on the shelf. "They are mainly Japanese cottons, with a few Russian ones. They have the best colours and designs. Look at this one," I pulled out a bale of Japanese cotton that I particularly loved and used often. It was a rich shade of midnight blue, scattered with delicate sprigs of violet, purple and pink flowers with pale green leaves. "Or this Russian one, which has a bigger pattern than usual."

"Oh, I love that," Mum said, "The red rose-buds on the black are quite dramatic."

"And feel the quality, it's so soft." Mum stroked the material between her fingers and smiled.

"So right now, I am measuring six metre lengths out, next I will match them up with pieces of velvet for the backs." I selected a piece of soft pink velvet to go with the length of blue material I had just cut. "See how this colour brings out the pink of the flowers?"

"Yes, it's a good match. Where do you get the velvet?"

"There's a market entirely dedicated to women's clothes, and one stall just sells velvet dresses. All the aid that is sent to Afghanistan from the West is sold in specialist markets. There's a market for everything in Kabul. I bought all Molly's clothes at the children's markets, lovely knitted dresses from Germany or Austria."

"Doesn't the aid get given to people?" asked Mum, surprised.

"It gets given to the stallholders, although I would guess they pay some baksheesh for it too," I laughed.

Mum looked shocked. "It's the system here Mum, every wheel that turns in Kabul is oiled with baksheesh. It works for the Afghans. Everyone makes a little bit along the way."

"Then I add a dress front," I said, opening a drawer and pulling out a closely embroidered panel. "I buy these in Chicken Street. There are so many colours in the fronts they match everything. And finally," I said, opening a wider drawer, "I choose a matching pair of cuffs. These are older than the fronts, and I find these in Chicken Street too, although I have to hunt them out."

Mum examined the finely embroidered cuffs; every pair was different and many looked like they had been removed from existing dresses.

"I prepare around twenty bundles at a time, then take them to Sajid to sew."

"What happens to the dresses when you get them back?" Mum asked, still playing with the embroidered cuffs.

"We export them home, and now to the US as well. The ones I collected yesterday will go to a shop in Portobello Road called Forbidden Fruit. Afghan dresses are getting very trendy. I can sell as many as I can get made, and now we're exporting colourful knitted socks, hats, and gloves. I'll show you some next time we go to Chicken Street. I've even found some embroidered leather boots, very soft and comfy, I think they'll go down well."

"You're becoming quite a businesswoman, Jo."

"Don't sound so surprised, Mum. You taught me book-keeping when I was twelve, remember?"

"Oh, yes, when I worked at that garage and you helped me over the school holidays."

"I think every child should learn simple book-keeping; I'm certainly going to teach mine."

"You're planning on having more than one then?"

"Yes, I'd like at least two, Molly needs a brother or sister. It must be a bit boring being an only child."

"Would you have a baby out here?" Mum asked, barely disguising her concern.

I paused to think about it. "No, I think I'd want to make a home if I had two kids. Don't worry Mum, we won't be here for ever. It's good for us now, and we're learning a lot, and making some money, but we will be home eventually. Maybe we'll even be able to buy a house."

Mum hugged me and I noticed the glint of tears in her eyes. "I can't tell you how happy I am to hear you say that, Jo."

The day after Bill and Matthew left, we drove into the foothills for a picnic. On our way out of Kabul we saw a Kuchi camp, a straggle of flapping black tents and tethered camels. A group of brightly dressed women squatted beside a smoky fire preparing food. Several thin-faced men with long beards stood around, chatting. A flock of scrawny goats grazed the scrubby rocks.

We stopped beside a lake and walked the short distance down to the water. I lay out a couple of cotton bedspreads to sit on. The lake was still and clear, a perfect mirror for the blue sky and brown mountains.

"It's so peaceful here," Mum said, "I hadn't realised how noisy Kabul is."

"Well, it is a city," Eddie said, setting down the basket

of food. "There's always some noise, horns honking, cartwheels rumbling, donkeys braying."

"The muezzin calling the faithful to prayer..."

"Street vendors yelling their wares," Eddie added.

"I quite like the sounds of Kabul," I said, "it's much less noisy than London. But it is really nice to hear the silence for a change. Who wants *khobbs* and cheese?"

"I do," Mum and Eddie said in unison. I passed around chunks of the dark flat-bread that Eddie had bought from our local baker that morning. Delicious when fresh, rock hard after a day. The cheese was Edam, which was the best we could find at the local supermarket. We washed it down with bottled water and then shared a flask of tea.

Molly was restless so I walked hand in hand with her to the water's edge and found some stones for her to throw in. Eddie joined me and skimmed flat stones over the sparkling water. Mum lay down, her jacket bunched up as a pillow beneath her head. It was nice to take some time out. Eddie put his arm around me as we stood beside the water, enjoying the stillness and the open horizon.

"Any more tea in that flask?" he asked, hopefully.

"Afraid not, but we could break open the melon." We sat down, and I pulled Molly onto my lap. Hearing a distant voice, we both turned to look at the hill behind us. Three men on horse-back were riding toward us.

"Slide the gun toward me," Eddie whispered.

Mum sat up. "What's happening?"

"Just stay calm, Mum," I said, as I edged the shotgun toward Eddie with my foot. "Eddie will handle it. Keep your eyes lowered though."

Eddie pulled the shotgun onto his lap. The steady clip-clop of the horses grew louder. Soon the three men were beside us. I could see the horse's hooves and the men's legs. I did not look up at them.

"*As Salamu Alaikum,*" Eddie said, fingering the gun and nodding his head to each man, meeting their eyes as he did so.

"*Wa Alaikum Assalam wa Rahmatullah,*" the elder of

the three men responded. There was a moment of tense silence as the men took stock of one another.

Eddie smiled. *"Hal e shoma chetore?"*

I glanced quickly at the group of men, trying to assess our danger. The leader looked down at Eddie, his eyes thoughtful. *"Hobhas, tashakur. Khodafez."*

As the three men ambled away, I released my breath in relief. "What was that about?" Mum asked, once they were out of earshot.

"They were just checking us out," Eddie said. "That's why we always travel with a gun in Afghanistan. I've never had to use it, but if you have a gun and act without fear they respect you."

"What if they hadn't?" Mum asked. I raised my eyebrows at her. We preferred not to think about that.

"Everyone we've met so far has been respectful," Eddie told her. "The Afghans are honourable people. If you show that you understand the concepts of respect and honour, they treat you well. They always treat me like a brother. And I always carry a gun!"

We spent Mum's last evening in Kabul having dinner with our friend Sher Segunda and his wife, Faiza. Sher was an important man in Kabul, he ran several successful businesses and was greatly respected. He was a tall, well-built man whose presence filled any room he entered. Something about Sher was larger than life. He was well-travelled and very well read and had been a really good friend to us. He was also quite envious of our Mercedes Benz and Eddie had promised to give it to him when we left Kabul.

Faiza, a petite and elegant woman, was second cousin to Mohammed Zahir Shah, King of Afghanistan. Her bright eyes missed nothing and she handled both her household and her husband with a quiet strength that really impressed me. She was the only female friend I had in Kabul, and I was delighted to see how well she and Mum were getting on.

"So how did you meet one another?" Mum asked, as we sat in Faiza's airy living room after dinner.

Faiza laughed. "My husband likes to know every Westerner who stays in Kabul longer than three weeks, and he loves the British."

"Our doctor introduced us, didn't he?" I asked.

"That's right," Eddie said, "he'd worked as a G.P. on the Isle of Skye, so we'd shared reminiscences. One afternoon we were in the Khyber restaurant and Dr. Hassan was also there with Sher, so he introduced us. Sher has taught me a lot about handling Afghan officials."

"And the dress-making and export business," I added.

"I think of Eddie, Joanna and Molly as part of my family now," Sher told Mum. "So don't worry. I will look after them in Kabul."

"Thank you, Sher," Mum said, "that means a lot to me. Although I am very impressed by how well they are looking after themselves." Eddie beamed at me. I remembered how doubtful Mum and Dad had been when they first met him, and a wave of gratitude washed over me to know that Mum trusted both Eddie and me now.

"So, Julia, what do you think of Afghanistan, now you have spent two weeks here?" Sher asked.

Mum looked thoughtful. "It's a majestic country. A land of contrasts. Vast, open spaces and magnificent mountains, dry river beds and deserts. Very different from home. But most of all it's the people who have impressed me. There is a quiet dignity to every Afghan I've met, rich or poor, it makes no difference. You are a proud and noble race. I love the way everyone walks tall, their heads held high. Even though I have not met any women, apart from you, Faiza, and I sense there is no-one like you, and even though all the women I see are wearing the burka, I feel that the women are also proud. I can see that from the way they hold themselves. No-one shuffles about, trying to be inconspicuous, or making themselves smaller than they are. Too many people do that in the West. I will never forget Afghanistan."

Sher looked at Mum, he was visibly moved by her words, and he touched his hand to his heart with great sincerity. "Thank you, Julia, you have truly seen us."

Man is a musical being. His origin is in the spoken word. By sound was he sustained and by music he evolved. One day he will recognise music as a vital factor in the physical, emotional, and spiritual evolution of the whole human race.
Corinne Helene (1882-1975)

PESHAWAR Summer 1972

Eddie drove the Mercedes out of Peshawar and into the mountains, Mohmeen sat beside him and Rahman was in the back seat, with the rifles. Eddie felt bad, always leaving Joanna and Molly behind at Mohmeen's place, but there was no way he could take them into the tribal area. She had assured him that she was okay. She had a good book and was happy to spend time with Molly. He shrugged to himself and decided to just enjoy the trip. There was no point in regretting something that he had no control over. This was a man's world.

They climbed higher into the wilder-land of the Khyber Pass. Here the only law anyone recognised was that of the gun. This was neither Afghanistan nor Pakistan. It was tribal territory, overseen by the strongest men of the different tribes, all extended families. All of them Pathan. Fierce, loyal and quick to take offence.

Far below, a mule-train wound around the mountain, each animal laden with bulging panniers, a few tribesmen at the front and rear. Every day goods were smuggled across the border like this. Sometimes camels were used, they could carry a larger load, but usually mules bore the loads, because their hooves were steadier on the treacherous mountain tracks. Nothing passed through this area without permission, at a price, from the tribal leaders.

They arrived in Rahman's village and climbed out. A dozen men approached them. Eddie was dressed like Mohmeen, in the traditional baggy pants and shirt that all Pathan men wore, a piece of cloth wrapped around his head to protect him from the fierce sun. Rahman handed them both rifles and bandoliers of bullets, which they slung over their shoulders and around their chests respectively.

Mohmeen greeted the men gathered around them and introduced Eddie: "This is Edward, son of Raj."

Several men slapped Eddie on the back. He was accepted. Mohmeen's friendship meant a great deal.

Rahman went to visit his mother and Eddie and Mohmeen toured the village, which consisted of a few small houses and a big shed where several men sat on the floor, surrounded by pieces of metal, wood and guns.

Mohmeen, Eddie and four of the men sat in the shade of a large tree and a young boy served them tea. Eddie understood little of what was being said. Every so often Mohmeen translated a story about a mule train or a government raid for Eddie's benefit. There were no women in sight.

Eddie knew Mohmeen liked bringing him to the tribal area and enjoyed the kudos of being driven around in the Mercedes. Eddie needed Mohmeen's help to transport the goods from Kabul to Peshawar, so they could be exported cheaply from Pakistan. Sher had introduced him to Mohmeen and suggested they move their export business to Pakistan because the authorities in Kabul had vastly increased export duties and were always greedy for more baksheesh.

In some ways Eddie enjoyed the spice of danger in the tribal area, and yet he often wondered what on earth he was doing there. The guys puzzled him. One minute they were laughing together, playful and simple, the next they were cold-eyed killers, ready to fight their neighbours over some perceived slight of tribal honour.

Once the business was done, they drove back down the mountains. "Tell me something, Mohmeen," Eddie said.

"Anything, my friend," answered Mohmeen.

"Why are so many of the men blind in their right eye?"

"Home-made guns," Mohmeen said, "Often unreliable and the kick-back can be lethal."

"Oh, they need better guns then."

"For that they need money to buy them, from the

Russians or Americans. For now, they'll keep making them out of whatever they can lay their hands on…. and if they lose one eye, they still have another and can shoot just as well."

As they were crossing the flat, desert-like land between the mountains and the frontier town of Peshawar a truck full of tribesmen passed them at great speed. Every man in the back of the truck had his rifle ready in his hands. "They look like they're going to war," Eddie said.

"They are," Mohmeen said, "one tribe is always fighting another here."

"What about?" Eddie asked.

"Land, women, honour, it doesn't really matter what the reason is." They returned to Mohmeen's office, a small, dilapidated building on the main street. This was the hub of Mohmeen's empire. From here he ran a dozen taxis and smoothed the way for the movement of a multitude of goods and services. Eddie had no idea how many pies Mohmeen's fingers were dipped in and had no wish to know. They had an uncomplicated friendship and he wanted to keep it that way.

Peshawar reminded Eddie of a wild-west town, with tuk-tuk taxis and bullock carts instead of cowboys and Indians. Every building was a ramshackle, temporary structure and the central street was a chaotic flow of gun-bearing men, goats, cows, trucks and horses, each intent on their own goals. He sat in Mohmeen's window, drinking tea and smoking, occasionally standing to shake another stranger's hand as Mohmeen once again introduced him as "Edward, son of Raj."

Not for the first time Eddie wondered about his own father, Auburn Freeman, who had been born in India. He had joined the British Army, travelled to England at the age of 25, married an Irish woman, fathered five children and never mentioned India again. All Eddie could remember about him, apart from his silence, was the way he sprinkled curry powder on everything his wife cooked. Son of Raj indeed. Yet Eddie recognised that his natural affinity for this part of the world was in part due to some cellular or karmic memory, passed on to him from his father.

"Let's stop a night in Jalalabad," Eddie suggested, it's getting late and I don't want to cross the mountains into Kabul after sunset."

"Sounds good to me," Joanna responded, wiping the remains of a chocolate biscuit from Molly's face. "We can stop at that one with the lovely gardens, what's it called?"

"Can't remember, but I know the one you mean. I wish there was one with a swimming pool though, I'm longing to swim."

"Me too, I would love to introduce Molly to the water."

"Ah well, it's not going to happen here, is it?" Eddie asked, turning off the main road from Peshawar to Kabul and heading for Jalalabad. Both Eddie and Joanna regarded Jalalabad as their holiday town. When the temperatures dropped below freezing in Kabul it was spring in Jalalabad. The town was less than a hundred miles from the capital, but its location on the plains meant it was much lower and a lot warmer. The snow could be over a metre deep in Kabul, while in Jalalabad spring flowers bloomed and trees sprouted fresh leaves.

Eddie parked up and entered the reception area to book a room. Five minutes later he was back, looking glum. "There's a festival in Jalalabad this weekend and every bed is booked," he told Joanna.

"Really?"

"Let's go for a walk round the gardens anyway. Maybe we can think of something."

"Okay, we need a stretch. I'm sure there must be somewhere we can stay." They walked around the lush gardens, enjoying the earthy smells and refreshing greenery. "I'm missing gardens as well as swimming pools," Joanna said.

"I wonder where there is a perfect balance," Eddie mused, "a place that's not too cold and wet, like northern Europe often is, yet not too hot and dry, like it is here."

"Must be somewhere like that, we just haven't found it yet. Although I suspect that we actually need seasons and change and that everywhere is perfect at some time of the year, especially to people who live there."

"You're probably right," Eddie said, "you usually are."

"True," Joanna responded, laughing. They rounded a corner and saw a large painted van parked under a tree. A guy sat on the step outside the van, playing a guitar, his face hidden by his long hair. At that moment he looked up and smiled, making them feel instantly welcome.

"Hi, come and join us," he called. They smiled back and walked over to him. "Hi, I'm Johnny."

"Hi, man, I'm Eddie, this is Joanna and Molly, who is fast asleep."

"So I see," Johnny said, standing up and leaning his guitar against the van. A young woman, dressed in a long patchwork skirt, came out the van, her face lit up when she saw the new arrivals.

"Oh great, visitors!" She exclaimed, "welcome, how lovely to see you. And a baby too. I'm Suzie. Where are you from? Would you like some tea?"

"We're from UK too," Joanna said, warming to her immediately, "but we're living in Kabul for now. And we'd love some tea."

"Really?" Johnny said, sounding surprised, "How long have you been in Kabul?"

"Just over a year," Eddie responded.

"Wow, cool man."

A blond woman with a blue-eyed child in her arms emerged from the van at that moment. "This is Alice and Brigit," said Johnny, kissing Alice on the cheek.

"Hi, I'm Joanna and this is Molly and Eddie," Joanna said, including both Alice and Suzie.

"Are there any more of you in there?" Eddie asked.

Johnny laughed, "No man, just us. We're travelling overland to Rajasthan and beyond. Been on the road for four months already and lovin' it. How come you're stayin' in Kabul?" Suzie smiled again at Joanna and disappeared back into the van. Everyone else sat down on the assortment of cloths and carpets that had been spread in front of the van, creating a colourful front lawn.

"We're working there," Eddie said, "exporting dresses and hand-crafts and taking care of our mate's interests. He has an Afghan carpet shop in London."

"Hey that's really cool. You must have gotten to know Kabul pretty well by now," Johnny commented.

"Bits of it, "Eddie responded, "it's a big city and we actually spend a lot of time just getting on with our lives."

"Yeah, I know what you mean, man. Me an' the girls seem to spend most of our time shopping, cooking, eating and playing with Brigit. Your priorities are different when you've got a kid to look after."

"How old is Brigit?" Joanna asked.

"Two and a half," Alice replied, she was born on Christmas day 1969. Quite a Christmas present." Alice buried her face in Brigit's soft belly and blew raspberries, eliciting peals of laughter from the child. The laughter woke Molly. Her bright blue eyes widened in delight when she saw there was another little person around and she wriggled in her buggy to get out.

Joanna untied her and set her on the carpet beside Brigit. The two girls stared solemnly at one another, then simultaneously reached out and touched each other's faces.

"Are you Swedish, Alice?" Joanna asked.

"Yes, what gave me away, my hair or my accent?"

"Both really," Joanna laughed, "and your blue eyes and tanned skin. How come most Swedes have better tans than the Brits?"

"Must be the mid-night sun I guess," Alice said, laughing. Suzie came out with a tray of steaming cups. By the time the tea was drunk everyone felt they had known one another for years.

"Are you heading east or west?" Johnny asked.

"We're on our way back to Kabul," Eddie replied, "We were in Peshawar to extend our visas again. Third time now, we only get three months at a time."

"We flew Ariana Airlines once," Joanna said, "never again! The plane was tiny so couldn't go above the mountains."

"We flew between them!" Eddie added.

"And the wings were shaking so much I thought they'd fall off." Joanna said, shuddering at the memory.

"Inshallah we will arrive at our destination in one hour," Eddie mimicked the pilot's announcement in a very bad accent.

"And everybody was praying as we landed," Joanna said, "then they all clapped once we were back on solid ground. And I joined in!"

"So we drive over now," said Eddie. "We were going to take a room for the night, but the hotel is full. I don't like driving at night here, anything could happen."

"Stay with us, man. There's plenty of room." Johnny said.

"Oh yes, please stay," Suzie added, "It's so great to have someone else to talk to." Everyone laughed. Eddie and Joanna exchanged glances and confirmed their agreement with one another wordlessly.

"Thank you," Joanna said, "we'd love to. And I know exactly what you mean, Suzie. I am so enjoying being with you all. And look at Brigit and Molly, how can we break those two up?" Brigit had brought out her toys and the two little girls were playing happily together, feeding bits of dirt to the dollies and creating masterpieces on scraps of paper with soft wax crayons.

After sunset Alice cooked a simple meal of vegetables and rice. "This is so yummy, Alice," Joanna said, "such a treat to eat fresh vegetables. Wherever did you find them?"

"We stayed on a farm in a valley near here and bought some veg from them when we left."

"The food in Kabul is terrible," Eddie complained, "bits of stringy meat floating in greasy gravy. Yuk! We eat a lot of bread and rice and baked beans and treasure the few veg we find in the supermarket."

"The only good stuff is the fruit," Joanna said.

"The food in India is great," said Johnny. "I can't wait to get there. Spicy curries and tasty dhal, crispy poppadum's and dosas. And carrot halwa!"

"Shut up, man, you're making my mouth water," Eddie said, playfully.

"You've been there before then?" Joanna asked.

"Yeah, two years ago, and I've wanted to return ever since," Johnny said. "I wonder how much it's changed. A lot more westerners have been travelling east since then."

"It's like a tidal wave," said Eddie. "Why are so many of us travelling east? What are we all looking for?"

"I think we're at a turning point in human consciousness," Suzie said.

"So do I," Joanna agreed, "our generation have rejected the values of our parents and we're looking for a new way to live our lives."

"A way that doesn't involve becoming a wage-slave and buying more and more 'stuff' to supposedly make us happy." Johnny added.

"I think we're looking to the East for answers about how to live closer to nature, closer to ourselves," Alice said.

"Yeah," Eddie added, "we 'tuned in, turned on and dropped out' in the sixties, and had a few glimpses of other realities or universes or whatever when we took LSD."

"Now we want to drop back in," Suzie said, "but we want a different world, one based on love and sharing, on looking after the Earth and one another, not on making war, fighting and fear."

"I reckon it's all about freedom," Eddie said. "That's why I love the naffers, they are free. They don't kow-tow to anyone, they never have."

"But they're not free from poverty," Joanna said, "and the women don't really seem very free to me, they can't even eat until all the men have been fed. What kind of freedom is that?"

"And what is freedom?" Alice asked. "Isn't it something that you find inside you? A person can be free in their mind, in their soul, even if their body is enslaved or imprisoned."

"Maybe that's true," Johnny said, "but it's a lot harder to feel free if you're locked up, isn't it?"

158

"But are many of the hippies we meet on the road truly free?" Suzie asked. "I mean aren't they just slaves to their addictions? Some of the people we've met lately have been so stoned they could barely speak. What kind of freedom is that?"

"The freedom to get off their faces?" Johnny said. "Maybe that's a necessary phase along the journey to freedom."

"The freest guy I ever saw was a Gnaui in Marrakesh," Eddie said. "He sat and played his instrument all alone, night after night, making beautiful music and looking so peaceful and happy. He didn't care whether anyone listened or gave him money. He just played for the sake of the music. That's true freedom."

"And what about the Gnaui dancers?" Joanna added, "Just watching them dance made me feel free. Such total abandon to the music. Such joy on their faces."

"So, freedom is an internal state," Suzie said with excitement, "attained through total absorption in what you are doing."

"The freest guy I ever saw was an old sadhu baba sitting on the bank of the Ganges," Johnny said. "His eyes held something I had never seen before, and just being near him made me feel peaceful and still. He had nothing, looked like a wild man with his long dreads and beard, yet he carried himself like a king. I can still see him now. He didn't need anything. He had it all inside him."

Nobody spoke. Johnny's description of the sadhu had somehow invoked his presence and a deep stillness fell over them all. "That's why we're going East," Suzie said finally, "that's what we want—the freedom to simply be."

Eddie and Joanna woke the following morning well rested. Suzie had made a surprisingly comfortable nest of sleeping bags and cushions on the floor of the van. Molly and Brigit were curled up together in Brigit's bed, while Suzie, Johnny and Alice shared a platform bed a few feet from the roof.

Even though the sun had only recently risen it was

too hot and airless in the van for Joanna. She dressed quietly and went out into the cool shade of the garden. Eddie soon joined her. "It's so great to wake to the sight and smell of greenness," Joanna said, kissing Eddie on the lips and hugging him. Eddie held her body close to his, enjoying the cool sweetness of her lips.

"It's like paradise this morning, the birds singing their hearts out, the fragrant breeze and the stillness... such a change after the noisiness of Peshawar."

"And the dryness of Kabul," Joanna added ruefully. "I wish we could stay here another night but we'd better get back. I have to get more dresses ready for the order for L.A."

"Let's just pretend we're in the Garden of Eden and no-one else exists," Eddie said, nibbling her neck.

Joanna laughed and pulled away, "Not even Molly?"

"Okay, Molly can exist," Eddie laughed.

"I think I can hear her, we'd better go in. Parenting is a full-time job, isn't it?"

"Worth every minute though."

Joanna's eyes shone as she looked at Eddie. He was such a kind and good man. She was still amazed how much he'd changed in the past eighteen months, fatherhood suited him. He was more focused and self-assured. But then so was she. "Definitely," she agreed as she clambered back into the van.

After a delicious breakfast of papaya, banana and yoghurt, eaten in the garden, and a final cup of sweet tea it was time to go their separate ways. "It's been totally amazing to spend time with you all," Joanna said," I really hope our paths cross again."

"I think they are sure to," Suzie said, "feels like we're family already."

"Take care, man," Johnny said as he hugged Eddie.

"Yeah, happy travels, Johnny. See you on the road or back in the UK. Thanks for the bed."

"You're welcome. man, anytime."

Joanna turned and waved one last time, then they rounded the corner and walked back through the gardens to the car.

As they were driving out of Jalalabad, they saw a huge crowd watching a group of men on horses. "It's a *buzkashi* game," Eddie said, "shall we watch for a bit?"

Joanna laughed. "Of course, how often do we get to watch *buzkashi*?"

They parked up and found a place near a group of women with young children, hoping the crowd would be calmer there. The game was in full swing, around twenty wild-eyed, turbaned men galloped wildly around a large area, sending up clouds of dust. The horse's ears were drawn back and when they weren't galloping, they shook their heads, snorted and pawed at the dust. The air was electric.

One man galloped ahead of the rest, dragging the headless carcass of a goat behind him. Another man, leaning sideways from his horse, practically parallel to the ground, approached the goat at full speed and attempted to pick it up. The first rider was too fast for him and yanked the goat away at the last minute, wheeling around at an impossible angle while reeling in the goat at the same time. The crowd made a tidal wave of sound, a roar that swept everyone along in the excitement of the game. Molly opened her eyes wide and looked around, more curious than afraid.

The horses surged down the field once more, hooves thundering on the dry earth. The rider with the goat was out of sight, yet the magnificence of the chase continued, now at one end of the field, now at another, the crowd calling out encouragement or criticism in a constant flow of noise. Another rider managed to grab the goat, performing acrobatics that would have put any circus act to shame. The chase began anew.

They would play like this for several days at a time, stopping when they needed to, starting again when they wished. Buzkashi was the national passion. Just being in a crowd of Afghans watching a game was like plugging in to the beating heart of Afghanistan. Wild and free, unfettered by rules and regulations. Totally magnificent.

My idea is that there is music in the air, music all around us; the world is full of it, and you simply take as much as you require.

Edward Elgar (1857-1934)

KABUL 1972

I felt too weak to get up. For days I had been feeling lethargic and nauseous. My brain felt like it was coated in mud. Everything was an effort. When I finally dragged myself from under the cover and looked in the mirror, I was shocked at how pale I was. Eddie came in with a cup of tea, Molly trailing behind him. "It's a beautiful day, do you fancy a ride into the mountains?"

"I wish I did but I feel awful," I turned to look at him. "Thanks for the tea, think I'll stay in bed for a bit."

Eddie looked closely at me. "You do look rough, and your eyes are a bit yellow, maybe you should see the Doctor?"

I groaned, "I don't want to get up."

"Well, you can't go on like this. It's been almost a week already and you're worse each day. Come on, you can do it."

"Oh, alright then, I suppose you're right." Molly stood beside my bed her brow crinkled in concern. Wordlessly she reached out her hand and stroked my arm. I took hold of her hand and squeezed it. "It's alright darling, Mummy's just not very well. We'll go see the doctor and he can make us better."

"Mummy."

The trust in her eyes re-ignited the flames of mother-love that had been burning inside me since before she was born. What was I thinking? I had to get well so I could look after her, there was no space to indulge in self-pity now I was a mother. I threw back the covers and took a shower.

"I'm sorry but you have hepatitis," Doctor Hassan told me.

"How can I have that?" I asked, surprised. I thought only junkies caught hep from sharing needles.

"Everyone in Kabul catches hepatitis sooner or later," he said, "it's in the air, like colds and flu are in the UK. As soon as your resistance is down, you succumb to it."

"Is it catching then? I asked, worried about Molly.

"You were more infectious before your symptoms started, but you should all wash your hands often to make sure."

"Is there anything I can do to get better?"

"Avoid fatty foods, dairy and alcohol, drink lots of water, rest and be patient. You will feel better in time." Doctor Hassan smiled kindly at me, yet I wanted more from him, I wanted a magic wand that would make me feel like myself again, not this jaundiced floppy version of me.

I sighed and stood up. "Thank you, Doctor."

I stayed in bed for the next three days, unable to eat anything and getting weaker by the day. My urine had become a dark yellowy brown, while the few stools I passed were almost white. Something was very wrong.

On the fourth day Sher and Faiza came to visit. "Here is a tonic I made for you," Faiza said, handing me a bottle full of a dark brown, viscous looking liquid. "It was my grandmother's remedy and has kept generations of us well."

"Thank you, Faiza," I said, "I don't think I've ever felt so ill. Have you all had hepatitis?"

"Most of us Afghans catch it before we are twenty," Sher said, "and many of us go to the healer for help."

"What healer?" I asked. "Can I go to him?"

"Of course you can go, but you have to have faith," Sher responded, looking at me seriously.

"I have faith," I said, "I'll do anything not to feel like this."

The following day Sher took me to a small room in a back street of Kabul. A man with grey hair, a salt and pepper beard and piercing, bright eyes sat in the centre of the room on a small stool. A dozen or so people sat on the floor around him. Everyone looked up at me when I walked in. I held my right hand to my heart, lowered my head in respect and greeted them with a salaam.

Sher spoke quickly in Farsi to the healer, then turned to me. "I must leave you now," he said. "You are safe here and he will help you. Just do as he says. I will send my driver to collect you in an hour, and he can bring you here again tomorrow."

"Thank you, Sher," I said, feeling somewhat nervous, yet instinctively knowing that I must do this alone. The healer indicated me to sit, and I sat on the floor beside a woman who was cradling one arm against her chest.

A young man sat on a wooden crate beside the healer. The man's right hand and wrist were very swollen. The healer gently held the man's hand, palm-upwards, and stroked it with strong regular movements, like he was brushing something away. He even flicked his hand at the end of each stroke. He sang quietly all the while he stroked.

Everyone watched. Nobody made a sound. It was quite hypnotic and I found myself totally absorbed by the motion of the healer's hands and the sound of his voice. The stroking and singing continued for around ten minutes. When the young man withdrew his hand from the healer it was noticeably less swollen and red. Although I didn't understand his words, I could hear the gratitude in his voice. He dropped a few afghanis into a basket on the floor and left the room.

The woman beside me took his place. I looked around, apart from a few pieces of sacking the floor was bare, packed earth. A small, metal bowl stood on the floor beside the healer, containing what appeared to be a dark liquid. A small knife, a piece of wood, and a large spoon lay on a cloth. Nothing was very clean.

The healer spoke quietly to the woman, and she unfurled her arm to reveal a big angry red boil on her forearm. The healer held his hand over the boil, murmuring to himself, then he took the knife and lanced the boil in one swift movement. The woman was completely still. Next the healer scooped a large, black leach from the bowl at his feet and slapped in onto the woman's arm. He indicated that she should sit on the floor and turned his attention to me.

I sat down on the wooden crate, surprised at how

calm I felt. My intention was to have complete faith in this man, because I knew that he would then be able to cure me. He placed a metal bowl, which contained a clear, oily liquid, in my hands and told me to focus on it. I have no idea how I understood him as he was speaking in Farsi, yet I knew what he was telling me to do. The healer stirred the liquid with a woody root, singing a slow, rhythmic song while he stirred. The oily liquid turned yellow as I watched.

The healer took two small squares of paper from a pouch at his waist and handed them to me. Each square of paper was divided into nine boxes with a number written in Farsi in each box. The healer told me to wear one piece of paper around my neck, and to eat one square from the other one each day. I had no doubts whatsoever that these were my instructions, even though they seemed totally bizarre. I put a ten Afghan note into the tray, thanked the healer and left.

I followed the healer's instructions to the letter. Each of the next three days I visited him. Each day the oil in the bowl became yellow. Each day I became less yellow. I felt that he was drawing the toxic effects of the virus from my body with his ancient and simple magic. By the end of the week, I was back to normal, although I had lost over a stone.

Two months later we drove across the Khyber Pass to Peshawar to renew our visas and arrange two big shipments to London and Los Angeles. One day Eddie, Molly and I went for a drive north of Peshawar. I had been cooped up for days in Mohmeen's house and I needed to escape. Eddie had completed all the work so we had time to play.

It was October and the weather was cooling. Autumn and Spring were my favourite seasons, every day was like a perfect summer day back home, a pleasant seventy degrees, constant sunshine and blue skies. The summers were always very hot, around ninety degrees, and winters in Kabul could get as cold as minus twenty degrees. Yet the dryness meant that both the heat and the extreme cold were bearable.

The scenery as we drove into the mountains was

breath-taking: streams of pure, sparkling water trilled over rocks; wooded valleys, coloured in a hundred shades of green and brown; vast horizons, crowned with snow-capped mountain peaks, disappeared into a misty purple distance that was both mysterious and enticing. The air was fragrant with herbs.

We passed farmers ploughing the fertile soil with bullocks or mules, as their ancestors had done for centuries. We bought juicy black grapes, fresh pears and peaches from a roadside stall, and ate our picnic beside a waterfall. "I don't want to turn back," I said, "it's such a beautiful day, and I want to go deeper into the mountains. Can we?"

"I don't see why not," Eddie responded, "we can always find a hotel and go back tomorrow. I think we are near the Swat Valley; it would be great to see that."

"Oh, yes, let's stay the night in Swat. I'd love that. We deserve a holiday don't we Molly?"

Molly was playing near the water, gathering all the rocks she could carry and creating a precarious structure with them. She was chattering to herself, oblivious of us. She was such a happy, self-contained child, and I loved these times when she could just play freely in nature.

I lay on my back and stared up. Sunlight filtered through the trees, making everything dance with light. The combination of swaying green leaves and the deep blue of the sky in the dancing light was hypnotically beautiful, like a gateway to another world. I was aware of my body's contact with the earth, yet I felt a sense of oneness with the sound of the water rushing over the rocks, the warmth of the sun and the soft air on my skin. Earth, air, water and fire. I lay in a bubble of perfect contentment, relishing my connection with the elements and the freedom I felt.

Then Molly toddled up and lay down on me, laughing and wanting to play. I grabbed hold of her hands and lifted her up with bent knees, playing aeroplanes. Molly squealed in delight and Eddie picked her up and swung her round, making her squeal even louder.

I stood and brushed the dust and twigs from me. "I

guess we'd better head on into those hills then," I said, packing up the remnants of our picnic.

"Yep, the adventure continues," Eddie said, putting Molly on his shoulders.

We drove for another two hours through the most stunning scenery I had ever seen. The Swat River flowed through a rich and fertile valley, studded with orchards of fruit trees and fields of crops: walnuts and cumquats, okra and tomatoes, corn, rice and lush, juicy peaches. And the flowers! Tiny flowers bloomed wherever they could find space to root, on roof-tops and rocks, crevices and between the shrubs. Stately pines and cedars flanked the hillsides like sentinels. And above it all the snowy mountains, magnificent against the cobalt sky. We stopped beside an enormous lake, revelling in the pristine reflection of mountains, sky and trees and the clear, fragrant air.

We found a hotel beside a smaller lake and checked in, then sat on our balcony and watched the sun set behind one mountain as the full moon rose behind another.

Later that night I stood alone on the balcony, looking at the moon. I breathed in the jasmine perfumed air and silently spoke my heart-felt prayer: "Oh, Diana, goddess of the moon, I honour you and give thanks for the beauty of this wonderful world. Please, if you are willing, let me conceive a child this night."

I knew when Eddie and I lay twined together in our hotel bed, that the goddess had answered my prayer.

It was early December and I woke feeling sick every morning. I tried nibbling dry toast before getting up, but it wasn't always successful. It was time to talk to Eddie. "I've got some news," I told him, placing a cup of tea in front of him.

"What news?" he asked, looking up at me.

"We're having another baby."

He stood and enfolded me in his warmness. "Great! Molly needs a brother or sister. When is he or she joining us?"

"July, I think, it's very early days but I recognise the

167

signs. My boobs are tender and I just know. I think we made him or her in the Swat valley."

"On the night of the full moon. Perfect." He kissed me and held me close against him.

"Thing is I don't want to have a baby out here. Not after the hep. I still only weigh seven and a half stone and I'd like to get stronger. I don't think I can do that here."

Eddie looked at me, silent and thoughtful. "I can understand that," he said, sipping his tea. "I do love it here, but maybe it's time to go home?"

"I think that's what I'd like," I said, taking hold of his hand, "I feel that I want to make a home now we're going to have two kids. It was fine to travel with one child, but maybe now we should try settling for a bit?"

He squeezed my hand. "I've been missing the greenness of home, to tell the truth. And the beer."

I laughed.

"And I could always come out here a few times a year, if needed."

"Of course you could, and maybe we can find another way to earn a living at home," I said. "I do love you, Eddie. Are you happy to have another baby?"

"Of course I am. Molly is the best thing that's happened to me, apart from you that is. You know how much I love you don't you?" We put down our cups and folded into one another, his arm around my shoulder, mine around his waist, my head against his chest. I felt so safe in his arms, like a ship come to harbour.

Three very busy weeks later we left Kabul. We gave our car to Sher, shipped our large collection of carpets, hangings, jewellery and dresses back to the UK and gave everything else away.

We arrived in London on December 23rd and drove to Cornwall on Christmas Eve. In the new year we would find a home and a new chapter of our lives would begin.

Do you know that our soul is composed of harmony?
Leonardo Da Vinci (1452 – 1519)

WEST WALES 1978-81

"It's snowing!" Joanna said, opening the kitchen door and stepping out into the soft white flakes.

"Can we make a snow man yet?" Danny asked, running out in his slippers.

"Maybe tomorrow darling," Joanna said, ruffling his curls. "We're going to Nana's soon for a sleep-over, come on, let's go back inside and get ready."

"Mum," Grace shouted, "I can't find my pyjamas."

"Have you looked under the bed?"

"Oh yeah, there they are."

"Molly, have you finished your home-work yet?" Joanna called, climbing the stairs to help her two girls finish packing.

Molly was bent over her desk, writing furiously, "Nearly ready, mum, just want to finish this story."

"Ok love," Joanna said, her eyes misting with pride at her daughter's diligence and enthusiasm for study, "we'll be leaving in around half an hour." Molly nodded and carried on writing. Joanna closed the door quietly and walked into Grace's room. The floor was littered with clothes, toys, crayons and books. Grace lay against a red beanbag in the middle of the chaos, plaiting her doll's hair and humming. Joanna smiled to herself and finished packing an overnight case for Grace and Danny.

Outside Eddie was loading the PA into the back of the van. The flurry of snow was lessening, which meant they could get down the track and out. He was looking forward to the gig tonight and really did not want it to get snowed off. Richard always threw a great party and he was renowned for the quality, and quantity, of his home-brew. The band were in good form, they'd rehearsed twice and everyone was getting on well, for a change.

He pulled down the tail gate and walked up the drive

169

from the yard. Llety always looked picturesque, but he especially loved it in the early evening, all lit up like a beacon of homeliness surrounded by Welsh wilderness. The wind whistled in the trees around the house, the sky above was dark and starless. He heard the soft murmur of the stream in the distance. An owl hooted mournfully as he opened the kitchen door and entered the warmth within.

Soon they were driving along the half mile of bumpy track and down the hill to the tiny village. The kids were dropped off at Nana's, excited about watching Dr Who. They had no TV at home and Danny always sat mesmerised by the flickering screen, no matter what was on. Molly and Grace enjoyed Dr Who, but hid behind the sofa when the Daleks or Cybermen came on.

"And now it's just us," Eddie said as he drove into the hills.

"Well, that makes a change," Joanna said, "I'm really looking forward to a good dance and to seeing everyone. It's been a long winter."

"How old is Richard today?" Eddie asked.

"No idea. Thirty maybe? It's a big party so it could well be a 'special' birthday. I think he's invited everyone." After driving for twenty minutes or so they turned off the single-track road and rattled up a steep dirt track which seemed to go on forever. "Look," Joanna said, "there are lights in the distance. That must be it."

"Thank God," Eddie said, "I was beginning to think we were lost." They pulled into the yard. All the lights were blazing in Richard's white-washed stone cottage and cars were parked haphazardly everywhere. Most of the action was happening in the barn, where Richard had set up a bar and created a small stage from pallet boards. The bar was free, with an endless flow of home-brewed beer, lots of wine and a few bottles of spirits. Richard was a very generous host.

Davy Jones, the best lead guitarist in west Wales, helped Eddie to unload and set-up the PA. Gary was already setting up the drums and January was standing around, drinking a pint of Richard's best home brew.

Joanna walked into the house. The kitchen was packed, people chatted animatedly in groups, juggling with drinks and plates of food. She moved slowly through the kitchen, hugging and greeting friends along the way. The table was lavishly spread with salads, quiche and slices of ham, olives, bread, pickles and cheeses. She filled a plate with food, avoiding the ham, and squeezed her way out of the kitchen. The living room was much quieter. A log fire blazed in the large hearth and a space opened up on the sofa which Joanna quickly sat in.

"Hi Anna," she said, greeting the long-haired young woman who was curled up on the sofa, feeding her baby.

"Hi, Joanna. Where are your kids?"

"Having a sleep-over at my mum's."

"Wow, you're so lucky your mum is nearby. I really miss mine. There's so much to learn about looking after a baby."

"True, and I'm sure you're doing great. Mum and Dad moved here from Cornwall when Grace was six months old. Dad died just before I had Danny."

"That must have been hard."

"Yes, I was eight months pregnant. Both his grandads died before he was born, so we gave him both of their names, Arthur for my dad and Everett for Eddie's"

"I wish my mum and dad would move here. But it's much too quiet for them, they like life in South London."

"Yeah, it doesn't suit everyone here," Joanna said, "but we love it."

"So do we," Anna said, "lots of our mates are moving here now. The air is clean, land is cheap and we can live closer to nature. I was so sick of the pressure of life in the South East. Everyone striving for more of everything and getting stressed and miserable along the way."

"I know what you mean." Joanna agreed, "the land feels unspoilt here, like it still holds its spirit. A lot of South England is covered in concrete and asphalt. We all came here for some peace and quiet, and space."

"It's not very peaceful tonight though, is it?" Anna

commented. "Looks like everyone I know is here. When are Jester Band playing? I want to get Seren asleep before their set. Richard has given us a room upstairs for the little ones."

"I think they'll start as soon as they're set up. I'll go over there now. Great to see you, Anna."

"You too, Joanna, call round some time with the kids."

The barn was packed when Jester Band began their set. There was a manic, euphoric, drunken insanity about the entire evening. Like a modern-day saturnalia. Eddie's face was red as a summer apple, his eyes overbright and slightly bloodshot.

Everyone was shouting yet no one really listened to anyone else. People danced and jumped around to the steady, heavy beat of Gary's drumming, the visceral notes of the bass and Eddie's driving rhythm guitar. Davy's fine guitar wove melodic patterns of sound over the carpet of relentless beat.

Outside the snow fell, soft, white and silent. Inside Eddie sang about revolution and Rock'n'Roll. And the beer kept flowing.

At times Joanna was lost in the rhythm, her body responding to every beat, her heart pounding in time with the bass. Other moments she felt she was looking down on it all from above, detached and disconnected, watching the gyrating bodies and wondering what on earth she was doing there. Eddie was wild, his eyes glowed, sweat poured from him and his hair was plastered to his face. He was one hundred percent immersed in the music. Singing with all his heart and soul, anger and vitality sparking off him like firecrackers. "He's like a punk rocker tonight." Richard said, enveloping her in beer-breath.

"Yeah," Joanna answered, "I guess he is. A super-punk!" She watched her husband and saw a stranger. Suddenly she remembered a time when she was thirteen, going to her first ever gig at Watford Trade Union Hall. On the stage that night had been a wild and sweaty rock singer with long hair and a guitar. It must have been the early sixties.

172

Could that have been Eddie? Yes, it probably was. She'd have to ask him.

The journey home was a nightmare. It was snowing heavily; the roads were slippery and dark as pitch. Joanna was not used to driving the VW van, but there was no way Eddie could drive. Every few minutes he rolled over onto her and she pushed him gently upright. She'd never seen him so drunk. He was completely in his own world, laughing happily to himself, or speaking unintelligible words to her. She had to focus on the sharp bends and navigate the steep downhill slope of the road, all the while praying she didn't go into a skid. She had no idea how to cope with one if she did.

Finally, thankfully, they arrived home and she guided her drunken man into the house and up the stairs. He had sobered up a little and managed to get undressed, but he stumbled on his way to bed and fell into the tamboura, sending it crashing onto the floor with a sickening splintering sound. "Oh no!" she cried, jumping out of bed and picking the precious instrument up. There was a big crack across the centre of the gourd. Tears prickled her eyes.

"I'm sorry," Eddie said. "Don't worry, I'll fix it tomorrow." Laying the instrument carefully down on its face Joanna doubted anyone could fix it. But there was nothing to be said. Within minutes Eddie was fast asleep, and snoring. Joanna lay awake for two hours, struggling with anger, grief and resentment.

Eddie woke late the following morning, his mouth dry as sandpaper. He tentatively raised his head from the pillow and groaned in pain. He tried curling back up under the blankets but felt nauseous and knew sleep would elude him, no matter how hard he tried.

Groaning again he sat up and saw the wrecked tamboura lying on the floor by the window. The crack in the gourd looked black and jagged. Guilt washed over him, along with another a wave of nausea. Clasping his aching head in one hand he stood up and staggered to the bathroom for a shower.

Later, when he walked into the kitchen the kids were all sitting at the table colouring in the books Nana had given them. Joanna was cooking lunch. "Afternoon. How are you feeling?" she asked, stirring the frying pan with a wooden spoon.

"Terrible! Like I've been poisoned." Eddie said, filling the kettle for a much-needed coffee.

"Who poisoned you daddy?" Grace asked, her blue eyes wide and clear as a summer sky.

"I did it to myself, darling," he said, "not real poison, just too much beer and whiskey."

"Why did you have too much?" asked Molly, practical as ever.

"Because it's hard to know when to stop when you've had a few drinks." Eddie said, spooning Nescafe into the cup. "Look," he said as he wrapped an arm round Joanna's shoulder, "as soon as I've recovered, I'll fix the tamboura. I'm sure I can use something to re-build the gourd."

"Really?" she asked, trying not to let doubt and anger seep into her voice and face. What was done was done, she could tell from his face he wished it had never happened. As she did.

"Promise. It'll be good as new, almost." True to his word, Eddie spent the following day working on the tamboura. He cut some plastic from a five-litre water container and slid it into the crack in the gourd. Then he re-shaped the symmetry of the gourd with epoxy resin. Once that had hardened off, he painted several layers of stain and varnish over it.

The whole process took three days, and during that time he did a lot of soul searching. He felt really guilty for harming this beautiful instrument. At first, he berated himself, telling himself he was a stupid clumsy git. He could hardly remember what had happened at the party. It was just a haze, yet every time he thought about it, he felt a tightening in his stomach, a sense of unease that he couldn't put his finger on.

He started thinking about what he was doing with his

174

life. Weighing up what he valued most, asking himself where he was going. He would be forty in three years. He had three gorgeous children and a wife he adored. The band was fun, except when it wasn't. The business was doing okay. Sure, it was hard work running a shop, and he would never get rich from it. At times it was hard, dealing with Joe public day after day. But it was never boring. And he had no-one standing over him, telling him what to do. And he met some great people. So why did he feel there was something missing? What more did he want?

When the final coat of varnish was dry, he cleaned and polished the tamboura, affixed new strings and tuned them up. As he slowly plucked the strings the resonance and beauty of the notes lulled him into a space of stillness. He placed his head against the neck and the vibration of each note entered him. It was soothing and comforting, like swimming in a warm ocean. His mind gradually settled and stilled. There was nothing but the music and a deep sense of peace.

He gently lay the tamboura down and closed his eyes. He was aware of the fading resonance of the notes, the effortless ebb and flow of his breath. Stillness embraced him like an old friend.

"It really is as good as new," Joanna said, stroking the smooth gourd of the tamboura, "you are amazing!"

"Yep. I guess I am." Eddie said, smiling. "I thought a lot while I was fixing it," he said. "I'm going to try meditation again."

"Really?" Joanna asked, surprised.

"Yes. I'll use the mantra we got when we signed up for TM, you know, after the Beatles went to see the Maharishi."

"Yeah, I still remember my mantra."

"We both have the same one," Eddie said, "we weren't supposed to tell anyone, but we told each other."

"Can you remember what it means?"

"Not really. But it worked."

"It did for you, I just remember sitting there thinking about what to cook for dinner or what I was going to do next. I'm glad you've decided to meditate again. What prompted you?"

"Well after I tuned up the tamboura I played it for a bit and then I just sort of sat and meditated. I felt so good afterwards that I thought I should do it more often."

"Great."

"I may stop going to the pub for a lunch time drink as well."

"Wow," Joanna stood up and threw her arms around him. "I think I love you Mr Freeman."

One day, after Eddie had been meditating for a couple of years, Reggie, a regular customer, came into the shop and the conversation led to meditation. "I've been using the Transcendental Meditation mantra for quite a while now," Eddie said, "I want to connect with others who meditate. I feel a bit stuck, like there is more to learn. I've looked up what TM are offering and all I can see is expensive courses in levitation. I don't want to levitate. I want to go deeper."

"Well, you could try using this mantra if you like," Reggie said, writing three words on a piece of paper. "It works for me."

"Om Namah Shivaya" read Eddie. "Okay man, thanks, I'll try it."

Several months later, a good friend, Gwen, told Eddie about an Indian Guru she had met in London in 1976. "He was totally free," Gwen said, "and just being around him made me feel that everything was perfect, exactly as it was. I even felt that I was perfect. I was so happy." She gave him a book and everything Eddie read in that book made sense to him. But there was no way he wanted a Guru, so he thought no more about it.

A few weeks later Joanna, Eddie and the kids were having dinner at Rupert and Rif's home. Eddie noticed a picture on the mantelpiece and picked it up. "Who's this?" he asked.

"That's Babaji," Rupert said. "I stayed at his Ashram in 1970. I was just travelling around India and came to this little village in the middle of the jungle, somewhere north of Bombay. Babaji was like a blazing light. He woke me up and changed my life. I learned to meditate there and chanted for the first time."

"Gwen told me about him," Eddie said, "What do you mean, woke you up?"

"Babaji is a sadguru," Rupert said, "A true guru. That means he is one with the life-force, the kundalini shakti, the cosmic energy that exists in everything in the universe. He teaches that we are all connected to that energy. We just don't realise it. So being around him wakes you up to who you really are. We go around thinking we're so small, when really we are all part of cosmic consciousness, God, the Life Force, whatever you want to call it."

"Wow." Eddie said. "I'd like to meet him."

"Well, I'm sure the Ashram is still there," said Rupert. "You could go to India and find him."

"Hmmm, "Eddie said, "Not sure I'm ready for that."

One day a middle-aged Australian woman walked into the shop. Eddie was behind the counter. "What brings you to West Wales?" he asked her.

"I've come to visit my mum, who lives near here in the hills," she replied. "After that I'm going to India to study yoga with my teacher."

"That's a long way to go to study yoga," Eddie said. "Can't you find a good yoga teacher here?"

"He doesn't teach Hatha Yoga," she responded, "he teaches the Yoga of Union with the Self of all. He's a sadguru." She opened her bag and took out a picture, handing it to Eddie. Staring up at him was the same joyful Indian man Eddie had seen on Rupert's mantelpiece. A surge of energy flashed through him, and his eyes filled with tears. He didn't know if it was déjà vu or destiny, but he recognised a deep inner connection with this man. He looked up at the

Australian lady. "This is Babaji. I'd like to meet him."

She smiled, "I think you will. Look, I'm going to a meeting in Bristol on Sunday. You can find out more there. Would you like to come with me?"

"Yes," Eddie said, without hesitation and handed her back the picture.

"You can keep it," she said. "My name's Lynne Jones, here's my mum's number. I can pick you up here at nine on Sunday."

"Cheers Lynne, my name's Eddie. I'm so glad you came in here."

"Oh yes," she said, "what did I come in for? Something for my mum, I think. I'm happy to meet you, Eddie. I think this was meant to happen."

When Lynne and Eddie arrived in Bristol that Sunday, they walked into a large sitting room filled with people sitting cross-legged on the floor, chanting. The air was fragrant with incense. They sat near the back and someone handed them a chanting sheet. Eddie listened to the unfamiliar words and looked around. There were around thirty people, mostly westerners, many of them brightly dressed, and a few Indians.

A large table, covered in a bright red and gold cloth dominated the front of the room. Pictures of gods, goddesses and elderly Indian men filled the table. Eddie recognised a picture of Babaji among them. Several vases of flowers adorned both the table and the area in front of it.

The whole event seemed very strange to Eddie, but it felt friendly enough so he decided to simply go for it and join in. The tune everyone was singing soon became familiar to him. He realised that the same two phrases were being repeated and the words were on his sheet. He tentatively joined in with the response. He glanced over at Lynne and saw she was also singing.

Eddie found himself relaxing and enjoying the rhythm of the chant, which gradually sped up. A young woman sat on the floor near the table, playing the melody on a small box with a keyboard and bellows, which he later found out was a harmonium. An older man played a barrel shaped drum, which had a head at both ends, and several others played small hand cymbals and tambourines. The whole sound was joyful and celebratory.

The silence after the chant was still and very peaceful. After five minutes or so an elderly woman, dressed in orange, approached the central table, knelt down, bowed in front of it and began an elaborate ceremony. First, she waved a tray bearing three small candles in front of a statue of a long-haired god with a snake around his neck. Then she began to drip milk slowly over the statue.

Eddie looked at Lynne, puzzled. "I think it's a statue of Shiva," she said, "She is worshipping him. Maybe it's a special Shiva holiday?"

Eddie shrugged; he had no idea what was happening. When the milk-dripping was finished someone stood up and said he would like to show a video of Babaji giving darshan. Eddie's ears pricked up. Ahh, so now he would see Babaji. Although he had no idea what darshan was, he was looking forward to finding out.

The image that came onto the screen was mesmerising. Babaji's face was so full of light. He seemed to radiate a kind of energy that Eddie felt in his body. His heart beat faster and tears sprang into his eyes. Babaji's eyes sparkled, he looked both infinitely wise, yet boyish and playful. For most of the short film Babaji simply sat. He sometimes hummed to himself. Birds sang in the background, and occasionally there was the sound of a vehicle passing by. A few people approached Babaji, knelt at his feet and bowed to him. Sometimes Babaji brushed them with a peacock feather wand. One young child knelt and simply stared directly into Babaji's eyes. Babaji looked back at him with so much love, and gently took hold of his hand. Tears ran, unheeded, down Eddie's face.

After the video everybody stood and sang a song, while someone waved lights to all the pictures and statues on the table. Then everyone filed into an adjoining room, to enjoy some snacks and drinks.

Eddie spotted the man who'd played the Babaji video and made his way over to him. "Hi," he said, "I really enjoyed seeing the video of Babaji. Can you tell me anymore about him? My name is Eddie, by the way. I've come here from West Wales."

"Hello," the man said, reaching out his hand to shake Eddie's firmly. "My name is Chandrakant Arora. I met Babaji when we lived near Bombay. Now we live in East London. What do you want to know?"

"Well," Eddie said, "really, I want to meet him. Seeing him has affected me. I can't explain it but I feel....... different. Like I'm more alive than I was when I walked in here."

"Yes, Babaji can have that affect. I think something in us recognises and responds to Babaji's state. He has merged with the essence of all, he has become Self realised while still living in his body. Just being around him, or seeing him like we did today, we get a glimpse of what it means to be truly alive, fully awake."

"How can I find out more?"

"Do you meditate?" Chandrakant asked.

"Yes," Eddie replied, "I've been meditating for around three years now. Mostly I just repeat a mantra and play hide and seek with the thoughts in my mind."

"Mantra is good. Babaji teaches us to use the mantra "Om Namah Shivaya. It means I honour Shiva, the Self of all."

"Wow," Eddie said, feeling goose bumps shiver over him, "that's the mantra I've been using. Someone came into my shop around a year ago and gave it to me."

Chandrakant smiled. "There are a lot of synchronicities around the sadguru. Maybe you'd like to buy a tape of Babaji singing the mantra?" he said. "Then you would be able to chant along with him."

"Do you have a tape for sale?" Eddie asked, excited at the thought of having Babaji with him at home.

"Fortunately, I brought a few with me. My wife and I have a small meditation group in our home. There is also an Ashram in London, so maybe you'll be able to come soon. I'll give you the address, and ours as well. I think we'll be seeing one another again."

"So do I. Thanks, Chandrakant."

Meditation became an adventure for Eddie. Every day he chanted the mantra along with Babaji, then sat silently, watching his breath move in and out, allowing the thoughts to ripple across the screen of his mind like clouds in a summer sky. Often his mind chased after the thoughts, becoming absorbed in plans for the future or regrets about the past. Then he remembered the mantra once again, and gently brought his focus back to Om Namah Shivaya. When he opened his eyes, he felt fresh and clean, renewed from the inside out.

He was also developing a relationship with Babaji. He felt so much love for this mysterious man, he was already an important part of his life, which really surprised him. He had never dreamed he would accept a guru, and now he knew that he had. Each time he looked at his one picture of Babaji love surged through him.

Very naturally he began to wake earlier and he loved his quiet time alone. He meditated in the small sitting room on the ground floor. Every old Welsh farmhouse had a 'parlour,' a room that was kept for special occasions. This room had been his music room, and now it was his meditation room. He no longer had any desire to drink at lunch times, and rarely went to the pub in the evenings.

Joanna tried her best to keep the children quiet when Daddy was meditating. She could see how much it meant to him, and was happy for him, if a little puzzled. She was glad he'd stopped drinking, and she wanted to encourage this new phase as best she could, although she had no idea where it would lead him.

After a couple of months Eddie went to the Ashram in London for a weekend programme. As soon as he walked into the Ashram, he felt he'd come home. A friendly woman welcomed him and showed him around. Everywhere was clean and orderly, there were big pictures of Babaji and his guru on the walls, the air was fragrant with incense and chants were playing constantly. It was so peaceful he just wanted to sit in the hall and meditate. He later learned that Babaji's guru was called Papaji, he was a wonderful and wild looking holy man, who wore a simple loin cloth and was apparently born self-realised.

Eddie stayed in a four-bed dormitory, with three other men. That evening they all shared their stories with one another. Each man had found Babaji through a series of chance encounters. One guy had discovered a book by Babaji in a second-hand book stall. No sooner had he finished reading the book than he saw a poster about Babaji and discovered he would be in the UK that week. So, of course, he went to meet Babaji and his spiritual journey began in earnest.

Eddie hardly slept that first night. He lay in bed, energy buzzing through him, yet his mind was stiller than it had ever been. The following day, during the first break in the programme, Eddie was surprised to be asked to help with the cleaning. He soon discovered that service was also an integral part of Babaji's yoga. The community supported itself by everybody doing their bit to help. Eddie found that the simple tasks of sweeping a floor or washing dishes could actually be joyful. He connected with other devotees while they worked together, and he soon felt a sense of belonging to the group that came from working together for the common good.

One stormy evening, shortly after Eddie had returned from London, he was enjoying some time with Joanna after the children had gone to bed. Outside, beech trees groaned in the wind and raindrops skittered on the windowpanes. He knelt beside the Jotul wood-burner, opened the door and inserted three long logs. Then sat beside Joanna on the sofa. "I really want to meet Babaji." he said, taking hold of her hand.

"I know you do, darling," Joanna replied, "we'll be okay. I can manage without you, though I'll miss you of course. It will be great for you to go to India. You've always wanted to."

"Yes, I have," he said, "we spent two years in Afghanistan and never once went to India, strange really."

"Not so strange. We went to Pakistan a lot, and I have always been a bit scared of going to India."

"Why?" Eddie asked, although he thought he knew.

"I always thought I'd die if I went there. I don't know why. It's no more dangerous than Afghanistan, less probably. Anyway, have you worked out how much money you will need to go?"

"Not fully but I think I'll need six or seven hundred pounds."

"Phew. How are we going to raise that?" Joanna asked. Money was always tight. They had enough, but very little spare. Any extra profits the shop made went straight back into the business.

"Il can sell my Strat. That should get about £200."

"Can you bear to part with it?" Joanna asked, "You won't have an electric guitar anymore, what will you play in the band? And it's a Fender Stratocaster, you were so happy when you bought it."

"I don't really want to play in the band anymore." Eddie said, finally voicing what he had been thinking for weeks. "No-one really listens to us. Everyone just wants to get out of their heads on dope or booze. The music gets louder and louder. Davy keeps turning up his amp, then January turns up his and it just becomes noise in the end. It doesn't feel like music and I am tired of it."

"Wow." I never expected you to say that."

"No, nor did I," Eddie said, shaking his head and looking surprised at himself. "I'm actually only just realising this is how I feel." They sat silently for a while, listening to the wood crackling in the fire while the wind howled outside.

"Well, everything changes," Joanna said, "I guess you are beginning a new phase in your life. Let's pray the money comes from somewhere and then you can go."

"You are amazing, do you know that?" Eddie asked, wrapping his arms around her and kissing her warmly on the lips.

What makes us feel drawn to music is that our whole being is music: our mind and body, the nature in which we live, the nature which has made us, all that is beneath and around us, it is all music.

Hazrat Inayat Khan (1882-1927)

WEST WALES 1982-83

We waved until the Swansea bus disappeared around the corner, then Grace burst into tears. I squatted down to hug her, my own eyes brimming. "Daddy will soon be home," I said, wiping away her tears while mine ran down my cheeks. "I'll miss him though."

"And I will." Danny said, his bottom lip trembling.

"Let's go and visit Nana," I said, "she'll cheer us up."

"Daddy's never been away from home for a whole month before," Molly said, her brow furrowing in a worried frown, "how will we manage?"

"We'll be fine, it will be an adventure." In truth a part of me was really looking forward to being alone, as alone as you can be with three young children. I'd lived with Eddie since I was twenty, and this would be the first time I would live independently. Yes, it would be a lot of work, looking after the business and the children single-handed, but I thrived on challenge and instinctively knew that the time apart would strengthen us all.

It was miraculous how smoothly the money had come for Eddie to make his pilgrimage to the Guru. Once he'd made the intention everything fell into place. A tax rebate of £300 arrived soon after he'd sold the Fender, which had doubled his money. The shop became busier, so we were able to draw a little more salary and now he was on his way. The image of his face in the bus window was still clear in my mind's eye. I mentally sent him my love, aware of the tender thread that connected us.

We walked up the hill to Mum's bungalow, huddling into our coats and wrapping our scarves round our necks against the sharp bite of the east wind. It was early February and there was still snow on the Cambrian Mountains.

As we rang Mum's doorbell, I noticed a group of snowdrops peeking up from the cold ground. Spring would soon be here; Eddie would soon be home and I must make the most of my time of freedom.

"Come in, you look cold," Mum said, hugging each one of us and taking Danny by the hand as she led him through to her sitting room. She looked lovely, as ever, dressed in a red jumper and soft, dark skirt, her silver hair swept up in a bun, her eyes bright and full of love. Sheba, her ageing and devoted dog, waddled over to us, tail wagging. She licked the children's faces which made Molly cringe and Danny laugh.

"He's gone then," she said, a question in her eyes as she looked at me.

"Yes, on his way to catch the airport bus at Swansea."

"What time will he get to India?"

"Some time tomorrow."

"Well good luck to him. How are you feeling?"

"Pretty good, we will miss him, but I'm looking forward to some time alone."

"It'll take you time to get used to it. After your dad died, I kept expecting him to walk back in. I'd wake up in the morning and miss him lying in the bed next to me. I missed having him to talk to in the evenings. I still do really and it's been over five years now."

"You've done really well, Mum. I know it was hard at first."

"Yes, and I took consolation in the whiskey bottle for a while. I'm glad I got over that."

"You were very strong. Anyway, Eddie is only gone for a month. As soon as I get used to him being gone, he'll be home again!"

"Can we watch some telly, Nana?" Danny asked, an angelic look on his face. There was nothing he loved more than sitting in front of the TV and I knew it was only a matter of time until we bought one at home.

"Yes, lovely, of course you can," Mum said, switching on the 'magic box.' "And would you like some lemonade and biscuits while you watch?"

"Yes, please Nana," they all chorused, settling down before the screen.

I smiled; happy they were already consoled about their dad's temporary disappearance from their lives. "Do you mind if I pop down the shop for a few hours, Mum?"

"No, of course not. Will you be back for lunch?"

"Yes, around one. Then I'll take them home. They should be okay in the shop without me this afternoon." I kissed each child on the cheek, their warm skin peach-soft. Grace hugged me, Danny barely looked up and Molly moved onto the sofa to sit beside her Nana. "Bye then, see you soon." And so, my time as a single parent began.

I bought a new radio/cassette player and the Police album, 'Ghost in the Machine.' I realised that I had not played music for years. Eddie didn't really like listening to 'other' music. He liked playing guitar, and, more recently, he'd been singing chants, but we spent very little time listening to music, something which I now realised I'd missed.

We danced around the kitchen table to Sting singing Roxanne. Pretty soon I knew most of the words and sang along while I was cooking, ironing or cleaning. I was busy from dawn to dusk, and then some.

The bathroom light pull-switch broke the day after Eddie left, and I was determined to fix it myself. I was an independent woman, after all. I didn't need a man to fix things for me. I sat with that light switch and my teeny tiny screwdrivers night after night, trying to fix it after I'd put the kids to bed. I got it all apart, but there were so many components, tiny springs and screws that I had no idea what to do with. I'd tried to take note of what went where when I'd disassembled it, but it defied logic and nothing seemed to fit anywhere.

After four frustrating evenings I admitted defeat and took it into the electric shop. "Oh, you can't fix them," Simon electric told me. "Just buy a new one. Here, it's only £2.50!" So that was a good lesson for me. And I was still proud of myself for trying.

I began missing Eddie after the first week. All the petty irritations of married life seemed less important. Who cared about toilet seats left up, or endlessly cleaning up breadcrumbs, or bits of cheese on the sofa after the late-night cheese sarnie?

I missed the sound of his laughter, and the way he made me laugh. I missed the sparkle of his blue blue eyes. I missed the feel of his arms around me. I missed his solid, supportive presence in my life. He was like a rock, steady, strong and totally reliable.

I'd heard nothing. I knew that phone calls were impossible and assumed the post would be slow. I'd written to him twice, enclosing little notes and pictures from the children, but nothing came back. And the work was relentless: up at 7.30, feed us all, get the kids ready; make packed lunches; ensure school bags had all the essential gear for the day, swimming costumes, homework, PE kit; drive the seven miles into town; drop the kids at school; work in the shop from 9.00 to 5.30, with barely time to eat or drink; collect the kids from Mum; drive home; cook, eat, wash up; help Molly and Grace with home-work and read to Danny; put the washing on; get the children to bed; complete any orders for the shop; possibly read for a while, head nodding and eyes drooping with exhaustion; then fall asleep myself.

And yet I was happy, I was learning to live in my own rhythm. I enjoyed the silence as I sat alone in the sitting room or read late into the night in bed.

One day I was cleaning the small sitting room, where Eddie meditated. I looked at the picture of Babaji on his altar. I felt Babaji's gaze on me, he seemed to be challenging me and I felt both intrigued and a little apprehensive.

"Who are you?" I asked him silently. I thought of Eddie being with this man in India at this very moment and a wave of love swept over me, bringing unexpected tears to my eyes. I took a clean duster and carefully dusted Babaji's picture. Then I went into the garden and collected a bunch of snowdrops, arranged them carefully in my favourite blue and white Greek vase and placed it in front of Babaji's picture.

I sat on a cushion on the floor and stared into Babaji's eyes. I'd been resisting having anything to do with Eddie's new found spiritual path. Partly because I was actually quite content with my life as it was and partly because I did not want to follow another man onto a spiritual path. After my experience with Adam and Subud in 1967, I'd vowed to myself that if I ever followed a path again it would be my choice and I would be in control of what happened to me. Now here I was with another holy man in my life.

Why was I resisting him? I was content with my life, and in touch with a kind of inner peace. When I worked in the garden, or walked in nature, or watched the sunset, or the endless restless motion of the sea, I felt connected to something greater, something eternal and I felt expanded.

I didn't feel a lack of anything, nor a need for spiritual sustenance. Yet I also remembered knowing as a child that there was more to life than I could see. I read and re-read the ancient myths and legends of Greece and Rome, somehow knowing that they contained information about something I knew, yet had forgotten. A treasure that had been buried and a map that had been lost. I had a sixth sense of sacred mysteries once known, like the mist of a melody that reverberated silently within me.

Could this man actually show me the path back to this deeper knowledge? As I looked into his deep brown eyes, I felt him gazing back at me, beckoning me to explore this new path. Suddenly I wanted to play the tamboura, which I hadn't picked up for weeks. I went to my bedroom, dusted it and carried it carefully down the stairs.

I sat before Babaji, cradled the tamboura in my lap, bowed my head to him and played the four strings slowly and with focus. The sound reverberated through me. The music of the tamboura resonated throughout the room, creating a harmonic bridge which somehow connected me to Babaji, to India and to Eddie. I smelt jasmine blossom and frankincense. I felt the balmy, tropical air on my skin and the tiny hairs on my arm quivered. And still I played on. Tireless and completely absorbed in the magic of the music.

Finally, I stopped playing, gently laid the tamboura down and closed my eyes. I sensed my awareness encompassing the room, the house, the land around and the vast, pulsating sky above. Stars twinkled and comets created rivers of light. I was all this. All this was me. When I opened my eyes Babaji was smiling at me.

In the days and weeks that followed I read one of Babaji's books and placed fresh flowers in front of his picture. I was still wary, yet I was intrigued, and wanted to learn more. Very, very gradually I opened just a tiny chink in my heart, and let Babaji's light shine in.

A letter arrived from Eddie in early March. We sat around the kitchen table and I read it aloud to the children.

Dear Joanna, Molly, Grace and Danny,

I love everything about being here in Babaji's Ashram, and in India. I love the burning sun and the cool shade of the mango trees. I love the warm-hearted people and the hot spicy food. Most of all I love Babaji. He is incredible, like a force of nature. He is full of energy and yet he radiates such stillness. Everything he does is whole-hearted and filled with grace. He is the most conscious and alive person I have ever met. I find him totally fascinating and could sit and watch him for hours. My bed is on the roof, as the Ashram is very crowded. Because it's so hot on the roof, I go to everything. The ashram daily schedule is wonderful, each day we chant different scriptural chants, as well as kirtans and the morning and evening arati. The days here are very full, from early morning meditation through to the final chant of the evening.

We are like a huge family, Babaji's family. We all help out with the daily chores to keep the Ashram running smoothly. So far, I have washed giant cooking pots with wads of coconut hair, worked in the gardens and cleaned rooms. No matter what I do I am really happy.

There are people from all over the world here, all sorts of people. Sometimes we don't speak each other's language, but it doesn't matter. We understand one another on a whole

different level, beyond words. When we chant and meditate
together, we are one.
I think of you all every day and send each one of you a big hug
and all my love. Look after each other and write to me soon.
I love you,
Your own,
Eddie Daddy.

"He sounds happy," Grace said.

"When is he coming home?" asked Danny, fidgeting on his seat.

"Well, I thought he was coming home next week," I said. "He was only going for a month and it's been over three weeks already."

"He doesn't say anything about coming home," Molly said, "and he doesn't mention our letters." Her forehead was furrowing again and I knew she was sad. She missed her dad but never spoke about what she was feeling. Molly carried her emotions close to her heart, always showing a strong front to the world. I wondered what had made her like that so young. I put my arm around her and kissed her on the cheek.

"He probably wrote this letter in the first week he was there. The post is slow in India. The letters have to travel a long long way, then go in an aeroplane, then get sorted and finally come to us in Wales. He could be reading our letters right now."

"Do you think he likes my picture?" Danny asked.

"I'm sure he loves it. Shall we go to the seaside today? Look, it's going to be sunny. I'll make us a picnic."

We drove across the rolling green hills to the coast. Bright, golden daffodils nodded cheerfully in the gentle breeze, heralding the arrival of spring. Lambs gambolled and frolicked in the fields, chasing one another, leaping into the air in delight, batting up against their mothers' teats for a drink of her milk.

We parked in the National Trust car park and walked down the hill to Penbryn beach. Fluffy pussy willow and soft green catkins dangled from branches beside the path. Gorse bushes were covered in yellow, coconut-custard scented flowers and the air was rich with birdsong. Danny and Grace skipped ahead, while Molly and I walked with the picnic basket and the buckets and spades.

Ancient ferns unfurled beside mossy stones and purple violets nestled in the grass. Then we rounded the last bend and saw the magnificent sweep of golden sand, blue-green sea and slate-grey cliffs. We all ran the last bit of road and threw ourselves onto the sand. Grace and Danny made angel wings with their arms on the sand while I lay and listened to the sound of the surf breaking on the shore and watched a few powder-puff clouds scud across the blue sky. Every muscle in my body relaxed and a smile spread across my face. I turned on my side and looked at Molly, her green eyes reflecting my own, her smile mirroring mine. When had her eyes turned green, I wondered. They'd been so blue as a baby. "It's so beautiful here, Mum," she said.

I nodded wordlessly back to her. Our family had always loved being beside the sea. We felt blessed to live so close to one of the wildest and most beautiful coasts in Britain. We climbed the windy cliffs in winter, swam in the sea as soon as it was bearable, watched fireworks in New Quay or Llangrannog, celebrated summer birthdays on sandy beaches and brought all our visitors to see the secret coves, or sail out on Cardigan Bay to watch the dolphins play.

We walked to the far end of the beach and found a spot in the shelter of a cliff. While the children played, I sat quietly and watched the sea ebb and flow, the waves swelling, cresting and curling, then crashing on the sand, the dance of foam and sunlight, the flight and swoop of seagulls. I felt peaceful and happy, yet I was aware of an inner niggling, a space inside where I did not want to go. And as soon as I was aware of it, I had to look at it, and name it—the absence of Eddie.

In one way I was fine, I was enjoying the peace and quiet, living at my own rhythm, making my own decisions. And I was also slightly irritated. Why? Perhaps I resented his freedom, the fact that he was able to immerse himself in his spiritual life, while I was working and taking care of everything here in Wales.

Perhaps I just missed him and wanted him home again. I was acutely aware of how much I loved him, something which surprised me as we had been together so long, I had lost sight of the bond of love in the daily routines of our busy life. I saw the truth in the old adage—absence makes the heart grow fonder.

As I continued to reflect on my feelings, I recognised a cold shadow of fear. Perhaps he would not come back? Maybe he would love it there so much he'd want to become a monk or something. He had been very obsessed with his spiritual practices and much less interested in our love life. I remembered reading something somewhere about saving the sexual energy for spiritual growth. Maybe he wanted to become a celibate???

I shook my head, dismissing that thought. He would be back soon enough. I should make the most of my time without him. But what did I want to do with it? I had so little energy left at the end of the week. I was saved from further reflection by the return of three hungry, wet and sandy children. We enjoyed our picnic, played a ball game, went for a long walk and drove home.

Two weeks later another letter arrived. Eddie had asked Babaji whether he should stay or return to his family. Babaji had told him to stay until his birthday and then return. Babaji's birthday was at the beginning of May.

I was devastated. He had already been gone for six weeks. He would not be home for another six weeks! I was exhausted and felt very alone. Although we had been sending letters to Eddie, the letters that came back had nothing to do with the letters we'd sent. There was no real communication. The link that I had been aware of between us in the early weeks had weakened. I felt I was having a one-way conversation. He was truly gone. He had been a part of my life for sixteen years and his absence was like a gaping, jagged hole. I sat alone in the garden and sobbed.

I went into the small sitting room and turned Babaji's picture around to face the wall. I was angry and frustrated and did not know where to go with it. So, I just got on with my life, accepted the situation and made the best of it. The anger soon dissolved. I turned Babaji's picture round and put fresh flowers on the altar. I played the tamboura sometimes and found some peace. I read Babaji's book, which alternately annoyed and inspired me. I bought more tapes and danced in the kitchen with the kids, and we fell about laughing together. Mostly I was just so busy I had no time to think, nor to miss Eddie.

By early May the trees had unfurled their vibrant, fresh green leaves and we heard the first cuckoo. I woke each day to the joyful call of the blackbird and the glory of the dawn chorus. Eddie was due home on May 11 and we were all excited. He called from the airport and we met him off the Swansea bus late that evening.

It felt good to feel the warmth of his body in the bed beside me. I lay awake for some time, happy that he was home, enjoying the feeling of all being right in my world once again. He'd brought us all presents: bright plastic cars and a bug-eyed fluffy monkey for Danny, janky jewellery and silken scarves for the girls and two silver anklets with bells for me. I tinkled around the house like an exotic belly dancer.

He also bought me a black and white picture of a young Indian woman with large, striking brown eyes and a shaven head. "This is Babaji's successor, Swamiji," he told me. "I was in the courtyard just after she took sanyas initiation with Babaji. Just me and an elderly Indian woman. She came out dressed in a simple white robe, her hair shaven. She looked like an angel, or a visitor from another planet. I just sat and cried. Swamiji stood perfectly still, looking at the two of us with so much love."

"Is Swamiji her name then?" I asked.

"No, she has a long Indian name that I can't remember, so I just call her Swamiji. Before she became a swami, she was Babaji's translator, she has been his disciple since she was five years old. Some people say since before she was born. Her parents are devotees and have been visiting the Ashram for years."

I held the picture in my hands. It felt precious. As I looked at the radiant, otherworldly face something stirred deep within me. "Thank you. She is really beautiful."

We smiled at one another and the three months of separation faded into the past. Eddie hugged me and I kissed his warm lips. "Did you miss me?" he asked.

"Just a bit."

As we settled back into our familiar routines, I noticed how much Eddie had changed. There was a new gentleness to him. He was calmer and more balanced. Whereas before his anger had been quick to spark into flames, now he was more measured in his responses. He rose early every day to meditate and chant. At first, he used the small sitting room, but the noise of the children disturbed him. So, he cleaned up the caravan and that became his meditation space. It was two fields away from the house and completely quiet.

By July I was so impressed with the changes in him that I decided to try meditating myself. I went to the caravan whenever I had a spare ten minutes, shut my eyes and repeated the mantra *Om Namah Shivaya*, trying to synchronise it with my breath. I enjoyed the quietness, and having time to simply sit, however I was mostly aware of the busyness of my mind.

It was amazing to me just how many thoughts fluttered about in my mind. As soon as I sat and started repeating the mantra, events from my day flitted past the screen of my mind: a conversation with someone; regret about something I'd said, or a re-playing of the conversation with improved input from me.

And then I'd remember I was supposed to be meditating. *Om Namah Shivaya. Om Namah Shivaya. Om Namah Shivaya….* and my mind would be off on another journey, thinking about clothes, or remembering something I needed to do, or planning the events of the next day. And so it went on. I found it somewhat frustrating and occasionally boring. The time passed very slowly. I would sit for my ten minutes, and when I looked at my watch only five minutes had passed. But I did at least try to meditate most days.

Eddie, on the other hand, stayed in the caravan for over an hour. I sometimes resented his absence, thinking of the endless list of tasks that were always waiting to be done. But I could see I was being petty. While he'd been away, I just got on with whatever needed doing; I knew no-one else would do it. I was glad and grateful that he was so happy, and I decided to accept things as they were.

I sat alone in my bedroom one evening, looking at the picture of Swamiji that Eddie had brought me from India. She fascinated me. Her eyes were like doorways to eternity. Her presence was almost tangible. As my gaze melded with hers, I felt drawn inwards. My head felt heavy, yet full of swirling energy. Suddenly prisms of light radiated from her face, filling me and the room with pulsating white light. Tears ran down my face and I focused on the steady flow of my breath, inwards and outwards, and revelled in the light that surrounded and suffused me. My heart was full of love. From that moment on I knew that I would meet Swamiji one day.

One windy and wet Sunday in October I was walking past the sitting room window, on my way to the caravan to meditate. The phone rang and Eddie answered it. I walked on across the fields. This time, as I sat to meditate and repeated the mantra to myself, I settled into a place of stillness and silence that was soft as velvet and deep as the night sky. I felt enfolded in a blanket of love, wrapped in peace. I felt I knew this place like I knew my own heart. I had come home. I was vaguely aware of the ebb and flow of my breath, but the warm stillness and silence that embraced me was all encompassing.

Over thirty minutes later I opened my eyes. I felt clean from the inside out. Fresh and alive. Awake. So this is meditation I thought. I like it!

When I walked back into the house Eddie was crying. He'd heard on the phone call that Babaji had taken mahasamadhi. He had left his body and merged into the great Universal Consciousness, something that only happens to a great saint.

I realised that my first experience of true meditation had been a gift of Babaji's grace. When a great being takes mahasamadhi their spiritual energy, their grace, pervades everywhere. People from all around the world told stories about experiencing the Self, the unity in all things, during the time of Babaji's mahasamadhi.

Everything changed. I meditated regularly. Eddie was invited to open a meditation centre by the resident teacher in the Ashram in London. In November we held our first chanting and meditation programme. Eddie played the melody of the chant on his guitar. Several of our friends joined us, people who were curious about meditation, or had noticed how much Eddie had changed since his visit to the Ashram in India.

There was Peggy, an elderly woman with a curiosity for life and a thirst for spiritual knowledge. Peggy was a physicist and a Catholic, and loved the energy that was created when we all chanted together. Carolyn and I had demonstrated at RAF Brawdy, on the Pembroke coast, against the siting of Cruise Missiles. We had chained ourselves to a post within the camp and the troops had threatened us with a water cannon. In the midst of the chaos, Carolyn had experienced something that she could not explain, like being in the eye of a storm. As a result, she wanted to learn more about chanting and meditation. And Grace, our dear daughter who was only nine years old, found that she loved chanting and was a natural meditator.

So, every Wednesday the five of us gathered in the caravan, read some of Babaji's words, chanted and meditated. Then we drank tea and chatted in the house. I found myself talking about Babaji's path to others and I was not even certain that it was my path. Yet those Wednesday nights soon became the highlight of our week, uplifting us and infusing my days with a sweetness and energy that I loved and wanted more of.

In March 1983 I went to a national programme in London. When the teacher said that Guruji, as Swamiji was now known, would be at the Ashram in India in October I knew I should also be there. All the way home on the bus I plotted and planned how to raise the money and create the space to go. On October 1, 1983, I set off for India.

Sounds are the echo of the 'Harmony of the Spheres,' which man took into himself when he came down from the divine spiritual world into the physical world.

Rudolph Steiner (1861-1925)

MAHARASHTRA 1983

We descended through rain-dense grey clouds and emerged over Bombay. Below I saw a vast, sprawling city with thousands of flimsy shanties; simple one room dwellings constructed from sheets of corrugated iron, flapping doors of plastic and random pieces of wood or cardboard.

As our plane taxied along the runway I saw men, women and children scything the long grasses between the runways, presumably to feed their animals. The shanty town bordered the entire runway and children played dangerously close to the planes.

I walked out of the airport and all my senses were assaulted at once. The hot, humid air felt dense and thick in my lungs. The smell of humanity, spices, smoke, diesel fumes and rotting vegetation was overwhelming. The noise of engines, honking horns, raised voices, radios and the distant ringing of bells filled my ears.

I took a taxi to Andheri Road Station, driving past many shanties. All of life was there: women squatted inside their tiny homes cooking on a small stove or an open fire; men in suits, briefcases clutched close to their bodies, walked briskly down the streets; beggars gathered at every car window as soon as there was a pause in the traffic, hands out, eyes wide and pleading for something, anything; hawkers strained to sell their goods, a man cleaned his teeth while standing in the gutter, another squatted to relieve himself. The rickety stalls and streets teeming with life reminded me of Kabul.

I boarded the women's carriage of the Virar train and soon we were on our way out of the city. Kind brown eyes stared at me from fine-boned, delicate faces. I smiled back and soon they accepted my presence. The women were dressed in colourful saris in soft, silky fabrics. Schoolgirls in neat white dresses smiled shyly at me. Big notices proclaimed: 'Please do not spit on the platforms.' 'Beware of Chain-Snatchers.' I pondered what a chain snatcher could be.

A rickshaw took me on the final leg of the journey, rattling along muddy, rutted roads in the pouring rain. Nothing had prepared me for this. There was a terrifying absence of road-rules. Everyone drove somewhere near the middle of the road, avoiding pot-holes and puddles whenever possible, and veering right or left at random. Mostly we just seemed to go head-on towards whatever was coming at us, be it lorry, car or bus. It was like playing chicken. We only moved out of the way at the last possible moment. Every time a lorry passed us, I was sprayed with mud. Pretty soon I was soaked. The only way I could hold on to a modicum of calm was to focus on the passing countryside and avoid looking at the traffic.

The monsoon rains were still falling and the lush, succulent green of new growth sprouted anywhere it could find a soggy foothold. Water lapped around the houses, filled the fields and ran down the hills. Water buffalo and wild pigs wallowed in the mud. Cows wandered freely. Dogs, bikes and women carrying huge bundles of wood vied with the traffic for road space. Children fished by hand in vast puddles. Frogs and crows croaked and cawed.

We rattled and bumped along for miles and miles until, finally, we arrived. My heart danced within me and tears filled my eyes. I was here, at the Ashram, at the threshold of something I knew would change me indelibly. Behind the hills to the west the setting sun cast a warm glow over the Ashram and painted the horizon in streaks of gold and red. The contrast of sunlight and the lowering clouds created a magical light.

With immense relief I paid off the driver, gathered my luggage and walked through the Ashram gates. Inside was another world. A world of peace and shade, of coolness and tranquillity. The very air appeared to shimmer. No sooner had I entered than a huge bell began chiming. It was time for the evening Arati in the Temple. This ancient ritual of worship with light, sound and praise was offered to a life-size statue of Babaji's teacher, Papaji.

A young Indian man, dressed in a red silk dhoti and shawl, waved a three-tiered brass lamp which bore many tiny flames. An older man beat a huge drum with two wooden sticks. The primal rhythm reverberated within me, calling me to worship also. I left my luggage beneath the stairs and entered the Temple. Someone handed me a small silver bell and I shook it, adding one more sound to the multi-layered music of drums and bells.

The wall of sound built to a crescendo as the pujari waved the lights. Then everyone stopped at the same time, and, miraculously, so did I. The lights were placed in front of Papaji. The pujari lit a tablet of camphor and wafted the purifying white smoke towards Papaji. The silence was palpable. The harmonium player began to play the Arati and everyone joined in. I was handed a sheet with the words on, but I decided to listen until the words and metre became more familiar. There was such a sweet sense of devotion as we all stood in the Temple, praising God and the Guru, the Self of all.

Later, after I had settled into my dormitory and unpacked, I ate a simple meal in the dining hall and returned to my room to sleep. I wanted to see and do everything, but I was so tired and knew I had to rest. I was here, in India, in the Ashram. Tomorrow I would meet Guruji!

Early the following day a twenty-four-hour chant started in honour of Babaji. It was one year since he had taken mahasamadhi, a very auspicious anniversary.

I joined the chant for an hour and was amazed to see four tambouras being played, along with the harmonium, drums and cymbals that formed the heart of the music. There were two big tambouras, similar to mine, and two smaller ones. I watched the graceful way the musicians played. Their posture was so erect and they played with their hands parallel to the strings, rather than across them like I did. I tuned into the sound of the tambouras during the chant. The harmonics created waves of sound that rippled off into infinity. Each note blended into all the other tones, creating music that was mesmerising.

This was my first long chant with a lot of people. I'd joined a short chant during the programme in London, but nothing like this. The group of musicians and lead singers sang a round of the chant first. Then we all responded. This gave me time to listen and learn the chant, which soon became familiar.

The tempo increased steadily, driven along by the drummer, who played a *mrdang*, a barrel shaped drum with a head at both ends. Each round of the chant lasted about an hour, starting slow and stately and gradually building to a joyful climax. The tambouras maintained a steady drone, neither gaining in speed, nor slowing down.

At first, I was busy looking around. The hall was built with cool marble, in shades ranging from cream to ochre. We sat facing the eastern end, sunlight flickered through the lattice wall and birds flew in and out. The Guru's chair was in the centre, with pots of greenery behind it. Two small tables stood on either side of the chair, each bearing a picture, Babaji on the left and Papaji on the right. Both pictures were garlanded with tiny white flowers. A single red rose stood in a vase on each table. Above the chair was a large picture of Babaji, the same picture Eddie had on his altar. I smiled at Babaji's familiar face and a sudden rush of joy flowed through me. His picture was adorned with a huge garland made from marigolds.

The hall was very crowded, yet every time someone else arrived people made themselves smaller and found a place for the new arrivals. Everyone was dressed in their best. Most of the women wore saris, in every colour of the rainbow. Many of the men were dressed in a lungi, a kind of skirt made from a length of material, and a shirt. I saw a few westerners, most of whom also wore traditional Indian dress. Some of the women wore a longish top over trousers, with a decorative scarf or shawl. I thought that outfit looked comfortable and decided to buy one when I had a chance.

The drum beat became more insistent. I focused on the words and rhythm of the chant, allowing myself to become saturated in them. I concentrated on being fully present, listening as the musicians sang, hearing every note of the harmonium, every beat of the drum, aware of the magnificent sound of the four tambouras. When it was my turn to chant, each syllable tasted like honey on my tongue. I gave myself whole-heartedly to the chant. All around me people were swaying and I found myself swaying too. Our voices were as one. Praising Babaji. Praising God, the one Consciousness that pervaded everyone and everything.

A stir of excitement rippled through the hall and the fragrance of gardenia and jasmine wafted over me. Suddenly Guruji was walking along the central aisle towards the Guru's chair. As she drifted passed me, I heard the soft swish of her silk robes and recognised that the fragrance was emanating from her.

With utmost grace Guruji stopped before the Guru's chair, looked up at Babaji, bowed, and then sat cross-legged upon the chair. Effortlessly she controlled the chant with subtle gestures to the musicians: a lift of her finger and the drummer increased the beat; a slight raise of one eyebrow and the lead singers chanted with twice as much energy. Her presence was electrifying. One glance around the room and I felt she knew all that was happening.
I bowed my head, honouring her, and when I looked up, she was looking directly at me. Her gaze filled me and tears sprang from my eyes. All I wanted was to stay in that moment forever, chanting with Guruji on this beautiful and auspicious morning.

All I knew was that I must chant with every part of me, just as Guruji was already doing. Her rich deep voice delighted and thrilled me. With each round the chant became more and more ecstatic. Tears of joy ran unheeded down my cheeks. My voice was liquid love, responding to her voice which was love incarnate. We had become one. One voice. One heart. United in love.

And then the chant reached its crescendo and dived

into perfect, pristine silence, perfumed only by the constant drone of the tambouras. And slowly, sweetly we began again. Each syllable a love song on our lips. Each note a golden prayer. This is the meaning of bliss, I thought. Every particle of my being was alive, vibrant with the power of the chant. Sunlight glistened in the air, life radiated from the flowers around the Guru's chair, love glowed on every face.

I looked at Guruji and was filled with awe. I had read in the Indian Scriptures that the Guru is the grace bestowing power of God. Now here I was in the presence of a truly perfect master—one who had walked the path and reached the goal and was here on earth to guide any who wished to make the journey to union with their own divinity.

I was blessed indeed.

Later that day I was taken on a tour around the Ashram, a journey of discovery and wonder. The courtyard was the heart of the Ashram: shaded by mature mango trees, and coconut palms, which had been planted by Babaji when he first founded the Ashram in the 1950s. It was a haven of tranquillity and beauty. The walls and floor were of the same mellow marble as the hall, soft golden sunlight flickered through the branches of the trees, the air shimmered with energy, a deep, still and meditative power that permeated everything and drew my awareness inward effortlessly. The gates of the Ashram opened on to a small courtyard, which led into the Temple, with a small entrance to the main courtyard. The hall was to the right of the courtyard and Babaji's Samadhi shrine, a sacred place which was the original meditation cave and in which his body was now enshrined, was to the left. Next to the shrine was Babaji's house. Near the doorway to Babaji's house was a raised area, made of marble, and upholstered in soft blue velvet, where Babaji used to sit. Beside Babaji's seat was another Guru's chair, where I was told Guruji sat.

Beneath one of the mango trees was a life-size black marble statue of Papaji. My guide, a young Indian woman called Radha, informed me that the final arati of the day was sung here in the courtyard, to Papaji's statue. I decided I would join this worship each day I was in the Ashram.

We then walked down the slope into the grounds, along a shady path, past exotic flowers— bright orange bird of paradise and scarlet amaryllis. I noticed large shrubs of coleus, which I had only ever seen in the UK as a small house plant, the long, glaucous green leaves streaked with brilliant red and yellow.

We rounded a bend and a white statue of Lord Ganesh, the elephant-headed deity who was said to remove obstacles and confer his blessings on new ventures, sat cross-legged amidst a profusion of gorgeous flowers and plants. A small group of Brahmin priests were worshipping this benign image of Lord Ganesh, singing ancient verses from the Indian Scriptures in the Sanskrit language, and placing flowers and fruits on and around him. Radha and I stopped to watch silently, and the sense of reverence I felt surprised me.

Every part of the Ashram felt holy, deeply cared for, respected and loved. The simple beauty of the gardens and buildings created a harmonious environment that was dedicated to spiritual life. And it all felt alive with an intense yet tranquil energy. I was used to sacred places in the West being redolent with history, distant echoes of past devotion. This Ashram was alive with love, saturated with the positive energy created by thousands of people performing focused spiritual practices, from before sunrise until after sunset, day after day after day.

Radha pointed out the entrance to the meditation 'cave', which was behind, and in fact under, Babaji's house. The entrance was reached via a small path, not far from the statue of Lord Ganesh. The cave was closed for cleaning, but I noted the opening hours and vowed to visit the following day. We walked past the dining hall and Radha showed me around the modern clinic, which was on the ground-floor of the new accommodation building.

"We have two resident doctors in the Ashram," Radha told me. "One is qualified in modern medicine, he is actually from the USA, and we are also blessed to have Dr.

Patel staying for a month. She is a highly qualified Ayurvedic doctor from Pune."

"Does the clinic treat local people as well as the ashramites?" I asked.

"Oh yes, the clinic is open for the ashramites for two hours each morning, here, you can see the opening times." Radha pointed to a notice board on a wall near the reception area. "Also, we have the mobile hospital, which travels to the local villages four times a week."

"Really, how great. Would it be possible for me to go with them while I am here? I would love to help anyway I can."

"We can speak with the manager and ask. Visiting ashramites often help out with the mobile clinics. Do you have any medical skills?"

"Not really but I'm sure I could make myself useful somehow."

"Look, here's the pharmacy. You can buy some electrolyte salts here when it opens again tomorrow morning. It's important to replace your salts and drink a lot of water, especially when you first arrive from the West."

"Yes, I've been really thirsty, and the humidity is very high at the moment."

"We are at the end of the monsoon. In a couple of weeks, it will be better. In the hot season we long for the rain. And now, when we have had rain almost every day since June, we are longing for it to stop. Why can't we just be content, whatever the weather?"

I laughed. "It's like that in my country also, Radha. In the UK the weather is always changing. Sometimes we can have all the seasons in one day. Cold and wintry in the morning, then it warms up and showers a bit, like a spring day, then the clouds can disappear, the sky becomes blue and it feels like summer, then a wind comes up and it could almost be autumn."

Radha laughed also, "We hear that the British always talk about the weather."

"We are famous for it."

"Come, I will show you the cow-sheds and the upper gardens now." We walked along in comfortable silence. I was impressed by my companion. She had a quiet confidence and I wondered how old she could be. She looked around seventeen, yet seemed very mature. Her dark hair hung in a single plait, reaching beyond her waist. She was dressed in the long tunic and trousers I had noticed earlier. Her eyes were stunning, warm, hazel brown with an amber light that sparkled when she laughed.

"Radha, could you show me where I could buy a tunic and matching pants similar to yours? They look so comfortable."

"Ahh, a salwar khameez you mean. Yes, they are comfortable. And much easier to wear than a sari. Yes, of course I'll show you. There's a lovely shop on the way into the village. I could take you there tomorrow. After lunch maybe? Do you need to sleep then?"

"Well, I'm still a little jet lagged, but I have one more rest day before I start offering to help. We could go after lunch and I could rest before. Thank you."

Radha showed me the cowsheds, which were sparkling clean and contained three very contented brown cows. "Babaji used to visit the cows every day," Radha told me. "I have heard that Guruji also loves to visit."

"It's certainly very peaceful in here. But then everywhere in the Ashram is peaceful."

"It is paradise here."

"Yes, I think you're right. My husband said it was like heaven on earth. Now I understand what he meant." We walked past the cowsheds. On our right was an expanse of green, which a group of local workmen were watering. It was not grass, exactly, more a collection of sturdy green leaves, but the effect was cooling and pleasing to the eye. Soon we were in a rose garden, complete with pathways and shaded seats. A tall western woman in a big straw hat was tending the roses. She looked up and smiled.

"Hi, welcome to the gardens"

"You sound English," I said, surprised.

"That's because I am. My name's Sarah, pleased to meet you.

"Hi Sarah, I'm Joanna." We both laughed. "This could be an English rose garden," I said.

"It could. Babaji loved roses and planted every single one of these. It's my great honour to look after them."

"Do you live here?"

"Well, my husband, Andrew, and I have been here for six months, and I can't see us going anywhere else for a fair while yet. We love being here. How about you?"

"I arrived yesterday, in the evening. I feel like I'm still landing, but already I love it. Radha here is doing a great job showing me around."

"You're in good hands. Lovely to meet you, I'd better get on."

"Cheers, Sarah, see you later." We walked through the gardens, stopping occasionally to smell one rose and admire another. Then Radha led me through an avenue of trees and we stopped to drink in the vista before us. A huge, open sided building crowned the hill. The roof rose in incremental layers, and glimmered golden in the afternoon sun. The pillars supporting it shone white. I climbed the steps leading up to it and peered inside.

"This is the Yajna Mandap," Radha said, "see the central area? When the Brahmin priests come and perform *yajna*, the sacred fire ceremony which purifies the world and brings untold blessings to all, a fire is lit in the central pit. The Brahmin priests sit around the fire, reciting sacred texts and offering ghee, honey, milk, sesame seeds and rice to the flames. Just to be present at a *yajna* ceremony is very auspicious."

"Will there be one soon?" I asked hopefully. I could imagine how glorious it would be to sit in this place, surrounded by nature and worshipping the element of fire. Just standing on the edge I could sense the power of the place.

"Maybe, if our Guru wills it." We walked around the Mandap to a small white temple. Radha led me past the statue of a bull and down a few steps into the temple. We sat on a stone bench. A small, rounded stone stood in the middle of the floor. "This is the Shiva Temple," Radha told me. "And that is a Shiva Lingam, a symbol of Lord Shiva."

I closed my eyes, focused on my breath and sat silently. The atmosphere in this temple was different, older somehow, charged with a potent energy that felt primal. I was drawn into meditation.

After some time, we looked at one another and smiled. I followed Radha out of the temple. Outside the beauty and sounds of the gardens washed over me: the bright sunlight, filtered through the green trees, the rustle of the bamboo grove, the joyful singing of the birds, the perfume of the flowers. A peacock called from somewhere nearby. "It truly is paradise here."

Radha smiled at me, her eyes sparkling. We followed the paths around the upper gardens, passing life-size statues of saints. I knew nothing about any of them and vowed to learn all I could about Lord Shiva, Ganesh and all the saints that were represented here. I felt a shiver of excitement and anticipation. I was on the first steps of a great journey of discovery, learning about this ancient and sacred tradition, and learning about myself at the same time.

The path led us downhill. By now we were at the southern end of the gardens and ahead of us was a huge statue, which was sheltered by a domed pagoda. As we approached, I saw the statue was of a Goddess. She was draped in a red and gold sari and rode a huge tiger. She had eight arms and looked magnificent, fierce and strong, yet compassionate and full of love.

We stood in front of her. My head was barely level with her feet. Radha bowed reverently before her, placing an offering in a box on the altar. "This is the Goddess Durga." Radha said. "She is the warrior who defeated all the demon army when the gods were unable to, bringing an end to the great war between gods and demons. We pray to her to destroy the negative energies within us, the limitations that conceal our inner light from us. Come, we will offer pradakshina."

Radha began walking in a clockwise direction around Durga, and I followed silently. Once again, I was aware of a shift in the energy. This area felt deeply female, the domain of the Goddess. This I recognised in my soul. I had felt an inner connection to the Goddess since childhood, when I had read and re-read all the ancient myths and legends that I could lay my hands on. I knew her by many names: Isis, Ceridwen, Aphrodite, Venus, Diana, and Brigit. It was to her I had prayed when I wanted to conceive another child, the night of the full moon in the Swat Valley in Pakistan. Nine months later Grace had been born. During our three circuits of the Goddess, I welcomed her in the form of Durga into my heart. Once again, I stood before her. This time I bowed my head at her feet, then spontaneously picked up the lit candle and the small tray and waved it to honour Durga. My head was swirling with energy and I felt intoxicated, in the best possible way.

Radha and I sat for a while on a stone seat in front of Durga. I had been in the Ashram less than twenty-four hours. A lot had happened. I felt settled into myself, acutely aware and alive in a way I had never experienced before. "Thank you, Radha, for showing me around. I love it here. And I think I will visit Durga every day. She is very special."

"Yes, I also visit her every day. Would you like to stay here for a while? I have to go and practice for the chant. I am playing tamboura this evening."

"Really? I would love to learn to play. I have a tamboura at home and, when I saw how it is played here, I realised that I've been playing it the wrong way for the last fourteen years."

"You have a tamboura? How come?"

"It's a long story."

"Well, I will be happy to teach you. We'll meet tomorrow after lunch, in the small courtyard, and I will take you to buy a salwar khameez. How long are you here for?"

"Six whole weeks. How about you?"

"I am here for a year. I'm taking a break from school

to study here and think about what I want to do."

"Wow, how brilliant your parents let you do that. How old are you, Radha? You seem so mature."

"Thank you, I am sixteen."

"Sixteen! I'm so happy that you were asked to show me around the Ashram today, Radha, you are amazing." I hugged her and she hugged me back. Already I felt close to her and was looking forward to learning more from her. Radha walked off towards the courtyard, turning to wave as she neared the end of the path. I waved back, then sat looking at Durga and writing in my journal until it was time for the evening Arati.

The following day Guruji was sitting in the courtyard giving darshan. I was told that darshan meant 'having sight of a holy person.' This was the time when people could go up to her and bow. Sometimes she would speak to people, or they would ask her a question, or give her a gift. People sat quietly in the dappled sunshine, as the reverent line of devotees moved slowly forward to greet Guruji and offer their respects. Instrumental music played softly, tabla, sitar, flute and tamboura. A gentle breeze rustled in the mango trees. The fragrance of jasmine and mogra blossom lingered in the air.

I was shy to join the line, and unsure about bowing in front of Guruji. So far, I had never actually got on my knees and bowed. I'd bowed my head the previous day, to Durga, but never a full and proper bow. It was not part of my culture and I felt weird about it. I knew that I had to really mean it when I did it.

I watched as families and individuals approached Guruji, knelt and bowed their heads to the ground. Sometimes a tender look passed between Guru and disciple, or a child offered a gift and Guruji playfully hugged them and gave them a lollipop or a cuddly toy.

Some people gathered around her on their knees and talked earnestly to her. She often laughed. Her laughter was full, free, spontaneous and very infectious. I watched as an elderly woman knelt before Guruji and bowed, when she raised her head Guruji spoke to her, reaching out her hand for the woman to hold. Then, she stroked the woman's cheek with her other hand. Tears sprang to my eyes. There was so much love in that simple and sweet exchange. And I wanted to be that woman.

The atmosphere in the courtyard was vibrant with love. It was a heady mixture of devotion and stillness, both meditative and tranquil. I found my head nodding forward, my eyes closed, diving inwards. And then Guruji's laugh, or the giggling of a child, would bring me back to awareness of the courtyard and the pageant of love that was taking place. I longed to simply stand up and join the line. But I was scared. I felt that she would see right through me, see all my flaws and weaknesses. I wanted to speak to her, but what would I say? What if she didn't even look at me? I'd noticed that many people simply bowed and moved on. We were here to see her, after all, not vice versa. Yet I craved her attention. I wanted an interaction with her. I wanted her to know who I was. Why?

My mind spun when I tried to work that question out. Agitation replaced the inner serenity that I was already getting used to and enjoying. My heart beat faster. My stomach churned. Was it ego? Probably, I thought, yet also something more, something I could not name yet. Perhaps I was longing for connection.

The line of people dwindled. Now only one or two people, late arrivals, who had been offering service in the Ashram, approached the Guru's chair. Most of us sat silently in the courtyard. Guruji sat with her eyes closed. She was perfectly still. I watched her and a wave of pure love washed over me. Warm tears began to roll ever so slowly down my cheeks. I took a deep breath in, wiped away the tears, stood up and walked toward my Guru.

As I approached her, I felt I was walking through a mist of silence. I was acutely aware of every breath, every step and every pulse of my body. I knelt before her and bowed my head to the floor. Love embraced me, surged through me like a cleansing wave. My head felt too heavy to lift. I wanted to stay right there, at her feet, forever. This was where I was always meant to be. Where I belonged. Slowly I lifted my head and looked at her. Her eyes were still shut. Close to she was even more beautiful. Her skin glowed. A warm light seemed to shimmer in the air around her. I rose gracefully and walked on, every particle of my body singing.

When I returned to my seat on the marble floor I bowed once again. Then sat relishing her presence. Happy to simply be. No thoughts rippled in my mind. Just a pulsating silence that shone within me, drawing me deeper and deeper into myself. I had entered a timeless place, which was as familiar to me as my own breath. A wave of immense gratitude swept through me and I opened my eyes to look at Guruji. "Thank you," I thought.

At that moment Guruji opened her eyes and looked directly at me. Our eyes met. My heart soared like a bird in the sky.

I woke early the next morning and walked the path to the meditation cave. The air was cool and thousands of stars sparkled clear and bright in the sky above. The waning moon, still almost full, was setting on the western horizon. I stood for a moment, drinking it all in: the silence and stillness, the potent atmosphere, perfumed with night-flowering trees and sacred with the resonance of mantra and the many names of God. I felt as if I was walking on air. Energy coursed through me. I was more alive than I had ever been. And yet more centred, steadier and more connected with who I am and why I am here.

I walked into the cool, silent darkness of the meditation cave. I couldn't see a thing. Afraid of stumbling over someone or something I stood still; eyes closed. When I opened my eyes, I could see well enough to find an empty cushion on the floor and sit. Although it was only 4.00am several people were already meditating. I looked at the altar, the puja as I had come to think of it. At the centre was a large picture of Guruji. On either side were pictures of Babaji and Papaji. I bowed my head to them all, closed my eyes, focused on my breath and allowed the sweet stillness of meditation to wash over me.

An hour later I opened my eyes. I was tingling inside and I felt a deep sense of peace and well-being, a sense of freshness and clarity. I smiled to myself as I bowed my head and rose from my seat.

Ashramites, wrapped in shawls against the pre-dawn chill, made their way silently along the path to the dining hall. Nobody spoke. We each quietly took a beaker of sweet, steaming chai and sipped it slowly. I took mine outside and sat beneath the stars, searching the skies for familiar constellations. I recognised the plough first, as always, and then spotted Orion. I loved seeing how differently they were placed, a heavenly reminder of how far I was from home. And yet I felt more completely at home than I had ever felt before. While I sipped my chai I reflected on my time in the Ashram. I had been here only a few days, yet I knew something profound was happening to me. I did not understand it, but I instinctively knew everything would happen in its own time and all I had to do was stay close to my heart, listen and learn. Above all I was revelling in the stillness and quiet joy that I felt.

At 5.30 the daily scriptural recitation began. This was a practice I had never done at home. I had tried, but the endless Sanskrit verses and difficult pronunciation were too daunting for me. My mind wandered and after a few attempts I had given up. Now I was actually an Ashram resident I decided to give it a go once more. It was part of the daily schedule and I wanted to give myself whole-heartedly to every moment. While I listened to the men sing the first two lines of each verse, I read some of the translation. Then I sang the last two lines, along with all the other women. It was like a conversation.

On that first day I became lost in the beauty of the rhythm and metre of the sacred verses. Occasionally I read a line, or a verse that was so full of love and devotion I was moved to tears. Sometimes my head felt heavy, the power of the recitation drawing me within. Yet I managed to stay focused for the entire hour, and, by the end of it, I felt a surge of energy and pure delight as we all stood to sing our praises to the sadguru, the Self of all.

During our recitation the sun rose, casting a soft golden light over everyone's face. Birds flitted in and out or sat on the beams above us. The silence after the recitation rippled with the sacred vibrations of the ancient words.

After breakfast I walked around the gardens, visiting the roses and the statue of Durga, pausing often to breathe in the tropical beauty that surrounded me. At 8.30 I went to find out what seva I would be given for my stay. Seva is the name given to the practice of offering service to support the Ashram. Apparently, it was also a spiritual practice. Eddie had told me about it, but I had not fully understood at the time. I was a little nervous. What if I was asked to clean toilets all day long? I did want to offer something back, but I also wanted to explore the library and learn more about this path of union with the divine.

I was invited to help with housekeeping for four days, and then go into the laundry. My heart sank. Cleaning, washing and ironing! That's not what I'd come to an Ashram for. I did enough of that at home. I tried talking myself into it as I walked to the housekeeping department. 'Yoga is about surrender,' I told myself. 'Be like a willow tree, bend with the wind.' But underneath the philosophical words I was silently speaking, my mind was seething. 'It's not fair. It's too hot to clean. I'll get my clothes dirty. I have a dust allergy. Why couldn't they give me something more important?'

The housekeeping department was little bigger than a broom cupboard. There was a big picture of Durga on one wall. Instead of holding weapons she held a duster, a broom, a dustpan and brush and a mop. I sighed in resignation and introduced myself. Malini, the department head, a warm and friendly Mexican woman, invited me to wave the arati tray for the morning puja. Apparently every seva session began with waving a light and singing mantras to the Guru.

After puja Malini invited a young Indian boy, whose name I hadn't heard properly, to read from a book she passed him. I can't remember the words exactly, but I do remember their effect. Seva was an offering to the Guru, to God. When we offer seva with a pure heart, with no expectations, then very soon we experience the divinity that is our true nature. Sounds good, I thought. I'll try it.

I spent all morning on my hands and knees scrubbing monsoon mould off stone steps outside the original accommodation building. It was hard work. I found a piece of carpet to put under my knees, which helped, but the mould was tenacious and required a lot of scrubbing. I remembered that I should be offering my seva to the Guru. How to do that? I decided to repeat the mantra to myself while I scrubbed. *Om Namah Shivaya*. Scrub scrub scrub. *Om Namah Shivaya*. I Honour the Self within.

'Is mould the Self?' I wondered. 'The Self is in all things and in all places, so it must be.' Gradually my mind quietened. I noticed the patterns the mould had painted on the smooth stone steps. I was in the shade of a huge tree with leaves that shimmered in the wind. A bird sat in the tree, watching me, chirruping occasionally. I scrubbed and scrubbed and by lunch time I felt peaceful and still inside. Maybe seva wasn't so bad after all.

After a delicious lunch of rice, bhaji and dhal, served with chapattis, I had a short siesta and returned to seva around 2.30. This time a group of us were invited to clean a family bungalow. We gathered our buckets, mops, brooms and cloths and crossed the road into the residential area where families and long-term staff lived.

Our group consisted of the young Indian guy, whose name was Prahlad, a slim French woman, Delphine, who looked older than me, and an American girl with striking hazel eyes and a southern drawl. "Just call me Nancy, honey," she said, "I love your English accent."

"And I love yours. Do you know where we're going?"

"Yeah, it's right here." Nancy set down the bucket and mop she was carrying and fumbled in her pocket for the keys. It was surprisingly spacious in the bungalow, with two bedrooms, a sitting room and even a small kitchen.

We had fun cleaning it all up and making it welcoming for the family. I enjoyed meeting new people and working with a team. By the time we'd finished I'd made three new friends and felt like I was part of the Ashram community, rather than a new arrival who was looking in from the outside. We were finished by 4.30. After a shower and change of clothes I walked the shaded path past Lord Ganesh, pausing for a moment to nod at him, then turned right into the courtyard.

Guruji was sitting on her chair. Once again, I noticed how the air seemed to shimmer. As people arrived, they walked up to Guruji, bowed at her feet, and then sat in the shade of the trees. I sat first, closing my eyes and feeling the inward pull. The energy felt thick and heady. I was tired from the day of physical work, yet I was also aware of feeling light and somehow cleansed myself.

I allowed myself to drift into meditation, the pull was too strong to resist. After some time, I opened my eyes. Guruji was looking directly at me, a gentle smile playing around her lips. Without a thought I stood and approached her. I had my chanting book in my hand. I knelt at her feet and bowed my head to the ground. My heart was thumping in my chest. I raised my head and looked at her. She looked back at me. Being this close to her was wonderful. She was radiant and beautiful. Her eyes were mesmerising and her presence all-encompassing. No-one else existed. Just Guruji and I.

"Hello Guruji. Would you sign my chanting book please?" I held my book out to her. She smiled and joy flooded through me.

Guruji took the book from my hand, signed it and offered it back to me. I held my hands out to receive the book and Guruji tenderly held my right hand, looking closely at it. "What are these?" She asked, lightly touching the blisters at the centre of my palm.

Her love enveloped me, washed through and into me. I had never known such love; pure, unconditional, accepting me completely as I am, and knowing me far better than I had ever known myself. Somehow, I managed to speak. "I was planting tulips in my garden before I travelled here."

She continued to hold my hand, and gently stroked my palm. Love flowed like a current of light between us. My heart melted in her love. I knew, with a deep and shining certainty, that every single thread that had been woven throughout my life, indeed in many lifetimes, had led me to be here in this moment, kneeling at my Guru's feet.

Guruji slowly nodded at me and smiled, still holding my hand. When she handed me my book I bowed once again, and somehow stood and made my way back to my place. I sat down and wave after wave of love washed over me. I was overflowing with love, radiant with light. There was no thought in my mind, just a perfect and complete joy.

I settled into the rhythm of Ashram life. I was intensely happy, yet very emotional. Tears came at unexpected moments: while watching the sunset, or walking in the gardens, or chanting. Each evening Guruji sat silently in the courtyard, and we all sat with her once we had completed our seva.

One evening I was sitting in the courtyard, quite near to Guruji. The meditative energy was so strong my head kept nodding forward and I could not keep my eyes open. I had a sudden inner prompting to go into the Samadhi Shrine, which was just behind me. I bowed, walked around three times in pradakshina, and then sat against the wall. I dropped into a deep meditation for a short while and during the meditation I found myself talking to Babaji. "If all this is real, Babaji, and not my imagination, nor a communal hallucination, please give me a sign."

I went back to the courtyard and sat down. No sooner had I taken my seat than Guruji looked at me. Her eyes seemed to see right into me. Then she turned and looked ahead. As I watched her something amazing happened. Guruji began to radiate a clear, golden light. The light was pouring out of her and saturating everyone and everything in the courtyard with a shimmering luminescence. I too was filled with this light, each of us was a part of this light, and it both connected and defined us. I knew I was seeing the light of all, the light of the supreme Self. I was filled with awe. And I knew, beyond doubt, that Guruji was a conduit for supreme Grace, to guide seekers back to union with their true nature, which is one with all. Tears of gratitude flowed down my face. My heart was overflowing.

Two days later, as I left the evening chant, I saw that Guruji was sitting in the courtyard, so I sat down close to her. It was dark and silent. Some people did not notice and walked away to their beds. Others came to sit with Guruji. Time passed and we sat quietly, absorbed in the tender sweetness of the night. A bell tolled in the distance. A bird called out. The scent of jasmine and mogra flowers drifted on the air.

Guruji stood and walked purposefully out of the courtyard, turning right and walking quickly toward the statue of Durga. I jumped up and followed her, barefoot and curious. A small group of us followed at a distance. Durga was dressed in a rich dark red sari which was covered in gold brocade. She looked magnificent. A group of brightly dressed Indian women stood in a circle in front of her. The women held short sticks in their hands. Two banana palms had been placed at the entrance to Durga Park, and a chair for Guruji was between the palms.

Guruji sat and we stood in a small group behind her. The women began to dance in a circle, clicking their sticks together, first lifting the sticks up to the left, then down to the right. As they danced, they sang and, deep in my soul, I recognised the song and began to hum along. Round and round they danced, their skirts and saris swirling, gold and sea-green, burgundy and saffron, azure blue and coral pink. Their dark hair swinging. It was hypnotic and exhilarating.

Above us sat Durga, astride her tiger, her dark eyes watching, regal and glorious. I looked at Durga, then I looked at Guruji, who was sitting in front of me. I thought: "Why are we worshipping a statue of the Goddess, when Guruji is right here?" Guruji turned around and looked at me. Her eyes seemed enormous and I felt her gaze enter me, filling me.

That night I could not sleep. I lay all night, Guruji's

eyes filling my consciousness. In the early hours a poem
arose, fully formed:

Paramahamsa, perfect swan,
how blessed am I to have looked upon
the glory of the Guru's form,
for this alone was I reborn.

As you gracefully glide o'er the waters of life
never a drop soils your pure white light.
By your grace we are freed from the deep nets of maya
hearts and minds filled with mantra – Om Namah Shivaya

You're the sun of my day, and the moon of my night,
just one look from your eyes fills my soul with delight.
From the lake of compassion flows the river of joy
and the current of love brings us safe to the shore.

I had my first tamboura lesson with Radha around two weeks
into my stay. She met me outside the dining room and took
me to the music practice room, which was in one of the
buildings surrounding the courtyard.

She showed me how to sit, how to hold the tamboura
upright, close to my heart. Then she demonstrated how to
play the strings, my hand relaxed, yet almost parallel with the
neck of the instrument. Play the bass string with my middle
finger, and the other three strings with my first finger. Slow
and sedate. Four notes, one after the other, then again and
again. The resonance building into a swell of sound.

At first it was hard for my fingers to stay in that
position. I was tense, wanting to get it right. "Relax," she said,
"to play beautiful music we have to be centred in our heart,
not in our head. Don't worry. Let the instrument teach you.
Breathe!" I consciously breathed in deeply and softened the
tension in my shoulders, neck, arms, fingers.

"Good. Don't play for a while. Just sit and feel the
instrument in your arms." I sat, one hand resting lightly on
the gourd, the other on the strings, my forehead leaning into

the neck.

When I started to play again my hands were soft and the music sounded much sweeter. I relaxed into the steady rhythmic flow of sound. It was like a river carrying me gently along. I felt my awareness drawn deeper and deeper. Radha played with me and we lost ourselves in the magical sound of the tamboura.

We smiled at one another as we both finished playing at the same time. We closed our eyes and sat in the resonance of sound that vibrated in the room and in our beings. After a few minutes of sublime silence Radha gently settled her instrument upright on its ring, ensuring it was balanced. She then lifted mine from my hands. "This is how we store the tamboura," she said, "each instrument has its own ring and it is important to make sure the tamboura is balanced, or it will fall and break."

"I noticed that you touched it before you played, and then touched your heart."

"I was honouring my instrument before I played it. When we play sacred music, we are walking the path to God through our music. Each instrument is also sacred. So, we treat them with respect. We never walk over them, or act carelessly with them."

"That is beautiful Radha, thank you for telling me. In the West we are quite careless with instruments."

Radha laughed, "I've noticed."

"I realised today," I said, "while we were playing, that it was while playing my tamboura that I first experienced the inner silence that I now know is the place I touch in meditation. In a sense it was the tamboura that brought me here."

"I understand, Joanna. I've been playing tamboura since I was a little girl. I've always loved it because of the way I feel when I play, the still place it takes me to. How come you have a tamboura?"

"A friend came to India and was given it here. Then he gave it to me. How come you were playing tamboura as a little girl? Are your parents musicians?"

"Very fine musicians. My mother plays tamboura and

harmonium, and my father plays sitar, as well as tabla and tamboura. He is also one of the best instrument makers in India."

"Really. So you grew up surrounded by music."

"Yes, I am very blessed. We live in Miraj, which is not too far from here. It is a town famous for music and fine instruments."

"Do all your family play?"

"My twin brother, Krishna, plays tabla like a maestro. He will be coming here in two weeks, so you may meet him. My little sister is learning to play the sitar, and she is very good already. We are a musical family. How about you?"

"Music is also very important to us. My husband plays guitar and is learning to play the *mrdang*. He met Babaji here last year. He bought a *mrdang* in Bombay. I'm not sure about the children. They all love chanting, and Danny, our son, seems to be very musical."

"How great that your family chants together. Maybe one day you will all come here, to the Ashram."

"Oh, how I would love that."

"Now we must go for dinner. You can come and practice here any time you wish. You will soon be a good tamboura player."

"Thanks, Radha. You are an excellent teacher."

We hugged one another and walked to the dining room together. A new moon had just risen, a shining silver crescent in the darkening sky.

During my stay at the Ashram, I took an introductory course on the philosophy and scriptures of India. One concept that really grabbed my imagination was that our minds are a form of Universal Consciousness, the same force that pervades everything. One afternoon I was reflecting on this thought, and walked the gardens repeating to myself, mind is consciousness. I decided to meditate and went into the meditation cave. I sat down and focused on my breath, breathing in slowly and deeply, then releasing my breath fully, without any tension. I had begun using the mantra *soham*, which means I am that. I repeated the mantra in alignment with my breath. I also held the awareness that mind is consciousness.

Gradually I became aware of the connection between the ebb and flow of my breath and the beating of my heart. With each breath, with each heartbeat, I was becoming more and more immersed in a divine pulsation that I knew was Supreme Consciousness. My entire being felt expanded. I was the pulsation, the throb of the universe. It was within me and all around me. My very breath, my heartbeat, the flow of blood through my veins were all in harmony with this divine pulsation. I saw that every cell and every star pulsed with the same beat. I felt blissful, euphoric, yet totally grounded. Each breath was a blessing. Each heart-beat a miracle.

I do not know how long I sat there. I do know that I never wanted to move. I wanted to stay in that experience forever. Finally, I did move. I stood up, walked over to the puja and lay my entire body on the floor in front of Guruji's picture, overwhelmed with gratitude. These words, from the Shiva Sutras, a scripture we had been studying, sprang into my mind.

Vismaya yoga bhumikah
The ways of yoga are filled with wonder.

I lay, stretched out on the floor for a long time, still immersed in the divine pulsation of all life, Supreme Consciousness. I emerged into daylight again and put on my shoes. I turned to go and saw that Guruji was walking straight toward me. She stood in front of me and looked deep into my eyes. Profound and radiant stillness. Total intoxicating love. In that timeless moment I was one with my Guru and the eternal pulse that sustains all. The faintest smile twinkled in Guruji's eyes, and then she moved on into her house.

For days I was in an uplifted, transcendent state. Every time I connected to my breath I also connected to the inner pulsation, the heartbeat of the universe. I did not speak about my experience to anyone. I cherished it and nurtured it, wanting above all to maintain my inner connection, my awareness, with the pulse of Consciousness that pervaded all and was my true nature. Yet I had to function, and at times I had to let go of the bliss, to be able to focus on mundane tasks. I wondered how Guruji did it, instinctively recognising that she lived in a transcendent state all the time.

I consoled myself with the thought that at least I had glimpsed that state. Now my life's work was to maintain that inner connection, so that, no matter what tasks I was performing, I was firmly anchored in the divine spanda, the pulsation of Consciousness.

Two weeks later I was home with my family. I was thirty-six years old and had opened a new chapter in the book of my life. Guruji had woken up my soul. She had opened my heart and shown me the true nature of love. The love I felt for her encompassed everything and everyone in my life, including myself. I had experienced such unconditional love from her. I knew that she recognised the divinity within me and in all. I had been given an amazing experience of that divinity and so now I must acknowledge that indeed I too was worthy. And I wanted to see that same divinity in everyone I met, including those I found difficult.

One day I turned on the kitchen tap, to wash some dishes. As the cold water gushed out it was filled with light. I was immediately re-connected with the divine pulsation of Consciousness. There it was, in the flowing, light-soaked water before me, in the sunlight on my back garden, in the dishes and in the eyes of my loved ones. I closed my eyes for a moment and gave thanks, then continued washing the dishes.

I sat one evening, shortly after my return, playing the tamboura. The children were all asleep and Eddie was out. I plucked each string with love. My mind was empty of thought. There was nothing other than the sound of the strings, the harmonic resonance that entered every fibre of my being. The sound swirled and danced around me, harmonising with the song of the stars, the flow of the waters, the steady throb of the earth and leaping flames of the fire. Music is both the doorway and the path.

Afterword

The effect of Indian music and spiritual philosophy on the minds and culture of western youth in the sixties was profound, and *Tamboura* opens a window on that effect from the perspective of people who lived through it. The Beatles', and other well-known musicians', stay in Rishikesh in 1968 with the Maharishi was historical, and affected many thousands of people. The prevalence of LSD in the late sixties, the psychedelic revolution, the process of 'turning on, tuning in and dropping out' led many people to begin the search for spiritual meaning and initiated the so-called 'hippy trail' to India.

Many people are still searching. Music, and sacred sound, can open the doors of perception within us. We know, in our hearts, that there is more to life. We catch glimpses of wonder and joy, of stillness and serenity. Hatha yoga classes, mindfulness and meditation are popular and help people to find some inner peace. There are many good teachers, and, fortunately for our world, there are a few living enlightened beings who have completed their own journey toward unity and illumine the path for others. My intention, in writing *Tamboura*, is to give an eye-witness account of what it is like to live in the presence of such a being, and, hopefully, to inspire others to explore their own inner realms.

Listening to, and telling stories is in our DNA. We were sitting around fires, hearing stories long before screens were invented, and we will be long after they are gone. Many tales, like this one, are based on truth and all storytellers will use the tools of drama and fiction to bring the facts to life.

Josie Smith
tambourathebook@gmail.com

Bibliography

Berendt, Joachim-Ernst, *Nada Brahma: The World Is Sound*.
Rochester, VT: Destiny Books, 1987
Bose, Ajoy, *Across the Universe –The Beatles in India*, Penguin
Gurgaon: Viking India 2018
Cooke de Herrera, Nancy, *All You Need Is Love*: An Eyewitness
Account of When Spirituality Spread from the East to the
West: Jodere Group, California, 2003
Lavezzoli, Peter, *The Dawn of Indian Music in the West*:
Continuum Publishing NY, 2006
Leitch, Donovan, *The Hurdy Gurdy Man*: Arrow Books,
London, 2006
https://en.wikipedia.org/wiki/Abdul_Karim_Khan
https://www.rikhiram.com/
https://chandrakantha.com/articles/indian_music/sitar/sitar_
making.html

- o 0 o -